Awaken My Heart

Awaken My Heart

DiAnn Mills

HARPER LUXE

An Imprint of HarperCollins*Publishers*

HarperCollins books may be purchased for educational, business, or sales promotional use. For information please write: Special Markets Department, HarperCollins Publishers, 10 East 53rd Street, New York, NY 10022.

FIRST HARPERLUXE EDITION

HarperLuxe™ is a trademark of HarperCollins Publishers

Library of Congress Cataloging-in-Publication Data is available upon request.

ISBN 978-0-06-147094-3

08 09 10 11 12 OV/RRD 10 9 8 7 6 5 4 3 2 1

To all those who love the history of Texas
and the romance of the era

I want to thank Louise M. Gouge
for her patience in critiquing my work,
Mona Gansberg Hodgson for her support,
and Dean, who understands my need to create.

And what doth the Lord require of thee,
but to do justly, and to love mercy,
and to walk humbly with thy God?

MICAH 6:8

Chapter 1

April 1803
The Colony of Tejas

Before the rooster had crowed three times, forbidden adventure had crept into Marianne's mind. In the shadows of her room, she quickly dressed and stole from her father's house to the outside. Cool air bathed her face, and a yellow-orange sunrise streaked the eastern sky. She made her way to the stables and peered inside the dimly lit building for signs of the servants before gathering up her skirts and squeezing through the latched entrance. Safely inside, she eased the heavy door closed and cringed at the creak, fearing its sound would arouse attention.

The smell of horses and leather met her nostrils, their familiarity breeding both comfort and excitement. She stopped and listened for voices. Her heart pounded furiously at the thought of being discovered. Glancing upward, she saw a glimmer of sunlight filter through a high window, illuminating a golden, straw-laden path to Diablo's stall.

Her father's sleek, milky-white stallion pawed at the ground and snorted as though defying any intruder to enter his domain. Weston Phillips, Marianne's father, owned the horse, but not his spirit. Only the stableman could groom him. Only Marianne could ride him.

Marianne gasped and hurried to his stall. "Hush, Diablo. Someone will realize I am here."

At the sound of her voice, the stallion ceased his complaints. She lifted the latch and stepped inside, being careful to gently close the door behind her. She eagerly anticipated the two of them racing across the dew-bathed hills dotted with live oak and juniper. How she yearned for the freedom of flying with the wind and being as one with the powerful Diablo.

She wrapped her arms around the stallion's neck. He neighed softly and nuzzled into her embrace. "Oh, I have missed you, too." She planted a kiss on his forehead. "And we have a long morning to ride."

The low rumble of male voices pricked her ears and paralyzed her. *Papa!* He and Clay Wharton, the hacienda's foreman, had entered the barn. She held her breath and glanced about the stall. If Papa found her, his wrath would echo across the vast expanse of the Phillips Hacienda.

When the voices of Papa and Clay grew closer, she slipped her hands from Diablo's neck and crouched against the wall next to the stall door. She prayed neither Papa nor Clay heard her heart slamming against her chest.

"Quiet, you devil." Papa stopped outside of Diablo's stall. "I would welcome the opportunity to blow a hole through you, but I need you to breed with my mares."

Clay chuckled. "Are you sure you want more horses with his temperament?"

"I will sell them to the Spaniards," Papa said. "Let them deal with it."

Diablo lifted his head. His notched ears lay back as though he understood Papa's contemptuous words.

Her father banged his fist against the side of the stall. "Remember, I still own you."

Marianne clasped her arms around her trembling body. She envisioned her father's penetrating, blue-gray eyes, framed with the many lines of age and Texas sun. The servants called them *relampago*, lightning eyes, for they flashed with his ravings and curses.

"Where are our horses?" her father shouted. "Lazy Mexicans. None of them worth their pay."

"My guess, all of 'em here are aiding Armando Garcia," Clay said. "That rebel needs a bullet in his head."

She'd heard the stories about the man who rallied the peasants to fight against Papa's demands to leave their valley. The young girls dreamed of him and proclaimed him more handsome than any man ever born. The boys and men sang Armando Garcia's praises— the hero who dared to defy the harsh treatment of her father.

"You get rid of him, and there's a bonus for you," Papa said. "I'm tired of dealing with his arrogance."

"You know what I want."

Papa seemed to ignore him.

"I plan to talk to Garcia today. Our cattle need to graze in La Flor. Those Mexicans can move closer to one of the missions along the San Antonio River and leave me their valley."

"Weston, they haven't agreed to leave in the past. What makes you think they will now?"

Her father laughed. "I refuse to give them a choice. They'll either clear out of there, or I'll force them out. We have more weapons than they could ever hope to steal."

"What about men to carry it out? The vaqueros will not fight against their own people."

"I've already sent for some friends of mine back in Virginia. Everything is handled." Her father spat tobacco juice against the side of the stall. The slap of it coupled with his gruff words agitated Diablo.

"Shut up," Papa said to Diablo, who snorted and tossed his head. "This isn't a good day to rile me." He reached for the stall's latch.

"Leave the horse alone. Let's saddle up and get out of here," Clay said. "The day's wasting away."

When the heavy door of the stable finally creaked shut, and the pounding of horses' hooves faded into the distance, Marianne struggled to her feet from her crouched position, trembling more from overhearing Papa and Clay's conversation than the fear of being discovered in Diablo's stall.

What did Papa plan to do? He had plenty of land without adding more from the villagers' valley. From what she knew about Armando Garcia, he'd not take Papa's threats lightly. She hoped the problem could be settled without a bloody battle, for she feared the Mexican peasants were no match for whatever Papa had in mind.

With a deep sigh, she stepped from the stall to fetch Diablo's silver-studded bridle from the tack room. Beneath a worn, carved leather saddle decorated boldly in orange and yellow mineral paints, she found her cotton skirt and blouse.

One of the servant women had given Marianne the clothes after she complained of having to ride in the cumbersome petticoats. Mama objected to her wearing the apparel of the Mexican women, especially the blouses that revealed her elbows. But Marianne loved the loose fit and the way the style made riding effortless.

Diablo pranced like a child eager to play. She laughed at his impatience and pushed aside the conversation she'd overheard between Papa and Clay. Later she'd ask one of the servants about the valley. She grabbed a sombrero and fitted its cord beneath her chin. Mama would banish her from any horse if the sun tanned her pale skin.

Leading her beloved stallion to the stable door, she pulled hard to slide it open. As a child she'd found the task impossible, but at eighteen she'd found the undertaking easier.

"Marianne," Mama had said. "You need to abandon riding and settle down. You must learn to act like a woman ready for marriage."

"Not yet," Marianne had replied, planting a kiss on her mother's pale cheek, "but soon."

Neither spoke of her father's threats to arrange a marriage with a Spanish-born cattle baron, Lorenzo Sanchez de la Diaz y Franco, who lived near the

Guadalupe River. She knew why Papa wanted the marriage. The Sanchez holdings promised to multiply Papa's power and influence among the Tejas elite.

Marianne detested the thought of marriage after living with the unpleasantness between Mama and Papa. Why put herself under the dominion of any man, especially one who was twice her age? Still, she knew her feelings meant nothing if Papa wanted the marriage. She would be forced to comply with his demands.

Shaking her head to rid herself of all the unpleasant thoughts, she raised her foot into the stirrup and swung her leg over the saddle. She turned her attention to the western pastures and the farther hills where her father's cattle grazed.

The stallion left a blinding cloud of dust behind them, and all around she reveled in the beauty of spring unfolding like the wings of a butterfly. Yellowish-white yarrow and nodding daisies with orange centers scattered the earth.

Yet, in all of this beauty, the Phillips Hacienda could not compare to the lush valley called La Flor. It bordered on the southern edge of Papa's empire and had been fed with underground springs. La Flor's inhabitants were Mexican peasants who had nothing but their valley. They were a mixture of the Spanish and the conquered Indians. Mestizos. A race of their own. A race that had no future except for the hope of their own land. Reports were the valley was green year-round. To them it was paradise.

The morning wore on. Marianne and Diablo stopped and basked in the shade beneath the leafed canopy of an oak tree. Another time they rested beside a cool, gurgling stream, and Diablo drank his fill. There, Marianne wove wildflowers for a wreath and placed them around the horse's neck. She loved the strong stallion, impressive with his perfectly aristocratic stance and his independent spirit. She allowed him to pick and choose his way. After all, he came from the Spanish mustang, intelligent and strong-willed. Perhaps the two of them had become friends because each respected the mind of the other.

Seated on a grassy knoll, she watched her stallion toss his head to the south.

"What is it, my prince?" She gazed in the same direction, but saw nothing.

They had ridden far, and a twinge of caution settled in the pit of her stomach. Marauding Comanches could be nearby. She stood and stared across the quiet, rolling landscape. It appeared peaceful, but at any given moment it could erupt. When the stallion's ears stood erect, she gathered up the reins.

"Señorita, there is no need to make haste," a male voice said in Spanish.

Fear gripped her heart, and she whirled around in the stranger's direction. All of Mama's warnings about the ways of men replayed in her mind, and she pulled the brim of her sombrero farther down over her face. From under a grove of trees, the man rode a dun gelding toward her. The quality of the horse startled her, uncommon for a man of threadbare dress. Few of her father's vaqueros owned so fine an animal.

"I must have frightened you. I'm sorry."

Gripping the reins and holding back Diablo, she realized he must not see her light skin.

"Your stallion protects you. That is good."

Marianne nodded and moved to mount Diablo. The man inched his dun closer, and the stallion screamed his protest. Though Marianne understood his Spanish, during Juan's lessons he'd made her promise to not tell anyone as it could put them both in danger.

"Shall I not see your face, señorita?" His voice rang like a soft breeze in midsummer, but Mama had warned her of falling prey to a man's charm. Marianne climbed onto the saddle. No man would assault her with Diablo as her guardian.

Holding back the reins, she stole a curious look at the man. He pushed his sombrero back from his head, revealing raven-black hair and a honey-colored face so handsome that it took her breath away. His genteel features best befit the Spanish noblemen who often visited her home. Deep, penetrating brown eyes, veiled in thick black lashes, stared back at her. And a slight cleft in his chin gave him a Spanish appeal. This was not a Mexican, a mestizo, a mixture of the Spanish and Indian. Or was he?

The stranger peered back, but not a line on his face revealed any emotion. "You have pale skin. Who are you? Tell me your name."

Marianne swallowed hard. The words she'd heard that described La Flor's rebel leader, Armando Garcia, fit this man. Surely he could not be her father's enemy? Mama had often said sin took the disguise of beauty. Paralyzed with the thought of danger, she couldn't force her feet to sink into Diablo's sides.

The man drew near, and Diablo lifted his front legs. The action propelled Marianne to her senses, and she urged her stallion into a full gallop and raced toward the hacienda.

She did not attempt to pull him back but sunk her heels into his flanks until the two were one with the wind. Who was the man who had momentarily captured her senses? The memory both frightened and thrilled her. The mixed emotions were foreign, and she didn't know whether to shove them aside or allow them to linger.

By the time Marianne and Diablo returned home in the noonday sun, Diablo heaved from the vigorous pace, and sweat glistened from his white coat. She'd thought of nothing else but the handsome stranger by the stream. Was she a fool? He could have meant her harm.

While she walked Diablo to cool him down, one of the servant boys hurried across the stable yard. "Hard run, señorita?"

"Diablo sensed something amiss. He wasted no time in getting us back here."

"Señora Phillips, she call for you." The young boy kept his distance from Diablo.

Instantly, concern for her mother's delicate condition alarmed her. "Is she ill?"

"I think not." His dark eyes peered up at her. "But I think you might want to hurry."

"Yes, of course." She quickly led Diablo to the stables and his stall. As soon as she spoke to her mother, she'd return to tend to her stallion.

Marianne's feet barely touched the stone entryway, shaded with huge palms, that led to the carved wooden doors of the adobe home. Pushing it open, she rushed past the reception room and its huge logged ceiling, down a hallway, and back to her mother's bedroom.

Marianne stopped for an instant outside the bedroom door and prepared for the worst.

Mama lay asleep against propped pillows. Her eyelids fluttered over cavernous pits that had once been a clear, azure blue, but now were dull and lifeless with the prolonged effects of her illness.

"There you are." Mama opened her eyes and gave a faint smile. "I don't have to guess where you've been, for the telltale scent of horse is wrapped around you. Is this my daughter dressed like a servant girl?"

Marianne glanced down at the blue skirt and white blouse. Her cheeks flushed warm.

"For a moment, I thought one of Carmita's daughters graced my room." She beckoned Marianne to come closer. "I envy your free spirit. I wish it could last forever."

"Yes, Mama, I do too. When you are better, we will ride together again." She tilted her head. "I might even use a side saddle."

"You are my best medicine. We must talk of many things, Marianne. Your father will be gone for a few days, and he has asked me to prepare you."

"Prepare me for what?" Immediately her thoughts flew to La Flor, but her mother would not have knowledge of such things. Papa kept his affairs to himself and Clay.

Her mother brushed back a lock of light brown hair. Not a single strand of silver wove through her tresses, and her features still bore the smoothness of youth. If only the spirit of good health surrounded her again. "He plans to visit Don Lorenzo Sanchez . . . to arrange your marriage."

Chapter 2

A chill raced up Marianne's arms. "When is the marriage to take place?"

"September." Tears pooled Mama's eyes. "I wish I had better news, my dear. I could not persuade your father to postpone it until next year."

Marianne inhaled sharply and fought the urge to weep. She refused to upset her mother. Still, her lips quivered as she lifted her chin. "I do not want to marry him. The don is older than Papa."

"He can give you fine clothes—more things than you possess here. And he has kindly ways."

"But I have no feelings for him." Marianne kneeled at her mother's bed. "How can I marry a man who is more like a father? Shall I be his daughter?"

"Your plight could be much worse." When Marianne failed to respond, Mama moistened her pale lips. "Clay has also asked for your hand."

Marianne shuddered. She knew exactly what her mother implied. She stood and walked to the window. Some called Clay striking with his deep violet eyes and chestnut-colored hair, but Marianne loathed him. The way he looked at her made her feel as though she hadn't bathed. Her hand in marriage might be what Clay wanted for killing Armando Garcia.

"Yes, Mama. Marriage to Clay Wharton would be a severe life."

"Perhaps in time, you'll learn to love the don. Come here, dear." Marianne obeyed, and Mama touched her soft hand to her daughter's cheek.

"Did you not dream of love?" Marianne knew her words were laced with desperation, but she could not stop herself.

Mama's dull eyes appeared distant. "Ah, yes. I loved your papa from the moment I first saw him, and I still do today."

"Papa?" *Was Mama delirious?*

She continued to stroke Marianne's cheek. "He courted me with the utmost tenderness, a perfect gentleman in every respect. I loved him with all my heart."

"What happened? I mean now . . ."

Her mother sighed. "My dear, your papa does have his tender side. Over the years, his ways have become peculiar at times, and I know you don't understand him. But everything he does is for you and me."

"And you still care for him?" Marianne found it difficult to imagine her father anything but demanding and harsh.

"My love for your papa has never faded. And each time I look at you and see his smoky-blue eyes and thick, honey-colored hair, I realize how blessed I am."

For several moments, Marianne studied her mother's face, unable to comprehend how she could love a man who openly voiced his disdain for her. He ignored Mama unless he had guests. "If you can endure Papa, then I can make the best of a marriage to Don Lorenzo Sanchez."

The stranger's face from earlier today flashed across her mind, but she pushed it away. The brief encounter could have been her demise. She had been foolish to tarry for so long.

Mama's face brightened. "How noble of you to not rebel against your papa. God will reward you."

"Yes, Mama. God will keep me in the shelter of His wings."

"Do not give up on your papa."

Again Marianne fought the urge to weep, but God loved all and she could do no less. "I won't. I promise."

Desiring a change in conversation, she glanced out the window overlooking the garden in its spring splendor. "Let's spend the afternoon together, and Carmita can prepare us a fine meal. We can eat with the smell of flowers and the singing of birds."

"Splendid, and we will talk no more about your marriage until the morrow. Today is for you and me."

Marianne gently grasped the hand caressing her cheek. "Rest for now. I must tend to a few things and bathe. Later I can read to you in the garden. The day is lovely, Mama."

"I will look forward to our time together." Her mother eased back onto her pillow. Her eyes closed, and Marianne stayed by her side until the sound of even breathing met her ears.

Oh, Heavenly Father, I do not want this marriage, and I'm sorely afraid that Don Sanchez is like Papa.

Once Diablo was groomed and Marianne had bathed and washed her hair, she again considered marriage to the cattle baron, a wealthy Spaniard who had inherited land and gold through his family. The man did have an amiable disposition. Surely her Heavenly Father knew best.

A short while later Marianne found Carmita grinding parboiled corn kernels to make flour. The dark-haired woman had beef simmering with onions, and in a separate pot she boiled seeded red peppers and wild herbs to make a thick sauce. All would be rolled into a warm tortilla and topped with more sauce.

Sensing hunger pangs, Marianne picked up a tortilla left from breakfast. Carmita glanced up from her work. Her earth-brown eyes twinkled. "You left the casa early this morning before breakfast, señorita," she said in English.

"I spent a glorious morning riding Diablo."

"And you are hungry?"

"Extremely, but this tortilla will do until later. Mama and I are spending the afternoon in the garden."

Carmita handed her another tortilla. "I see hunger on your face." She smiled and went back to grinding corn kernels and humming a familiar tune.

Marianne swallowed a lump in her throat and wondered how she could ever get along without Carmita and her husband Juan, whom she fondly called *tia* and *tio*, aunt and uncle. She loved them and their children. Spending hours with their family showed Marianne that a true family, such as what God wanted, was possible. Wealth had little to do with happiness; love could not be measured in gold, but in open hearts.

The afternoon with Mama sped by, and a hint of color returned to her mother's cheeks. Marianne read aloud from William Shakespeare. Thoughts of marriage to the don settled uneasily in her heart and mind as she read from the great love story *Romeo and Juliet.*

The sun slowly traversed across the horizon, and Marianne glanced up from her book. "Are you sure you feel well enough to eat?" She had asked Carmita to forgo the normal afternoon meal for a later one in hopes Mama would have an appetite.

"I am weary." Her mother closed her eyes and smiled. "But I do want to spend this time with you. Let's enjoy the garden a while longer. Come September, these days will be a fond memory for me."

"For me, too." Marianne allowed Shakespeare to fold in her lap, and she took her mother's frail hand. "Mama, please get better. I need you."

"I will try, for your sake. And I think your papa needs me too."

Armando Garcia allowed his dun gelding to pick its way along the water's edge. Beneath the cool canopy of overhanging cypress trees, he drank in the tranquility which often escaped him. He allowed his mind to wander beyond the needs and responsibilities of his people to the señorita who rode the white stallion. At first he'd thought she was a dream, a beautiful angel sent upon a magnificent beast to give him a revelation about the problems of La Flor. Never had he encountered such a stallion. Never had he seen an animal with such fierce devotion.

A smile tugged at the corners of his mouth. The señorita appeared frightened, but it was he who fell captive in her presence. He'd caught a glimpse of her before she detected him and lowered her sombrero. Her beauty gripped him. She stood a little taller than most women and graceful in her walk. He could not recall ever seeing a woman with light brown hair spun with tendrils of gold. The color was like that of a young doe poised in a ray of sunshine. He wanted to study her face, to ask where she lived, but she had touched the sides of the stallion and raced away.

He turned his gelding toward La Flor. The mere gesture reminded him of his people's sad plight. How could he keep the gringo Weston Phillips from their land? Armando's refusal to leave the valley made him a rebel in the eyes of the two Americans but a saint in the eyes of the poor. He detested his people's homage, but his failure to acknowledge their praise only encouraged them to designate him as their fearless leader.

The Spanish control of Tejas was nothing more than a way to ward off the United States from extending its borders. So why had the Spaniards allowed Weston Phillips to settle so close to the San Antonio missions?

Armando recalled the many sick children, lonely widows, elderly, and hopeless men who needed help to survive. He'd rallied the villagers together and initiated a genuine caring for all its people. Now, no one went hungry or suffered alone.

The villagers had an opportunity to secure a meager living in the beautiful valley of La Flor. From Phillips's herds, they had bred cattle and had begun breeding their own stock. They had captured wild mustangs, broken them, and built their own herd. Sheep had provided wool for the cold months, and chickens had supplied eggs. The rich earth fed by underground streams produced fertile gardens and abundant pastures. Here his people had an opportunity to thrive.

But guilt was always hovering over Armando. He knew it was wrong to steal from the Phillips Hacienda, but at the time, his people were hungry. To him, it was more important to give his people an opportunity to raise their own cattle and become self-sufficient. Many times he'd considered driving the animals he'd stolen back into the Phillips's herds. He desired to owe no man.

And now the lord of the Phillips Hacienda laid claim to their valley. Weston Phillips would kill for the fertile land; earlier today he had stated so. Why should Armando be surprised? The wealthy had always oppressed the poor. That was life.

"Get out of La Flor unless you want a blood bath," Phillips had said in Spanish. "Take your people to the missions."

Phillips had leaned on his saddle and spit at Armando's feet, daring him to protest. Anger had seized him, but women and children were about, and he did not want the gringos to open fire. Besides, Armando needed time to find a solution to his people's problem without the shedding of innocent blood.

"This is your last warning, Garcia. I've tolerated you for as long as I intend," Phillips had said before leaving La Flor.

Armando had spent the morning and afternoon thinking about how the villagers could oppose Phillips's intentions and not get themselves killed in the process. Although Armando didn't have a strong plan, he still needed to assure the villagers that their valley was secure. Sharing the pastures might temporarily solve the dilemma, but how long before Phillips decided he needed all of their land? Presenting the situation to the governor in San Antonio de Bejar held little merit. The high-ranking officials always took the side of the landowners. In their eyes, mestizos were an annoyance, something to deal with like pesky flies. As long as they worked hard and did not interfere with the Spanish aristocracy, the poor mestizos were tolerated.

Even so, Armando had vowed on his mother's grave that he would not relinquish La Flor. He'd gladly give his life, but he was afraid that, with Phillips's irrational behavior and demands, more lives than his might be sacrificed.

Chapter 3

Marianne sorted through an ornate, walnut-stained chest containing her dresses and searched for a particular one that would please her mother for tonight's dinner. She recalled Mama telling of ladies in the States who changed gowns according to the time of day and scheduled activities. What nonsense. Marianne felt perfectly content in wearing the cotton skirts and blouses of the servants.

An unpleasant thought occurred to her, and she frowned. Would the don expect her to dress lavishly when they married? And would Papa allow her to take Diablo with her? Perhaps as part of her dowry?

With a sigh, she pulled a pale green gown from among her other frocks. Fitted high at the waist, the dress gathered and flowed to the floor with lace trim around the neckline, cuffs, and hem. Carmita's daughter Josefa, a dark-eyed beauty of fourteen, helped Marianne slip into the garment.

"Will you arrange my hair?" Marianne asked. "Mama enjoys seeing it pinned up, and I lack patience to do it myself."

"I will make you more beautiful than you already are."

"I love you, Josefa. If I had ever enjoyed the company of a sister, she would have been just like you."

Moments later, they viewed the effect in a handheld silver mirror. Marianne's hair looked decisively Spanish, complete with beaded combs.

"*Gracias*, Josefa." She laughed. "Now, if I could find a lace mantilla." Suddenly remembering her upcoming marriage, Marianne turned to her. "Do you believe a father should always arrange a marriage or should a woman marry for love?"

Josefa's huge eyes danced. "Señorita Marianne, a woman must always fall in love before she marries. I think it's the best way."

"I did hope for love, but now I have no choice but to marry the man Papa has selected."

"I'm sorry," Josefa said. "Maybe you will learn to care for him. I'll light a candle and say a prayer."

What more could Marianne ask of one she loved so dearly?

Down the long hallway to the dining room, a dozen candles flickered in the iron chandelier above a pine table. The Phillips's adobe home stood as tribute to the Spanish. Every room held carved furnishings decorated with bright colors of mineral paint. Mama had originally added touches of Virginia, her girlhood home, but Papa had them removed. He claimed Tejas was their home, and they would honor the Spanish, who allowed them to live in their country, and the Phillips Hacienda to prosper.

Although Papa had sworn allegiance to the Roman Catholic Church in order to purchase his land, he and his family did not attend any of the five missions set along the San Antonio River. The priests were too busy tending to their duties to enforce the religious laws. This concession allowed Mama and Marianne to privately worship according to Protestant beliefs.

Upon the table sat tortillas, beef stew, and vegetables for many more than the two women, who dined alone. Seated across from each other in leather bound chairs, they talked freely, without Papa there to silence them.

"Mama, you look lovely tonight," Marianne said. "The deep purple gown is fitting for a queen." She felt reluctant to comment on her mother's health.

"Thank you. You are my medicine. You have always been my joy, just as Jesus is my strength." Mama's face saddened. "When your baby brother was born dead, after we had lost so many children before him, I wanted to crawl into the grave too. But I cannot live in the past another day. I am determined to be strong again."

Marianne smiled. She had prayed earnestly for her mother's health, but until recently, there had been little improvement. Perhaps God had not forgotten Mama after all.

She glanced at Mama's untouched plate. "Aren't you hungry?"

Her mother folded her thin hands primly in her lap. "I am extremely tired, but I want to spend every minute with you."

"Mama, it's important that you eat something."

"For you, I will have a little—"

Angry voices resounded from the rear of the house. Startled, Marianne strained to hear every Spanish word while she studied Mama's blanched face.

An unfamiliar male voice barked for Carmita and Josefa to step aside. The two Mexican women screamed, sending Marianne to her feet. Pottery crashed onto the tile floor, and she realized the intruders must have turned over the massive cupboard, the *trastero*, that held their finest dishes.

With Papa and several of his men away, only the women servants presided in the house, and Marianne knew she could not get to Papa's weapons fast enough. Before she could gather her thoughts, four men burst into the room waving pistols and muskets while pushing Carmita and Josefa ahead of them. Dressed in simple clothing and tattered sombreros, the men looked more like farmers than evil men. But the weapons and the grim looks upon their faces gave them away as criminals.

"*Por favor,* leave," Carmita said in Spanish, "Señor Phillips will return soon."

A man laughed. "I know he's been gone from the hacienda since early morning."

Terror gripped Marianne, but at the sight of how shaken Carmita and Mama looked, she gathered her courage.

"What do they want, Carmita?" She rushed around the table to her mother's side and bent to embrace her shoulders. Marianne's mind spun at the gravity of their situation, and her gaze swept across the table. Where once the tantalizing aroma of food rose pleasantly, now she smelled desperate men.

Please, Carmita, do not let these men know I understand them, for I fear it will not go well for any of us.

Again Carmita asked the men what they wanted.

"To take Señora Phillips with us," the same man said. The apparent leader, he wore a silver dagger at his waist in addition to carrying a fine pistol. No doubt stolen.

"Why?" Carmita asked. "What has the señora done?"

"The woman is nothing. We need her so Señor Phillips will know we refuse to leave La Flor. It is our valley and not his for the taking." His dark eyes flared.

"Kidnapping the señora will not help the people in the valley." Carmita reached for Josefa and pulled the young woman into her arms. "It would only make the situation worse."

Marianne turned to Carmita. "Please, tell us what he said." *Papa's greed has caused this. God help us!*

After Carmita's translation, Marianne stood from embracing her mother's shoulders. She stiffened and curled her fingers into her palms. She faced the leader, a harsh-featured man who looked to be in his twenties. "Tell him my mother is ill. She cannot go anywhere."

Carmita translated the message, but the man issued a sardonic laugh.

"Tell him Señora Phillips could die without proper attention," Marianne said. "Then they all would face my father for murder." She hoped none of them could hear her fluttering heart or see the lack of courage in her eyes.

The pleading for her mother proved useless, and nothing Carmita said dissuaded them. "Let me go in her place," Marianne finally said. "Tell them I am Señor Phillips's daughter."

"No, you can't." Mama grasped Marianne's hand.

"There's no other way, Mama," Marianne said. "Ask them, Carmita. I beg of you."

Against Mama's protests, Carmita translated the request. Marianne stood between her mother and the men. They would not take Mama without a fight. She glanced down at the knife resting beside Mama's plate. Would God forgive her if she purposely plunged it into the leader's heart? If only she could speak directly to him, reason with him, but that was foolish and she dared not risk angering the man. The other men waited stoically with their weapons aimed at the women.

"We'll take the daughter," the leader said a moment later, and Carmita relayed his words. "Tell Señor Phillips that Armando Garcia and his followers hold his daughter in exchange for La Flor. He will kill the girl in five days, unless he rides to our valley unarmed and alone to talk. Any sign of his men will result in the señorita's death."

Carmita gasped. "You act in Armando's behalf? He would never attempt such treachery."

Marianne pretended ignorance until Carmita could translate the ultimatum. Even then she refused to show any signs of fear, but her emotions swelled.

The moment two of the men clutched Marianne's arms, Mama's hysteria echoed through the house. Marianne glared at the leader, wanting to shout at him for his absurd scheme. For a moment she considered spitting into his arrogant face.

"Mama, I will be fine until Papa returns and gives these men what they want." Papa would never give in to their wishes. The man should simply end her life now, but caution curbed her tongue. Mama didn't need to endure the pain of witnessing her daughter's murder.

"Tell them to release me," she instructed Carmita. "I go willingly."

When Carmita informed the leader, he seized Marianne's upper arm. He squeezed it sharply until she bit into her lip to keep from crying out. The pain aroused a sense of panic for what surely lay ahead.

He pulled her toward the kitchen. "We need horses." He nodded to two men standing nearby. "Search inside for weapons and meet us at the stables."

Juan! He'd surely put up a fight, even with a crippled leg. *Please, Tio, don't be a hero. Let these men have anything they want.*

In the blackness of night, save for two torches held by the vicious men, she saw several others awaiting their leader. Juan held onto Diablo's bridle.

"What is this, Felipe? I thought you wanted horses, and now you have the señorita. Armando will not approve of this." Her *tio's* anger echoed across the night.

"Be quiet, old man, or you will taste my wrath. I see you have my stallion."

Marianne hoped her stallion stomped Felipe to the ground. Diablo would never allow her captors to seize him.

"No one can ride the stallion," Juan said. "Not even Señor Phillips can tame him."

"Juan," she said in English. "Tell him the horse is mine."

Juan wiped his brow. "No one can touch the horse, Felipe, but the señorita. Try if you must. Your men have gotten nowhere."

From the torch, she saw Felipe's seething glare. Haughtiness and contempt ruled his countenance.

Feeling her world collapsing about her, Marianne turned to Juan. "If he must have Diablo, then allow me to ride him." If she had learned anything from observing Papa, it was his fearlessness.

Juan translated, but Felipe grabbed the reins. The stallion lifted his front feet with more fury than she'd ever seen. Felipe held tightly, but Diablo's twisting and prancing broke free the leather straps. A moment later the proud animal stood at Marianne's side.

"For now, she can ride him," Felipe said. "But the stallion is mine. Armando will reward me with the horse for bringing him the señorita."

With Juan's final translation, she mounted Diablo, and his powerful muscles relaxed. A word from the leader, and the others found their horses. She watched Felipe mount a swaybacked mare. The horse suited him.

Marianne took one last look at Juan. She longed to see his familiar smile. "I love you, *Tio*. If I do not see you again, take care of Mama. Tell her I love her."

No more words passed between them, for Felipe ordered his men to leave the hacienda at once.

Through a blanket of deep indigo, the band of nearly a half dozen men pushed westward on to the rocky hills and hiding places known only to the followers of Armando Garcia. The band skirted hills and twisted around low places until Marianne knew for certain she'd lost her way. Even if she could break free, she'd be lost in the black maze.

Diablo easily kept pace with the abductors' horses while Marianne did nothing to hinder her stallion's stride. His speed and agility against the other horses made her wonder if she could escape. But where could she go that wouldn't put Mama in danger?

The sorrow etched into her mother's face with their farewell held her more captive than the Mexican rebels. Mama, her treasure, her friend. She knew her mother's state of mind. With Papa's impassiveness and Marianne no longer there to encourage and love her, she worried about her mother's will to stay alive.

She turned her attention to Armando Garcia, her father's enemy and now hers. She wondered how much more cruel he could be than Felipe. Confusion seared Marianne's mind. Her friends had spoken highly of the Mexican leader and his love for his people, but any man who ordered the kidnapping of an innocent woman deserved a hangman's noose. Until her abduction, Marianne had sided with their leader. The people of La Flor deserved their own homes in a fertile valley where they could provide a good living for their families. She had seen a few of the children and their shy mothers when they came to visit Juan and Carmita. Mama had given them leather for shoes and clothes when Papa was away from home.

At last Felipe slowed the men, and they rode single file through a narrow opening carved between two hills of steep rock. Up ahead she saw a glimmer of light. This was clearly not La Flor but rather a wayside place meant to keep her hidden.

"What is going on here?" A man emerged from the shadows. "Where did you go? I didn't give you permission to take these men and ride out."

"Armando." Felipe carried himself as though he'd just ridden in from a victorious battle. "I have done you a favor."

Marianne's gaze flew to the infamous Armando Garcia. Just as the voice sounded like the man she'd encountered earlier today, the face matched the mysterious stranger. Revulsion for her earlier musings about him added to her confusion.

The man stepped to the side of Felipe's horse. "What have you done?" His very words commanded attention. He glanced up at Marianne. "And who is this?"

Felipe swung his leg over his horse and jumped down beside Armando. "I have Señor Phillips's daughter so we can bargain for our valley. I left instructions with Señora Phillips that unless our demands are met, you would kill their daughter."

"You kidnapped his daughter? That makes us look like barbarians." Armando's words were low, meant only for Felipe. But Marianne heard and understood every word.

Felipe whirled around and pulled her from Diablo. His hands dug into her waist, but she refused to cry out. Diablo snorted and reared. Two other men tried to seize the stallion, but the horse kicked its front legs, sending them sprawling to the ground. This time she did not offer to settle her horse. Let them taste Diablo's wrath.

She heard the sound of a whip and struggled to free herself from Felipe's hold. "No!" she cried in English. "Diablo, let them take you." Her stallion calmed enough for the two men to lead him away.

"Let her go," Armando said. "I fear you have made a terrible mistake this night." He strode toward the fire and snatched up a narrow log as a torch.

Felipe released her, and she stood defiantly before the famed outlaw leader. If he hadn't sent Felipe to raid the hacienda, he should apologize and send her home.

"Take a look at the señorita." Felipe laughed. "She is beautiful and not afraid."

The torch blinded her, and she prayed he did not recognize her from earlier in the day. Armando released a labored breath. "Felipe, we must speak in private. Now."

"I have done a good thing. This is the right way, amigo." Felipe clenched his fist. "We have the power now to get whatever we want from Señor Phillips."

"You have acted lower than our enemies." Armando said. "This will cause the death of our people and bring down the Spanish and the Americans on us. Are you sure this is not about what Wharton did to your sister?" He turned to a man behind him, one Marianne had not seen before. "Emilio, take the señorita to my hut. See that she is not harmed. Put her stallion with the other horses."

Marianne breathed hope. Perhaps she'd be taken home before the night was over. She glanced about but failed to see any women, and her stomach churned. She dared not think of home until she felt her mother's arms around her. These men . . . Who knew what they were capable of? She'd fight to her death before she'd allow them to touch her. She could feign bravery, but they held the weapons, and she was their prisoner.

Emilio took her arm and urged her along. As they passed the fire, smelling of mesquite, she saw the man's features. Anger crested the face of a typical farmer, young, darkened by race and sun. Nothing distinguishable. He could have been any of so many Mexican men. Was he angry because of her father or because Felipe had gone against Armando?

Emilio led her to an obscure lean-to where he flung open the door and ushered her inside.

"Much trouble tonight," he said in his native tongue.

Oh, how she wished she knew what he meant. Marianne stumbled and fell as the door closed.

Sitting on the damp earthen floor, she attempted to focus her eyes on the surroundings, but utter blackness met her. Massaging her arms, she wondered what manner of insects and animals inhabited her cell. The weariness of the ride settled over her. It must be after midnight, and although she craved sleep, she dreaded the unknown.

Drawing her knees to her chest, she sought to pray. Every noise alarmed her, as though at any moment Armando would return with evil intent. At least she understood her abductor's words. Juan's patient instruction had given her insight to what was happening around her.

After what could have been hours or minutes later, for she dozed between her prayers, the door squeaked open and Armando strode in. He closed the door and rested a torch in a corner. At last Marianne could see about her. The makeshift shelter was indeed small, a single room large enough for only a few people.

"Are you resting well?" he asked in Spanish.

She ignored him for fear he might realize she understood his words.

"Let me look at you." He stepped forward and cupped her chin. "I recognized your stallion, señorita. Twice we have met today, although these circumstances are not as pleasant as the first time."

With his vile hands upon her, Marianne's agitation erupted. She swung at him, but he caught her wrist, clutching it until her eyes filled with tears.

"Pretty, but full of rage. Not that I blame you. Felipe may have caused the death of us all." He grabbed her other wrist and forced both arms behind her back. Quickly, he wrapped a rope around them, as easily as a vaquero bound a calf. "I don't like doing this, but I don't want my throat cut while I sleep."

All thoughts of his releasing her vanished. She struggled against the bindings. "Let me go," she cried in English.

Armando smoothed a long, black sideburn on the left side of his face. "I don't understand you, señorita, but I'm sure you are not pleased. For now, you'll have to be tied. I cannot offer you a grand room, but a dirt floor may tame your spirit. You and the stallion are a matched pair."

Removing his sombrero and bandanna, Armando waved the cloth in front of her face. "If you choose to annoy me, I'll gag you."

She did not need Spanish to comprehend what he meant, and the idea of a sweat-soaked bandanna across her mouth tugged at her stomach as much as the idea of his filthy hands upon her.

Marianne turned her attention to the door. Already her arms ached from the tightness of the knotted rope.

How foolish she'd been earlier today when his handsome face invaded her thoughts. Armando Garcia would not think twice about killing her when Papa refused the rebel's demands.

Armando extinguished the torch, and she heard the rustling of his straw pallet. Moments later, his even breathing caused her to believe he had fallen asleep. Her wrists were bound too tightly to lie comfortably, and her attempts to find a less painful position failed. She wanted to give in to tears, but she fought them with a vengeance.

"I'm truly sorry," Armando said. "This is for my people. I will do anything for them, but I'd never considered murder, and neither do I relish the idea now."

Her heart seemed to leap from her chest.

He rose from his bed. She couldn't stop her body from trembling. To her amazement, he loosened the ropes, then laid his blanket over her. "I've made a terrible mistake by allowing Felipe to manipulate me," he said. "But until I find a way to make him see his foolishness, I will guard you myself."

Chapter 4

Armando lay awake on his pallet while his mind spun with the evening's events. In the past, he'd been bold in openly defying the gringo's threats for his people to abandon La Flor. But kidnapping the gringo's daughter?

Tonight he'd stepped into dangerous territory by not returning the señorita to her home. This maneuver would force his enemy to choose between his lust for land and his own flesh. For Armando, a choice would not be necessary; for the gringo, he wondered. Reports came to him of Weston Phillips's ill treatment of his family and how the señora and señorita gave generously to the people of La Flor when the man wasn't around.

Armando had thought about the señorita all day. Never had he suspected her to be Señor Phillips's daughter. Now she lay within a few feet of him, frightened and alone. This was not how he envisioned a second meeting with her.

The longer he lay on his pallet and begged for sleep, the more his thoughts whirled in his head. How did one young woman tame such a wild horse? Had she bewitched the stallion? And the name Diablo—devil. The sound of her voice soothed the animal's wild spirit—sweet, gentle, almost musical, like the lull of a guitar on a star-studded night. Armando confessed the fair-skinned maiden tugged at his senses, and he did not like her effect at all.

What father would not trade his ambitions for a gem such as this? A part of him wanted to know her name, but he saw a weakness in such intimacy. She looked too much like her father not to have his evil heart. Armando must keep his distance and use sound logic in dealing with her.

The dispute with Señor Phillips involved a way of life. The matter with Felipe involved honor. If Armando returned the señorita, he looked like a coward, not earnestly seeking the betterment of his people. If he kept her in captivity and waited for Phillips to render a decision, he risked the gringo summoning the soldiers at San Antonio de Bejar to settle an uprising. No matter the outcome, the people of La Flor faced losing their valley and their lives.

Apprehension seized Armando's thoughts. This afternoon, when he attempted to gather the men together, he had learned Felipe had disappeared with five other men who believed violence was the best way to handle Phillips's threats. No one admitted knowing where the men had gone.

Armando forced himself to consider Felipe. No longer could Armando discount him as a mere irritation. Felipe possessed an ill temper along with cleverness and cunning. He befriended those who sought a blood price for the unfairness mandated by those in authority, and he persuaded them to his way of thinking. Armando realized Felipe craved power, but his shortsighted tactics would get them all killed.

Marianne heard Armando stirring and realized morning had arrived at last. Such a long, dreadful night. It had trickled by endlessly, a black prison. Sometime during those hours, she'd grasped the meaning of life without God. Without Him, every hour would be like the night. Once, a furry creature crawled across her foot, and she bit her tongue to keep from crying out. Her entire body hurt as though she had been beaten and left to die. She'd attempted to focus her mind on other things, even marriage to the don. Perhaps being treated as a beloved daughter, a rarity for her, meant a more pleasant life. Oddly, she'd never considered marriage as a substitute for a father's affections. At this moment, she even craved the face of her father. Would he come?

Marianne wet her lips. She tasted dirt and desired privacy. How could she convey her needs to Armando?

Choking back a sob, she clung to the only hope left in her miserable state—that of God. Mama had said that God reached out to her when she was truly broken. And Marianne definitely felt broken and alone.

Armando rose from his pallet and stepped outside, leaving the door open for a cascade of light to flow into the small hut. Morning. A new day. By now her mother would have sent someone after Papa, if he came at all.

Within moments, her captor returned. He peered down at her, emotionless, reminding her of the dispassionate Mexicans who toiled at the missions.

"We have a new day." He untied the loose ropes binding her. The release sent tiny needle pricks from her arms to her shoulders. She was more determined than ever to mask any uncomfortable feelings. Massaging her throbbing wrists, she avoided his gaze.

He helped her to her feet and nodded toward the door. Together, they stepped into the light of dawn. She blinked until her eyes grew accustomed to the light, and she could view the campsite, an array of brush and scattered timber against the rocky hillside. A strong wind could blow it away like chaff, and it reminded her of the wicked people in Psalm 1.

Armando led her beyond the site to a remote area several feet away. He pointed to a heavy growth of brush and rock jutting from the cliff.

"Do not try to run away, señorita," he said. "I know this land far better than you."

For the second time, Marianne realized she did not need to understand his language to conceive what he meant. His tone had spoken fathoms. She slipped behind the heavy undergrowth while humiliation flushed hot in her cheeks.

She vowed to be grateful for all God's blessings. He was beside her on this perilous journey. He held her hand and guided her with His presence. She had prayed most earnestly for deliverance, but this might not be in God's plan.

A few moments later she emerged from the brush.

"I'm sure your father loves you very much," Armando said, as if she understood. "You have more courage than any woman I have ever known."

I am not brave at all. I am terribly frightened. I must cling to God and hope He remembers me in my time of need.

Back in the hut, Armando left her alone. He closed the door behind him and imprisoned her in the dark. She wanted a glimmer of sunlight. Was this how she must spend the next five days while they waited for Papa's answer?

He returned shortly carrying a small plate of stew, a tortilla, and a cup of water. Armando watched her eat with a curious frown upon his face. Avoiding his scrutiny, she concentrated on the food, a bit watery with few vegetables, but filling. Her next meal might be a long time from now.

"We leave for La Flor in an hour," he said. "My lovely *prisionera*, I hope the people of La Flor see that nothing will be gained by Felipe's foolishness. Perhaps we shall see how your father reacts to our demands."

Marianne watched Diablo pace the perimeters of the stone-walled corral in search of an escape. The stallion caught sight of his mistress and stopped abruptly, his stance proud and erect. His ears lay back flat, and he tossed his head, snorting his disapproval. She held her breath as the stallion lifted his forefeet and slashed the air. Diablo sensed her danger and could scale the gate if provoked. Envy nudged at her. *Oh, to be free from these horrid rebels.* Marianne grieved with Diablo's distress. She knew the same frustration as her beloved horse. She stepped forward, but Armando clutched her arm.

"Wait to see if my men can calm him," he said in Spanish.

Enraged with his hands upon her and exhausted from the night's ordeal, Marianne attempted to pull herself from her abductor's grasp. How she loathed this man. And these poor people looked to him for leadership? One of the decorated combs that Josefa had skillfully placed the evening before slipped to the ground, sending a lock of hair across her forehead.

"I have done nothing to warrant this treatment." She challenged him with an angry gaze. "And you are sadly mistaken if you think my father will give up his demands for La Flor in exchange for me. I matter nothing to him. Nothing." Immediately, caution sealed her lips, for the consequences of inciting Armando could be deadly. One of his men might speak English. Then Armando, Felipe, and the others would know that she understood their every word.

Marianne took a ragged breath and swallowed the rash words threatening to erupt. She ceased to struggle against him and forced herself to relax. With her free hand, she lifted the remaining combs from her hair and released her thick tresses to fall about her shoulders. Her defiant glare shifted to the ground where a fat, black spider crawled across the tip of her slipper. *Captured in a tangled web of power.*

Marianne knew that impetuous actions could get her killed, and logic demanded that she dispel her indignation. She raised her head to meet Armando's dark scrutiny, but found amusement lingering in his eyes. Oh, how the frustration battling inside her longed to be unleashed.

Instead, Marianne focused her attention on the men retrieving their mounts. Armando's horse stood poised while a man whom she recognized from the evening before saddled the animal. But the men assigned to Diablo made no progress. She observed their futile efforts and basked in the satisfaction that her stallion refused to allow any man to approach him.

"Is no vaquero brave enough to bridle the señorita's white stallion?" Armando chuckled.

"You can ride him," Emilio said to Marianne, leading the dun to Armando. "We value our heads."

Armando threw back his head and laughed. "I agree. We will insist our captive prepare her own horse and ride the devil."

Marianne listened to the men banter and tease. Their leader obviously had a strong following; he knew when to become one of them and when to issue orders. Yet she questioned why Armando chose to live among these people when his light skin, an obvious marker of his Spanish blood, could have gained him a higher social status.

Once Diablo was ready, Armando's gaze captured hers. She attempted to appear unafraid, but her trembling body would not still. He beckoned her, but she refused to move. He lifted his chin and silently demanded her presence.

Obey the man.

But Lord, he is evil.

Obey him.

God did know best. Didn't He? Marianne patted the stallion's neck. "Stay here, Diablo." Every step in submission to her captor left an uneasy sensation in the pit of her stomach.

Armando removed his bandanna. "You cannot see where we are going, señorita." He whirled her around and tied the cloth firmly over her eyes.

The nearness of him, his hands upon her flesh, and his scent reminded her of the horrors that possibly lay ahead. She shivered. How could she trust God with these vile men surrounding her? And with her eyes covered, how could she ever find her way back home?

Throughout the morning, Marianne rode alongside Armando, but not at the maddening pace of the previous night with Felipe. She recognized the rebel leader's deep, resonant tone as he talked with his men. At one point, he sang a song she remembered hearing from Juan.

"My heart dwells with a pretty young maiden
A maiden fair who loves me not.
She cast her dark eyes upon another
And left me weeping—alone, and lost."

Marianne thought it was a sad song, especially the way Armando sang it. She decided he must feel about La Flor the way the song depicted lost love. For certain, he knew not the meaning of compassion, or he would have returned her to Mama's arms the preceding night.

Grasping Diablo's mane and reins, she tried to ignore the thought of toppling over her stallion's head at any unexpected drop along the trail.

How desperate Mama must be. But Carmita loved Mama, too. Her *tia* helped Marianne the night Mama labored with the baby and comforted her when she cried in the loss and wanted to die with him. Papa was gone that night, too. Certainly, God granted provision for one faithful woman who knew not the destiny of her only daughter.

I am always with My children.

Once again, God had spoken to her, or had she gone mad?

I am here with you.

Marianne startled. The whisper had draped a protective cocoon around her heart.

Lord, thank You for Your holy presence. Hope inched across her heart. A portion of Psalm 23 came to mind. *Yea, though I walk through the valley of the shadow of death, I will fear no evil; for Thou art with me.* Marianne took a deep breath. With God, she could endure anything.

I have always been here for you.

How she treasured the soft whisper. Gentle as the spring rain and soft as a flower petal. Her eyes moistened, and she quickly blinked back tears. The Lord of the heavens now surrounded her with His love more completely than her mother's arms.

Oh, God, I do love You, and I do ask Your forgiveness for all those times I have not been faithful, yes, even stubborn and rebellious. Calm Mama's heart as You have calmed mine.

Marianne heard not another sound except the beating of her heart, the men conversing, and the rhythmic gait of the horses. No matter what the future held, she was not alone.

Chapter 5

Armando halted his gelding to view the valley of La Flor breaking forth in green and bright colors. He loved this time of year, when the cold of winter was forgotten in anticipation of new life. He sensed a strange peacefulness. This seldom happened in his tumultuous life, and he took note for those times when the pressures of his leadership left him restless and unsure of his decisions.

La Flor stretched out in small thatched roof huts. Beyond the village, sheep, cattle, donkeys, and a few horses grazed. Lush fields ripe with newly planted corn, beans, squash, tomatoes, and peppers insured the people of plenty now and provisions for next winter. He longed for the laughing children, crowing roosters, and barking dogs. He envisioned women grinding corn for tortillas, and pretty señoritas seeking reasons to stroll near the center of town. Old men recounted days of youth, while the young dreamed of heroic deeds. He inhaled the aroma of cooking pots filled with simmering chili peppers, and he drank in the delicate perfume drifting from the flowers growing around the huts.

Here, the water had a different taste, as though it held a magic potion for happiness—sweet, like droplets of honey. Yes, La Flor was Armando's home. He had been born in the sleepy village, and he would most likely die defending it.

Armando reached over to untie Marianne's bandanna. She recoiled at his touch and lifted her chin in defiance. After blinking several times, she peered out at the enchanting scene.

"La Flor." A hint of recognition settled in her blue-gray eyes. But, when he drew closer, her stallion leaped in protest.

"Calm your steed." He gestured to show exactly what he intended, and she obeyed.

The mere gentle words from her lips eased the stallion's anger. Armando stood in awe of this young woman. He studied her delicate features and looked to find fault in her appearance. She was exquisite even with a smudge on her cheek and her tousled hair.

The elegant pale green gown displayed patches of dirt, and the hem had frayed about the edges.

Frustrated with his straying thoughts, he jerked his gelding down the winding path to the valley. There he would show his allegiance to the people and decide what to do about Felipe's rebellion and the fate of the señorita.

Soon the shouts of the villagers rang about them— excited, cheering voices beckoning the heroes to enter and make merry. As the band entered the town, Armando waved and feigned a broad smile. He should feel victorious, but instead he faced the truth. He had handed them more trouble.

Emilio rode up beside him. "They are happy to see us, my amigo."

Armando nodded grimly. "They believe I wanted this kidnapping. Felipe has succeeded in manipulating me for now."

All traces of joy vanished from the young man's round face. "I agree that Felipe has done a bad thing. But *Dios* is with you. I can feel it. The gringo will leave our valley to us now that we have his daughter."

Armando stared into his friend's face and noted Emilio's familiar seriousness. "I hope so, for if he refuses, I'm afraid I must kill her."

"No father would willingly have his daughter murdered," Emilio said. "When he returns to his hacienda, he'll gladly find other grazing pastures for his cattle, far from us."

"Of course." If only he shared the same confidence as Emilio. "But we cannot keep her here. Tonight we celebrate. Tomorrow we must ride back to the campsite, for it is too dangerous to remain among our people. Señora Phillips could send spies to La Flor while awaiting her husband's arrival."

"Who would dare spy on us?" Emilio's face reddened. "Surely not my brother Juan?"

Armando shook his head. "None would willingly, not Juan or the others working at the American's hacienda. Understand this, my friend, the gringo could threaten them with their families' lives, as we have done with his daughter . . . something I'm sure Felipe has not considered."

Emilio set his jaw. "*Si,* a vicious circle." After a moment's hesitation, he lifted his gaze to the cloudless sapphire heavens. "I pray we have *Dios* on our side."

Armando chose not to expound on his disbelief in God. After all, the affairs of men were governed by flesh and blood, not an invisible spirit sought after by frightened men and fragile-minded women. Unfortunately, his mother, as much as he loved her, believed *Dios* watched over them all. She died not knowing he had renounced the faith of the padres.

The two men rode silently on each side of Marianne, while laughter and cheer rippled behind and before them.

"Where are you going to keep the señorita while we are here?" Emilio asked.

Raising a brow, Armando glanced at his friend, but quickly discarded his distrust. He could trust Emilio with his life. "She will stay with me," he said a moment later. "And she'll not escape."

"Unless she gets to her devil stallion before we can stop her." Emilio pointed back at Diablo.

Armando chuckled. "I have no intentions of letting Diablo carry her away. She will not be out of my sight."

"Do you think your *tia* and *tio* will object to having her at their home?"

"Probably, but I must keep the señorita with me. No harm can come to her, unless I'm forced to do it myself."

"You speak wisely. I have heard some of the men talk."

"And?"

His friend sighed and glanced at Marianne. "She is beautiful."

Armando's thoughts had also been consumed with the beauty of the young woman and he wondered about the temptation of his men. Something he'd never do nor allow to be done.

"We are, above all, men of honor," Armando said. "If her father does not value his daughter, then circumstances may change. Listen to my words. None of you will have the blood guilt on your hands." *It is not what I want. There has to be a better way.*

Emilio observed the girl between them. "My brother thinks highly of her. The señorita and Señora Phillips are the only reasons Juan and Carmita have remained at the Phillips Hacienda and not joined us in La Flor."

"Why?" Armando wondered why this information had not been passed on to him before now.

"Señor Phillips is not a good husband or father." Emilio paused before continuing. "I have ignored that fact since the kidnapping. But both women have been good to our people, offering gifts of food and clothing in his absence."

"I know of the things the Phillips women have done—good things, which cause me to regret Felipe's impetuous actions."

"The señora has been ill for some time, and she asked my brother and his wife to look after the señorita as a *hija*, daughter, even to bring her here rather than to have her under the care of her father."

The news of Juan and Carmita caring for the señorita frustrated Armando. The more he learned about the situation at the Phillips Hacienda, the more he was determined to free the young woman. Armando had promised to keep the valley from Weston Phillips, but if the man did not care for his daughter, her death would mean nothing.

"When did you learn of this?"

"The last time my brother and I talked. I should have told you this last evening. I, too, wanted this to be our opportunity to save our valley."

Armando stared into the dark eyes of his friend. "What is your allegiance?"

"To you and you alone," Emilio replied without a trace of hesitation. "I told my brother I must follow you. You know what is best for our people."

Armando breathed an inward sigh of relief. Above all, he needed his men's loyalty—even death if necessary. *Gracias.* He glanced back at his captive. It made no difference if she were innocent of her father's greed. The mere color of her skin and her name sealed her fate. Still, regret stabbed at his heart. Like himself, she suffered because of her *padre.*

For a moment, Marianne wished she didn't understand Spanish. Ignorance of her dire situation could easily be interpreted as a blessing. The ways of men frightened her—Papa, Clay, Felipe, and Armando—except for Juan, dear *Tio* Juan. He endured Papa's ill moods and incessant demands because of Mama and her. She loved him and Carmita. Sometimes she wished Mexican blood flowed through her veins. Too many times she felt responsible for the difficult plight of the Mexicans because of the color of her skin.

As the voices from the people rose and fell, dread swept over her. She recalled Armando's words that he planned to keep her with him, and he obviously lived with his relatives. Marianne desperately wanted her captor to have a wife and children. With a family, he had more to lose by killing her. Just when she felt a glimpse of hope, she plunged deeper into the nightmare. She sighed and held her head high.

They rode to the center of the village. Armando nodded to passers-by, but he didn't join in the gaiety. He reined in his horse in front of a small hut and dismounted. An elderly woman stood on her toes to embrace him.

"La Flor's *héroe* has returned." The woman touched his cheek. "I prayed for your safe return."

"The most beautiful señora in all of the valley." Armando lifted her off her feet.

"Nonsense." She appeared to scold, but Marianne saw the smile playing on her lips.

Armando whispered something in the woman's ear. She scowled and wagged her finger at him.

"No. Take your captive somewhere else." Her wrinkled mouth pierced to a bird-like beak. "With the horses, perhaps?"

Armando laughed. "No, *Tia* Rosa. I have to keep her with me. It's only until mañana, then we move back into seclusion."

"That soon?" All traces of agitation slipped from her leathered face. "Your *Tio* Manuel and I looked forward to your coming home."

He took her veined hand into his. "Just a few more days. This time next week, we'll be rejoicing."

"I hope so. Violence frightens me. I'm an old woman, and I want my husband, my home, my handsome nephew, and no worries about Señor Phillips taking our valley."

"Patience," he said. "I will not let my people lose their homes or their lives."

Marianne studied the delicate carvings of Diablo's saddle as she listened to the conversation. The orange and yellow paint glistened in the sun. Oddly enough, she felt a strange kinship to these people. They wanted to keep their homes for their families; she wanted a family to make a home. As much as she hated Armando, she sympathized at least with his cause. Not enough to die for it, but enough to understand. The compassion she'd felt for the people of La Flor had not changed. Her confusion must come from exhaustion. How could she respect Armando and despise him in the same breath?

Perhaps my mind has grown ill with this turmoil. Papa could right this ugliness, but would he?

Chapter 6

Manuel and Rosa Garcia's thatched hut reminded Marianne of the familiar surroundings at Juan and Carmita's home. But unlike the lively dwelling at the hacienda, which resounded in love and laughter and the antics of six children, these walls imprisoned Marianne. No warmth radiated from the meager furnishings, even though within this room sat the same simple pottery, and the smells of cooking wafted through the air. In the corner were stacked red, blue, yellow, and orange blankets, and on a small table sat a crucifix—common in the homes of those practicing Catholicism.

Marianne's gaze rested on the carving of Jesus on the cross, a reminder of the many times Mama had told her how He had died for her sins. Juan repeated the same story to his children with the same passionate love for the Lord. The crucifix caused her to ache for home and those she loved. Granted, these people's ways of worship were different, but they prayed to the same God and knew His Son. The quandary of doctrine and the right way to worship, whether Catholic or Protestant, had entered Marianne's thoughts on more than one occasion. How did God decide whose prayers to answer?

God had spoken to her heart two separate times since the kidnapping and assured her of His presence and His peace. Surely He did care for all of His children.

Marianne twisted against the leather knots binding her hands. Her shoulders ached, but not her wrists. When Rosa complained about being alone with Señor Phillips's daughter while Armando and Manuel talked with the men of the village, Armando had pushed Marianne into a chair and tied her to the wooden back. Now her shoulders ached from the awkward position, but he had not bound her too tightly. Odd, how some concessions became small miracles.

Hunger had given her a headache. Typically, people ate in the hottest part of the afternoon, and today would be no exception. She smelled vegetables and chicken stewing together, and her stomach growled. Armando had given her a cool cup of water before he and Manuel had left, but the drink did not satisfy the empty space inside her—or the fear.

Rosa waved a wooden spoon in front of Marianne's face. "Are you hungry, señorita? I may let you eat after we are finished." The old woman tilted her silver head and studied her. "You're young, perhaps too young to be a part of such evil."

Marianne wanted to talk to Rosa, tell her she hoped the villagers were able to remain in their valley, but she dared not. What good would it do to sympathize with the peasants of La Flor if her knowledge of their language got her killed? With a heavy sigh, Marianne gazed into the deep brown pools of Rosa Garcia's eyes, a reflection of Armando.

The old woman wobbled closer to her and bent down to peer into Marianne's face. "You are frightened. I, too, señorita. We women suffer much for the affairs of our men." With those words, she returned to her stew, muttering complaints against the Spanish rule, Weston Phillips, and the hard peasant life.

Observing Rosa helped to occupy Marianne's weary, anxious mind, and the worries surrounding the next minute, hour, or day temporarily subsided. Rosa reminded Marianne of a mother hen, fussing over this and that. Her body toddled back and forth when she walked as though her legs might give way. If Marianne were not a captive, the entire scene would have been amusing.

When Armando and Manuel finally returned, they were in high spirits. They talked of music and singing that evening and took turns pulling Rosa into their arms for an imaginary dance.

Celebrating a victory that will never be theirs. I wish they did hold some power over Papa. Then I might be able to dwell on freedom from this. I'm so grateful that Mama is not in my place.

While they ate, Armando fixed his gaze directly at Marianne, but he refrained from any comments.

"She's hungry," Rosa said. "Untie her so she can have something to eat."

Armando pressed his lips together, visibly annoyed at his *tia's* suggestion. He stood and untied the leather straps binding her. "Remember where you are." How strange his words were, as if he knew she understood what he was saying.

"Does she speak our language?" Manuel asked. His lean, narrow face held fewer lines than Rosa's, but his shoulders stooped as though he'd given up holding onto his youth.

"No, *Tio.* She has expressed her anger more than once and has always spoken in English." He dragged the chair to the table and motioned for her to sit.

Once seated, she watched Rosa fill a warm tortilla with the chicken and vegetables. She laid it in a chipped bowl and placed it before Marianne.

"*Gracias,*" Marianne said.

"Well, at least the señorita knows her manners," Rosa said. Since the men had returned, her animosity toward Marianne had resurfaced.

Marianne kept her focus on the bowl before her. The food tasted wonderful with the blend of spices she'd grown to love. She chewed slowly, savoring every bite. As it disappeared, she noticed the chip in the pottery had formed a jagged, cracked line all the way to the other side.

Broken, but still useable. She felt the same way.

Armando set a cup of water before her, and it too refreshed her.

"*Gracias.*"

Armando chuckled. "This is the second kind word I've heard from her."

Manuel joined in the mirth. "What did you expect as her captor?" He picked up a knife and studied it closely. "Given the chance, she might try to use this on you. Be careful that she doesn't use kindness as a means to escape."

Marianne felt their eyes upon her, and her cheeks warmed. They viewed her with such curiosity. Perhaps in better circumstances, they might have been friends.

With the meal complete, Armando wasted no time in tying Marianne to the chair once again. Her shoulder muscles hurt the moment he wrapped the bindings around her wrists, pulling the rope tighter than before. Fighting the tears threatening to betray her, she fixed her gaze on the earthen floor.

But Armando must have sensed the suppressed emotions, for he cupped her chin and met her gaze. "Such a pretty señorita should not be so unhappy." He hesitated and loosened her wrists, as he'd done the previous evening.

Marianne didn't want his pity, and she battled the urge to spit into his face. Let him charm the señoritas with his dashing looks, but to her he resembled Satan.

"I see the anger in your eyes, stormy with flashes of lightning. *Relampago,* much like your father . . . Such unfairness for the innocent." His voice softened. "I regret the unpleasantness between us. You are a precious gem, and I hope for your sake Señor Phillips yields to our demands." Armando breathed deeply. "It is good you do not comprehend my words."

A few hours later, when the sun had dipped behind the hills, Rosa, Manuel, and Armando made ready for the village celebration.

Armando had stepped behind a partitioned corner of the hut and changed into a clean white shirt and black *calzoneras*—fitted trousers that were wide-legged at the bottom when left unbuttoned. He stepped from the partition and snatched up a bright red sash and tied it about his slender waist before donning a short, black jacket, trimmed in blue and red. The jacket's delicate needlework across the back and silver studding down the front distinguished him as a vaquero. Armando was handsome, yet Marianne believed his heart to be as black as a crow's feathers. After all, he allowed Felipe to dictate her demise. *The great Armando. Huh! The great coward.* He proclaimed himself a leader, but he didn't have the courage to set her free when he believed her kidnapping was wrong.

"And what of her?" Manuel nodded his white head toward Marianne. "Shall we leave the *cautivo* here?"

"She shall go with us and stay within my eyesight."

"And how will you dance?" A bit of luster sparkled in Manuel's brown eyes.

Rosa offered a near toothless smile. "The señoritas will be disappointed. So many are vying for your attention."

Armando placed a quick kiss upon his *tia's* cheek and picked up a black sombrero, trimmed in bright purple braid. "Next week I will join the merriment. Tonight is for me to relax and enjoy." He pointed to Marianne. "And I already have a pretty señorita to keep me company."

You could untie these wretched ropes.

A wayward lock of hair fell onto her forehead, and Marianne shook her head to drive it away. Utterly miserable, she wished for a basin of water to wash her face and a brush to smooth her tangled mass of hair. Catching sight of her soiled dress, she surmised a clean frock was also in order.

Most of all, she desired to flee from this place and its stench of impending death. She feared the morrow and the next, while these people anticipated music and merrymaking.

Oh, God, my strength is waning, and I want to break down and cry until there are no more tears. If I have placed all of my faith and trust in You, then why am I tormented and afraid?

Immediately she regretted her impetuous words. *Please forgive me, Father. I know You are here.*

Armando untied her to walk with him to the center of the village. His aunt and uncle had gone on ahead, leaving them alone in the twilight. Marianne wished the walk took them past the corral and Diablo, but the lively sounds came from the opposite direction. The throng of high-spirited people and singing guitars seemed to beckon Armando, for he urged her to walk briskly.

"This is in my honor and to celebrate your captivity." She detected a note of melancholy. "Ah, I wish another led this poor band of farmers instead of me. The responsibility and the weight of my people's expectations burden my waking and sleeping hours." He turned to her in the shadows, and a glimmer of a smile tugged at his lips. "When you are gone, to whom will I pour out my heart? I will miss your quiet, yet comforting spirit."

Marianne kept her gaze straight ahead. She dug her fingers into her palms to keep from screaming at him. She was not his amiga, friend. He held the power to set her free, and her destiny lay in his hands. How could he speak as though he had no choice?

"My people," he said, "mean more to me than my life, but shedding innocent blood is not the answer—not their blood or yours."

Her heart pounded against her chest. A few times before he'd relayed regret, but now she heard remorse. She already knew he wasn't assured of the wisdom in her kidnapping. Now he'd confirmed that he thought it foolish . . . even a mistake, perhaps. Armando Garcia did not take his position lightly. His people and their welfare were his lifeblood. This revelation startled her, and Marianne wondered if she must reconsider her evaluation of him. She feared what it might mean to be held hostage by a man that she might learn to respect.

A vivacious young woman lifted her bright green skirts and raced toward Armando. Her large, brown eyes, veiled with long, black lashes, sparkled at the sight of him. "Armando, would you dance with me?" Her full lips pursed into a smile. "*Por favor*, please. I have turned down the others while waiting for you."

Armando shook his head. "No, Isabella. I have come only to watch the festivities tonight. My joy is to see my people happy."

Isabella tilted her head and pouted prettily. "Such sacrifice, except I am one of your people, too. *Por favor*, a single dance to begin the celebration."

He gathered her slender hand into his. "If I choose to dance this evening, I will look for you." He winked at her. "Perhaps you will be in the arms of another vaquero by then."

"Never. I shall wait for you." She glanced at Marianne. Her eyes changed from glimmering jewels to daggers. "Tell me, is this Señor Phillips's daughter?"

"*Si*. She is our gold." Armando's stare fixed on the young Mexican woman's flushed face.

"When this is all over and we have no need to worry about La Flor, will you find time for me?" Isabella asked.

"We shall see. No one knows what tomorrow will bring." He brought her hands to his lips. "Isabella, you could dance for me. No other señorita can make her body whirl to a guitar like you."

Isabella laughed. She flung her arms around his neck and kissed his cheek. "I will dance with eyes only for our *héroe*, Armando."

Swinging away from him, she rushed to the man strumming a guitar. Armando hooked his arm into Marianne's and pulled her to a spot away from the circle of others.

"I won't tie your hands." He chuckled. "Unless you try to fight me."

Pretending indifference to his warnings, the only way she knew how to exhibit her rebellion, Marianne studied the fire. The clamor of music and laughter from the others prompted her attention to Isabella, who circled the fire and twirled her skirts in perfect rhythm to the guitar. As she had promised, her gaze captured Armando's, leaving no mistake as to her thoughts.

The strum of the strings quickened, and the dancer hastened her pace. Faster, even faster. Her body moved gracefully, like the lithe vine of a young tree. Raven hair whipped across her face and cast a seductive aura above the cheering crowd. The excitement that erupted moments before suddenly hushed to a breathless lull. Spellbound, the onlookers fell under the hypnotic trance until Isabella collapsed in front of Armando at the last note.

Silence continued over the crowd as though the passion in every man must quiet. Ceremoniously, Armando rose to his feet and applauded. He stepped to take Isabella by the hands and helped the breathless young woman to her feet. Others joined in the clapping, severing the dance's bewitchment.

"Well done," Armando said. "Who shall take the beautiful Isabella for a cool drink?" Glancing about, he pointed to his men gathered near the guitar player. "Emilio, Isabella needs a handsome man to tend to her."

Emilio emerged wearing a wide grin. He offered the young woman his arm and led her through the crowd.

Armando moved closer to the fire. He appeared to struggle with the right words, as though this was not the time or place to challenge Felipe. "While I have your attention, I want to say how proud I am of my men's loyalty." The crowd roared with enthusiasm. When they quieted, he continued. He looked at his men grouped together, all but Emilio. "Each time Señor Phillips and his foreman order us from our valley, you stand behind me and act bravely. No general could ask for more. I want to thank you. The danger is not over yet, but soon we will rejoice that La Flor is still our valley. Show these *valiente* men the praise they deserve." When the cheers subsided, Armando waved to them all.

"*El Dios* bless Armando," someone in the crowd said. Another repeated the cry. Soon shouts rang over the village, resounding like mission bells. "*El Dios bendice a Armando.*" God bless Armando.

Marianne shivered. *Please Lord, must I die for this cause?*

Chapter 7

Armando nodded at the circle of faces lit by the fire. He forced a smile. Praise. Shouts of jubilation. He detested this part of leadership. Chants about his heroism rang across the night air and praises for the blessings from God echoed around him. Some even declared him a saint. Too many times they entwined his name with deity.

How wrong of his dear friends, especially if they knew how he defied *Dios*.

Do you not see? I covet the end of tyranny and injustice—not fame or glory. I am only one man seeking to help my people keep their homes. I offer you little but a strong will, and the education I received from the padres. And what if I fail? What will your chants be then?

If he were to die in the midst of this battle for La Flor, who would lead them? Emilio shared in Armando's vision for his people, but Armando feared his friend's devotion to *Dios* weakened his determination. And Felipe. He cared only for himself.

There had to be a way to return the señorita and still keep La Flor.

The visit earlier this afternoon from Juan Torres caused Armando even more turmoil. He remembered every word and the agonizing grief on Juan's face as he pled for the señorita.

"I have come to talk to you about Señorita Phillips," Juan had stated, interrupting Armando's instructions to his men about leaving at daybreak.

Armando glanced up, surprised to see the head stableman of his enemy's hacienda. It was too soon to receive word from Phillips. "I have nothing to discuss. You know our purpose."

"Can we talk in privacy?" Juan asked, his tone respectful yet forceful.

"I'm busy." Armando sighed. "I have more important things to do."

Emilio stood beside his brother. "*Por favor*, for the sake of our friendship, listen to what my brother has to say."

Armando felt the scrutiny of his men. They respected Emilio and often looked to him for guidance. Armando studied Juan's face and saw the telltale signs of worry etched around his eyes. Although the man had refused to spy on Señor Phillips, Armando knew him to be as stalwart as Emilio.

Kicking his boot into the dirt, Armando deliberated a moment more. "Let's take a walk, and I'll listen."

Together the two men headed away from the ears of the villagers. Juan kept pace with Armando, not allowing his crippled leg to slow them down. At first they spoke of an early spring, mustang herds beyond their valley, and the increasing amount of sheep and cattle around them.

"My friend, I am ready to hear what you have to say," Armando said. "I apologize for my rudeness earlier."

Juan nodded, and they ambled toward the winding path leading to the hills away from the valley. Both men wiped perspiration from their faces in the heat of the afternoon.

"Your *prisonera* is like a daughter to me." Confidence laced Juan's words. "For me to ignore what is happening is to desert one of my children. We both know Señor Phillips may not be found in time to bring word to you."

"Are you saying Señora Phillips has not sent a rider after her husband?" Armando asked. "Have they no love for the señorita, especially since she chose to take the place of her *madre*?"

At that moment, Juan looked much like Emilio, wide-set eyes revealing the weight of his heart. "*Sí*, she did send a vaquero after him."

"Then Señor Phillips will return home in time to save his daughter."

Juan peered out to the hills and leaned on his straight leg. "I fear many things, Armando. Señor Phillips can be a harsh man, and he may decide to destroy the whole valley for what you've done to his family."

"I have my spies."

"Maybe so, but you could help guarantee the safety of our people by allowing me to take the señorita home." Juan's voice was edged with emotion.

"No, I must fulfill my vow." Armando stiffened with his reply. "This is the way I have chosen."

"Have you asked *Dios* for help?"

Armando thought through his words carefully. To deny God when his people worshiped Him meant losing their esteem. "Have you not heard my people? All of them seek *Dios* for our success. I am not one man imploring *Dios* to grant us victory, but many men, women, and children lifting prayers to the heavens."

Juan fixed a steady gaze into Armando's face. "Our *Dios* does not condone murder—"

"The padres have told us the stories of King David and his mighty armies. I read them while studying at the missions. Many people were killed."

"And you are comparing yourself to King David? This is not the same. You have kidnapped an innocent young señorita to hold as ransom for your demands, a young woman who already sides with your plight."

Armando tapped his boot against the ground to contain his fury. "How easy for you to judge. You live in the safety of Señor Phillips's Hacienda. Your children have food to eat and clothes to wear. My people," he waved his hand back toward La Flor, "will have nothing if we are forced to leave the valley. Our children will starve. The señorita is sympathetic to us? How easy for the rich to throw crumbs to the poor."

Juan's face flushed red. He wet his lips before speaking. "The missions are there to help."

"The missions, humph. One more ploy of the Spanish to keep us under their thumbs. They make laws to benefit themselves then have the padres dictate to our people how they should live as though the mandates were from God."

"Let's not argue, Armando. I did not come to arouse your anger, but to plead for the señorita. I believe *Dios* always has a better way, one that does not involve killing the innocent."

"The innocent are the ones I'm trying to protect." He slowly gained control of his anger. "I will keep her to bargain for La Flor. I believe her father will allow us to live on our land."

"I don't understand you; neither do I accept your decision. The thought of the señorita dying or losing my friends and family here grieves me. I wish I could make the situation right, but my *Dios* holds the power in His hands. Prayer is the best weapon I can carry . . . and I will use it night and day."

Tense, heavy silence settled upon them.

Armando sighed and laid his hand upon Juan's shoulder. "Stay with us, eat, and rest before you journey back."

"If I'm missed, there may be trouble for my family. May I see the señorita before I leave?"

"No, *mi amigo*. It would not be wise."

Juan narrowed his eyes. "You would deny a father the right to see his daughter?"

"Perhaps, if she were really your daughter." Armando forced a slight smile. "It's better this way."

Juan turned and limped back toward the village. Armando watched him secure his horse and ride away without a word to anyone, even Emilio.

Now, as Armando steadied his gaze into the flickering firelight, he regretted denying Juan the right to visit the señorita. Juan considered her as one of his own. He even believed the señorita sided with the villagers. Tomorrow he planned to tell Emilio of this poor decision and apologize to Juan at the first opportunity.

After all, Armando possessed honor among the people, and he intended to maintain his position. Juan had been right. Shedding innocent blood was not the way to secure peace for his people. But how?

I am nothing but a poor man leading a ragged troop of farmers, a man who loves his people. I desire only to see them live in peace and watch their children grow.

He studied his captive, who also seemed to engage her thoughts in the flames lapping at the fire's logs. He wondered about her fear, and if she truly felt her father was wrong in his plans to take the valley. Juan said she sided with La Flor. Again remorse nudged at him—for too many things.

Marianne sensed Armando's gaze upon her, but she maintained her musings and stared into the fire. What thoughts rippled through his mind when it came to her? Was he considering how Papa would get revenge for her kidnapping? Until she had heard Armando speak his heart, she'd hated him. Now she better understood his reasoning and determination, but he was terribly misguided.

The soft sounds of the guitar soothed the chaos in her spirit. She inwardly smiled. Mama had insisted she learn to play the piano, and Marianne had practiced with fervor. The sweet lilt had comforted her when Papa's stern words and actions had torn at her heart, and the music of tonight held the same effect.

Papa . . . how wonderful if he would ride into La Flor and demand that Armando release her.

"She is my daughter, and I love her," Papa would declare.

How foolish of me. Still dreaming of things that will never happen.

Exhausted, she fought the stinging in her eyes to keep from weeping. Oh, for a whole night's sleep without the painful ropes. She didn't care where—she'd even welcome the hard dirt floor. Leaning her head back, she closed her eyes and massaged her neck and shoulders. The pounding in her head had grown worse. Mama would have suggested a cup of tea with a hint of honey.

Marianne started. Something touched her side. At first she thought it was a dog, but a quick glance revealed a small boy had snuggled beside her. He peered up into her face, and a tousle of thick, dark hair rippled across his forehead. Instinctively she wrapped her arm around his shoulders. He smiled and nestled closer. He couldn't have been more than three years old, trusting, warm, and so little. She kissed the tip of his nose and delighted in the child-like smell of him. It didn't matter that he needed a bath. Carmita once said children should play as hard as their parents work.

The child laid his head upon her lap and drew up his knees to his body. She brushed her finger across his soft cheek. How good of God to bring her this glimpse of Him. Marianne swallowed a sob.

Heavenly Father, forgive my selfish ways. How could I ever have doubted You? I do not deserve Your mercies, Your love. I know You are here, as You have always been. I surrender my fears to You. No matter what becomes of me.

The child's hand slipped into hers, confirming to her His presence. A wave of peace settled about her. Armando, still seated at Marianne's left side, bent forward. She felt his scrutiny penetrate the shadows, and she met his gaze. Nothing audible passed between them, but she sensed the sight of the child resting in her lap softened his austere disposition.

She turned her attention back to the child and continued to stroke his face. With her head bowed, she wept for more reasons than she cared to list.

Armando reached across her lap and stirred the child. "Little one, where is your *madre*?"

The little boy pushed himself up and looked about him. Confusion etched his angelic features.

"Rico?" Armando lifted the child's chin and studied his face in the shadows.

The little boy's lips quivered.

"Where is your *padre*?"

Rico looked into the crowd then back at Armando and Marianne. He shrugged and laid his head down without releasing her hand.

Armando stood and scooped Rico up into his arms. He walked to the guitar player and silenced him with a nod. The crowd also hushed. "Little Rico is looking for his *padre*. Pepe, where are you?"

A man exited from the shadows. "*Mi hijo. My son.*" He opened his arms to the child, and the boy leaped into his father's embrace.

Jealousy stirred in Marianne. She had relished the child's touch and did not want to let him go, even to his father. But she knew Rico had been sent to her on the wings of an angel.

Armando raised his arms to the people. "This is why we fight for La Flor, so our children will have a home."

The villagers roared in agreement, and the music continued. Firelight illuminated Armando's high cheekbones and upturned lips. Standing erect and clothed in a vaquero's finest, he possessed a general's bearing. With a wave of his arm, he gestured to his men and incited their zeal for the valley.

Marianne marveled at the power Armando held over the villagers, and the way they clung to his every word. For a moment she felt the passion for his cause. No wonder his tattered army obeyed him, and the women craved his attention.

Marianne's father did not have an inkling of Armando Garcia's leadership.

Chapter 8

When the music and laughter from the celebration faded, Marianne watched the villagers return to their homes. Parents carried sleeping children, and couples knit together as one. Armando remained alone among the dying embers. He paced back and forth in front of the still crackling fire, reminding Marianne of a wildcat her father had once caged. Snarling, incensed, the animal simply wanted to be free.

He motioned for Marianne to stand. With a deep breath, she did his bidding and hid her reluctance. For a few precious hours, she'd masked her despair with the sights and sounds of the festivities. The truth of her plight now brought a weariness that crushed her spirit. *Where was her faith? God must think her fickle.*

Alone in the shadows, Armando seemed too preoccupied in his thoughts to leave.

Finally he ceased pacing, and they silently began the trek to Manuel and Rosa's hut. Armando grabbed her upper arm and pulled her away from the path. Marianne shivered and resisted his hold.

"Don't be afraid," he said. "I have no plans to hurt you. Sleep will evade me this night, and you can accompany me while I contemplate what I must do."

She willed her trembling body to relax and abandoned the useless struggle. How long before he realized she understood his every word?

"Ah, my voice calms you," he said. "I wish the nearness of you did not affect me so strongly."

Marianne dwelled on the tenderness in his voice. She could tell he wrestled with his decision to kill her.

"But my desires are selfish," he said. "The welfare of my people is most important."

Her spirits plummeted farther than before. She wondered if she relinquished her promise to Juan and tried to speak to Armando, perhaps she could convince him to abandon his resolve.

They began the slow ascent of the path that led away from La Flor.

"Ah, did you notice Felipe in the shadows when the others left for their homes? I wonder what treachery he plans next? If he were not my mother's cousin, I'd throw him from the valley." Armando breathed deeply and turned to view the village.

He stood close enough for her to feel his warm breath upon her neck. A strange sensation crept over her. She was bewildered. When the time came, this man would kill her. Had the toll on her emotions driven her insane? How could she feel anything but repulsion for her abductor?

"I do not know what is best," he whispered.

Suddenly she noticed a flash of fire rising from one of the huts. Marianne gasped and tugged at Armando's arm. He, too, detected the consuming flames.

"*Dios Santo*, remember the prayers of Your people." He grasped her hand, and together they raced toward the village.

Marianne worked alongside every available man, woman, and child to fight the fiery monster that consumed first one then two huts. The people formed two lines and passed buckets of water from the village well to the flames threatening to devour their homes. She heard their prayers to Mother Mary, pleading with her to bring their cause to God. The raging fires must halt before La Flor was nothing but burning embers. Marianne offered her own silent supplications for the innocent.

She looked for an opportunity to escape. No one would come after her as long as they battled the blaze.

The muscles in her shoulders and arms begged for release, but she still swung the pail of water on down the line as the fire persisted. None of the villagers slackened for fear their homes lay next in the treacherous path.

Several young children clustered near the fire, some were stunned by the devastation and others crying for their mothers.

"The children," a woman said to the left of Marianne. A mixture of perspiration and soot streamed down her face. "Someone needs to tend to the children before they're hurt."

Rosa broke from one of the lines to gather the little ones about her, but they were too frightened to follow. Another old woman attempted to help, but amidst the shouts of those battling the inferno, the children refused to move.

A gust of wind blew the flames onto another rooftop and immediately ignited the dried grasses. Marianne stole a moment to catch a glimpse of the children. A small boy escaped Rosa's grasp. He looked like Rico.

Marianne searched for Armando, but she knew he must be at the front of the line combating the fire. With his permission, she could help with the children. Alarm grew for the fate of the little ones. Rosa and the other woman had them under control, all except the one small boy who had inched closer to a hut that sat in the path of the blaze. A spark caught the rooftop.

As though spurred by an invisible demon, the child raced toward the burning hut. Rosa screamed a warning, and the other woman grabbed the closest two children. Without heeding their cries, he ran inside as the roof went up in flames.

The women could not leave the children alone. Neither could they go after the boy. Their cries brought the attention of an old man, but the fire had gathered momentum and had spread over the entire roof, deterring him. Giant yellow tongues snatched up and ingested every twig and dried leaf in its way.

Marianne rushed from the line toward the burning hut. The image of Rico stayed foremost in her mind, the small boy with a sweet smile and a gentle touch. *Oh, God, help me to get to him in time. Not a child, Lord, please, do not take this child.*

The intensity of the heat took her breath away, and the smoke billowed from the doorway as though it defied her entrance. She lingered a moment, but the shrieking child propelled her inside the raging furnace. Glancing up, she saw the weakened roof shift and a sputtering of fiery dried grass drift to the floor. She had to find him before they both were smothered by the flames.

Smoke stung her eyes and throat and swirled about her face. Flames leaped and lapped up a chair in the center of the room. In a far corner, she saw the child. It was Rico, surrounded by a wall of fire. He cried out.

Shielding her mouth and nose from the suffocating smoke, Marianne fought her way to him. She prayed the roof wouldn't collapse before she had time to carry him out. Her fingers stretched to latch onto his extended hands. She snatched him up into her arms, his tiny body hot and trembling. He laid his head against her shoulder, and she placed a protective hand over his face to help him breathe.

The path to the door stretched endlessly as she dodged falling fire sticks and burning debris in her path. An invisible crushing weight pressed upon her chest. She choked and coughed, fearing the worst.

Oh, God, help us. She could no longer hear anything for the roar and sputtering of the fire.

She strained to keep her eyes open, afraid to shift her focus from the door. They must escape the fire . . . only a few more feet. Rico must make it to safety.

Suddenly, Armando stood in the doorway.

At first she thought him a vision. "Armando!" He rushed inside and wrapped his arms around her and Rico, leading them through the fiery maze to fresh, clean air.

Once free of the flaming mass, Marianne felt her knees give way. She convulsed for air, afraid she would fall and injure Rico. Someone lifted him from her arms. Needle-like smoke filled her eyes and blinded her vision. Her chest hurt and tears welled her eyes.

"Here, drink this water." Armando took a bucket from Rosa. Marianne obediently sipped water from his cupped palm and wet her parched lips.

Her throat burned like a lighted torch. Again she coughed and struggled for air.

"Easy." His voice was gentle above the fiery inferno.

After several minutes, the overwhelming sensation faded, and her breath returned in less painful gasps. Marianne thanked God for deliverance, but when she tried to murmur a word of gratitude to Armando, she choked.

A droplet of water fell upon her head. She peered upward and felt a sprinkling of rain dot her cheeks. Its pace quickened, and she closed her eyes, allowing the steady stream to cleanse her face. Another miracle and answered prayer to a land that received little rainfall.

Shouts rose from the villagers. Marianne began to laugh. With wobbly legs and torturous wheezes of air, she attempted to stand. Armando's strong arm encircled her waist and supported her. If her body had been strong enough, she'd have danced for joy. Never had rain given such pleasure.

My Lord and my God. Thank You!

The cool water penetrated her hair and clothes, washing away the dirt and smoke. Glancing at Armando, she saw a smile creep across his face.

She smiled in return. *"Gracias."*

The heaviness of sleep tugged at Armando's eyelids. Nearby, Manuel and Rosa slept on pallets as did his captive. The women's even breathing and his uncle's snoring sounded peaceful after the turmoil of the past few days. All of them rested but him.

He knew he needed to rest, but his mind failed to release him. Thoughts of the evening whirled and spun with everything from the celebration to the fire, and always settling on the señorita. Staring at her small figure, he wrestled with what he must do now.

Oh, he knew what he wanted—to never set her free, to keep her with him. He wanted to know her heart and to find a way to talk to her. Perhaps discover a paradise where they could live without want, without prejudice, without fear. Armando sighed. No place existed, except in the minds of dreamers and foolish men at best.

When did this happen? Armando rubbed his temples in an effort to stop the ache across his forehead.

Sleep promised to deliver a respite, but not yet. He had to work through his obsession with Señor Phillips's daughter. Although he knew the depth of his feelings went far beyond lust or power, he could not put words to his unsettling emotions. He, Armando Garcia, the man of logic, had fallen prey to the daughter of his enemy. Somewhere in the blue-gray depths of the señorita's eyes, he had discovered a calming of his own restless spirit. Peace. Courage. Bliss. Strength. Odd, he didn't know her name, but he'd called out to a woman like her in his dreams for as long as he could remember.

What happened to his strategic plans? What about the people of La Flor? And what about the vow he'd made on his *madre's* grave? Did his commitments no longer hold meaning? He leaned back in his chair and recalled his mother and father's relationship. The similarities between his parents' tumultuous times and his staggering response to the señorita appeared ironic . . . even cruel.

His mother had lived among the people of La Flor. His father, Joseph de Garcia, the son of a Spanish nobleman, dwelled among the elite. When the elder Garcia had learned about the relationship, he forbade his son to see the peasant girl. The demands did not dissuade the young couple because she was to have a child. Armando carried his father's name, although his parents never married. As a boy, he'd often wondered if his father had loved his mother or him. Joseph used to visit them in the village, and later he insisted Armando secure an education at the Mission San José y San Miguel de Aguayo.

In those days, Armando had desired to enter the priesthood and cling to the faith of the dedicated padres. He had embraced the *Dios* who loved him and the sacrificial death of *Jesús*. Then, when Armando reached sixteen years of age, his father disappeared. No one knew where or why. Within two years his *madre* died. He blamed Joseph Garcia—for breaking his *madre's* heart. Armando left the mission and denied everything that represented *Dios* or Joseph Garcia. Later he learned his father had returned to Spain.

Armando pushed those old memories from his mind. They only served to depress him and fuel his hatred for those who were responsible. The years had hardened him against the Spanish and of late, the gringo, Weston Phillips.

Which was why tonight he despised his feelings for Señor Phillips's daughter, the object of his confusion. Fate had cursed him as well, and he saw his wretched family history replayed as he sought the affections of a woman who could never love him because of his stature in life.

Armando's heart wrenched when he relived those agonizing moments when he feared she might perish in the fire with Rico. He'd glanced up at the same time that she hurried into the burning hut.

In the darkness he shook his head, silently dispelling the horror of seeing her holding Rico surrounded by flames. Somehow he fought the blaze to pull them from the hut before the roof sank into the burning remains. She had no knowledge of her dress igniting in their escape or how he had shielded her hair from the hungry flames. If he still believed in *Dios*, he would attribute it to divine intervention.

Rising from the chair, Armando made his way to his pallet. The steady rhythm of rain continued outside. Tonight, everyone had been drenched, but no one had dared to leave until the last flicker died. He remembered the sight of his bedraggled señorita, her clothes clinging to her in shreds. One of the young women had presented her with a skirt, another with a blouse. A smile tugged at the corners of his lips. The tawny-haired señorita had wept at their gifts.

Armando now realized that most of the villagers did not desire their *cautivo* killed. Yet neither did they want to lose their homes. Who could find a solution?

He eased his tired body onto his pallet and under a blanket. As exhausted as he felt, he knew sleep would continue to elude him tonight.

A **rooster** crowed, then another, and Marianne stirred from her slumber, but she soon drifted back to sleep. Later, as sunlight filtered through the doorway, she opened her eyes. Voices hummed around her. For a moment she thought she'd spent the evening with Juan and Carmita.

"The señorita wakens," Rosa whispered. "She will be hungry."

"Your tone is much kinder to her this morning." Manuel laughed.

Rosa scowled at her husband. "She is different from Señor Phillips. She is like one of us."

"I agree, Rosa, and I feel sorry for Armando. He has a serious decision to make about her future and the future of our people."

The old woman sighed and silence filled the hut. "I believe life is more important than land."

"But what is life if one does not have a home or a place to plant a garden?"

Marianne swallowed against a raw throat. Manuel spoke the truth. Nothing had really changed.

Chapter 9

The morning dragged on with no sign of Armando. Marianne assumed he was making preparations with his men to depart later in the day. She dreaded his return. The thought of riding to the secluded campsite and waiting for word from her father was futile. At least here in La Flor, she could distance herself from reality.

Had it been only three days since the kidnapping? It seemed like much longer since Felipe had snatched her from the security of her father's home. She felt old before her time. And so confused.

While she helped Rosa grind corn for flour, Marianne allowed her thoughts to drift back to the evening before—the fire and Rico. The pungent smell of smoke still clung about her, nesting in her nostrils and irritating her chest.

Some aspects of the night were best forgotten, especially the way Armando had treated her. After he'd saved her and Rico from the raging fire, he'd behaved as though she were one of his people. His comforting words and tender embrace had eased her hysteria.

Her own response to Armando also unsettled her. She'd allowed him to calm her, and she'd even relaxed in his touch. She felt like a fool, deceived and judged by her own emotions. *This man will kill you for his people.*

The morning moved to afternoon, and Marianne continued to busy herself with Rosa, assisting her in chores and shaping dough into tortillas. Bold sunlight streamed through the doorway and coaxed her to venture outside, but she feared alarming the old woman or agitating Armando. She rubbed her wrists where the ropes had chafed the skin raw. The painful reminder halted any ideas of stepping from the hut.

Rosa chattered on as though Marianne understood every word, and Marianne fought the urge to reply. But she knew the danger in revealing her knowledge of Spanish. So far, Armando had heard nothing from her family. Although he'd given Papa five days to act upon his demands, Marianne feared a surge of anger or panic from Armando's men could bring about a hasty reaction.

Yet she couldn't deny that a twinge of hope nudged at her. Could her rescue of Rico have moved Armando to reconsider her fate?

Armando leaned against the corral gate, his worries consuming him. He had worked since sunrise alongside the villagers repairing the four homes destroyed by fire, but now everyone had taken time for water and a moment's rest. Two of his men had families living in those huts. Naturally, they wanted to stay in the valley until they'd completed the work on their homes. One more item to complicate his weary mind.

"The men are ready," Emilio called from behind him.

With the chaos twisting inside Armando's head about the señorita and his commitment to his people, he could not face his friend. Instead he fixed his sights on the horses, wondering if he dare reveal the secrets of his heart.

Emilio rested his arms on the gate. "*Mi amigo*, I see you are troubled."

Armando slowly nodded. "The men will not like what I have to say. Although I have no choice. Perhaps they need a new leader."

"No, Armando, you are the one we follow." Emilio pushed back his sombrero and turned toward

Armando. "Let them hear you first. They want your guidance through the dispute with *Señor* Phillips. Felipe may arouse their anger, but you arouse their faith in God."

The sincerity in Emilio's dark eyes spoke of his devotion. "You have known me a long time, and you're closer to me than a brother. How can I explain the circumstances that make me feel like a traitor to our cause?"

"Is this matter so grave that you can't discuss it with me?"

Armando's grayish-brown gelding nuzzled his hands. He stroked the horse's neck. "I can not put it into words."

Emilio pulled a piece of brush from the horse's mane. "A man's emotions are a difficult thing."

Armando sighed and studied him. "You know, don't you?"

"*Si.*" He laid his hand on Armando's shoulder. "I sensed it from the beginning."

"When? How could you know?"

Emilio gave him a wry smile. "When Felipe pulled her from her horse and she stood before you with no fear. I saw respect in your eyes. And later when you learned she alone could control Diablo, I saw admiration. When she tried to pull Rico from the fire,

I saw your passion. There, I said to myself, is a señorita who can tame Armando."

"How can a man find his beliefs and values changed in so short a time?"

"*Dios* does not care about time," Emilio said. "He holds our days in the palm of His hand."

"I gave up on *Dios* years ago. You know that."

"But perhaps *Dios* hasn't cast you from His graces. I remember when the joy of serving Him shone in your face."

Veering his attention back to the corral, Armando contemplated his friend's words. "The man you knew then doesn't exist any more."

"Oh, but he does." Emilio's words flowed with more power than a gifted teacher. "Sometimes I think your greatest struggle is within yourself."

Armando chuckled. Oh, the truth stung. "You know me too well, Emilio."

"I pray for you every day. Come, I will stand with you while you talk to the others."

"Your loyalty is more than I deserve." The two ambled toward a gnarled oak outside of the village. "I don't even know her name," Armando said. "Neither do I have the words to explain my decision to the others."

"Remember your first love? He will give you the words."

As much as Armando treasured Emilio's friendship, the talk of *Dios* bristled him. A man should choose his own destiny.

Beneath the shade of overhanging branches, Armando glanced from one familiar face to another in his trustworthy band. They looked tired, worn from fighting the preceding night's fire and taking charge of the reconstruction this morning. A tired man often possessed a short temper.

He began by praising them for their devotion to friends, families, and to the cause of securing their valley. Today they planned to return to the campsite. Some of the men were to remain behind to guard the village and help rebuild the homes, while the others joined Armando.

"I have given much thought to our original plan," he said. "And I have a confession to make." Armando took a deep breath. "We all want to keep our valley, even if it means giving of our lives. And we are all desperate men, for we are standing on our future. The night of the kidnapping, I felt it was wrong to put an innocent woman in danger. We are honorable men who do not need to resort to desperate means."

He hesitated, then willed the words from his troubled mind. "After the fire last night and witnessing how the señorita saved little Rico's life, I cannot hold her any longer. I must make this choice. To me, killing her makes me . . . us . . . no better than her father. We are not murderers, but farmers and ranchers who desire to live in peace. I have decided to let her go."

"What about our valley?" Felipe rose to his feet, his fists clenched. His quick temper had challenged Armando many times before.

"I do not want her to be killed." Pepe Sanchez spoke up, a short man with a round stomach and a boyish face. "If not for the señorita's bravery, *mi hijo* would be dead. I have already lost his *madre*, and I cannot bear the thought of losing Rico. If need be, I will take him to the mission." He glanced about him as though he dared the men to defy his position.

A burst of grumbling arose and divided the men. Finally, Emilio raised his hands for their attention. "All of you know I believe *Dios* will guide us in the right paths. In the beginning, I didn't agree with Armando and his methods of keeping the valley, but I supported him. I can do no less now. Murder is wrong, no matter what the reason, and I beg our Holy *Dios* to forgive me for my part in the kidnapping. I suggest two things: first, we return the señorita, and second, a few of us visit the padres at one of the missions and tell them of our difficulties."

"The gringo will not listen to a padre." Felipe stepped to face Emilio.

"I agree." Confidence edged Emilio's words. "But the Spanish will listen to a padre."

"I'll go to the Mission San José y San Miguel de Aguayo before being a part of a murder," Pepe said. "*Dios* heard our prayers last night and saved my son and brought the rain. He will not abandon us."

Three more men volunteered to accompany him.

"Armando." Pepe stood and faced the men. "Will you lead us to the mission and speak in our behalf to the padres?"

Armando swallowed his surge of emotion. Never had he imagined this loyalty. "My faith is not as strong as yours."

"But you are our leader, and we need a man to represent us," Pepe said. "And you are familiar with the padres."

A hush fell over the band as Armando deliberated the request. He glanced at Emilio, who nodded. "*Sí,* I will go," Armando replied. "I cannot promise the padres will help us, but I will try."

The burden of the responsibility before Armando left him uneasy. At the missions, the demons of his past would surely ensnare him.

Marianne continued to help Rosa prepare the day's meal. She wondered about Armando, and the old churning fear in the pit of her stomach rose to her throat and threatened to make her ill.

Rosa, too, watched the door. Manuel had been gone since early morning to help with the rebuilding. Neither man had returned to the hut.

When the tantalizing smells of meat, peppers, and corn rose from the cooking pot, Manuel returned and soon afterward, Armando appeared in the doorway. He avoided Marianne's stare and appeared sullen and preoccupied.

"I must leave today," he said as they sat down at the table. He motioned for Marianne to join them.

Manuel asked *Dios* to bless the food and then he and Rosa crossed themselves. So did Armando.

"When will you be back?" Manuel took a warm tortilla from Rosa.

"I'm not sure," Armando said and concentrated on his food. "Possibly late tonight or in the morning."

Manuel raised a questioning brow, but said nothing. Marianne's heart beat so fiercely that she feared the others could hear. This had to mean her father had refused Armando's demands. He would be rejoicing if his demands had been met. Could she be so despicable in her father's eyes that he desired her dead?

Silence rested on the remainder of the meal. Unable to eat, Marianne prayed her suspicions were wrong. *Oh*

God, give me the courage to endure whatever is about to happen. If this is the end, please have Carmita help Mama through this. And help Papa understand he needs You.

After the meal was completed, Armando left again. To Marianne, time stood still, and she wished the end would simply come.

Within the hour Armando entered the hut and disappeared behind the partition. He changed into vaqueros' attire then stood in the doorway blocking the sun, his face crimped with worry lines.

"I am taking the señorita back to her hacienda." Armando's voice sounded distant or perhaps it was the meaning of his words.

Marianne bit her tongue to keep from weeping. She glanced away and blinked back the tears. *Thank You, God. Thank You.*

Rosa stared at him, her face a mixture of approval and saddened emotions. "I believe you've made the right choice." She stood on her toes and hugged him. "We are not killers here, Armando. We just want to be left alone in our valley."

Armando glanced down at her wrinkled face. "I do not know what will come of La Flor, but I can not harm the señorita." He kissed Rosa's cheek. "My *tio* already knows of my decision. We'll speak more about this when I return."

"Maybe you can rest then. You always look so tired and unhappy." Rosa picked up the water bucket. She hesitated in the doorway and turned to give Armando one more tender look. "I want to see the boy who played at my feet, the one who dreamed of fine horses and carried a stick for a sword."

"That boy is now a man. Those days are gone forever."

Armando beckoned Marianne to follow him.

The truth. Armando needs to hear the truth. A soft whisper spoke to her heart as she smoothed her deep blue skirt and moved toward him. He reached for the door, and she stared at the top of his hand where the fire had burned and left an ugly blister. No one had bandaged or applied medicine from the aloe plant. As the latch slowly lifted, her gaze traveled upward to his muscle-laden arm, shoulder, neck, and on to his finely etched features. She remembered how tightly the man had held her last night and the comfort of his embrace. She hadn't noticed before how perfect he kept his pencil-thin mustache or long sideburns. Trembling, she moistened her dry lips.

"If I were a man, I would beg you to let me stay," she said in Spanish. "For your cause is noble, and I see the great love you have for your people." Marianne hastily turned away and stepped into the sunshine. She dared not look into his eyes. With her heart pounding, she walked toward the corral.

Armando strode beside her, no doubt angry at her confession. They walked on in silence, and she tried to think of more pleasant things. Home with Mama, Juan, and Carmita. Her deliverance and the importance of God in her life.

Once they reached the horses, Diablo rushed from the opposite side of the corral. His bridle, saddle, and blanket lay near the gate. As she led her stallion from his cell, Marianne felt Armando staring at her, yet she could not allow herself to acknowledge him.

"The *diablo* and the *ángel*," he finally said.

Confused, she whirled around to see what Armando meant.

"If you were a man," he said, "I would ask you to join us."

Chapter 10

Marianne took a ragged breath and lifted her chin. "I apologize for deceiving you. I . . . I promised Juan when he taught me your language that I would not speak it without his permission."

Armando stiffened. "And why have you done so now?"

"You have made a great sacrifice in allowing me to go free. I want you to know my gratitude, and to be honest."

"You have heard every word." His words were devoid of emotion.

"*Si.*" She hesitated. "Without the knowledge, I would not have known your compassion for La Flor." She glanced down at Diablo's bridle in her hands and attempted to focus on the pendants dangling from the leather straps. Fighting her inner turmoil, she met his dark eyes. "Never have I seen such unselfish devotion." As Armando stepped closer, the stallion raised his head and snorted. "Hush, Diablo," she said in Spanish and stroked his neck.

Armando ceased his stride, and he smiled. "Does he not care if you speak to him in Spanish or English?"

Marianne smiled in return and relaxed slightly. "No. He knows my voice."

A cloud of silence fell about them. She wanted to finish saddling Diablo before someone or something changed his mind.

"There are many things I would like to say to you," he said. "Many things I would like to ask. I should be angry that you know so much about me, for now it's harder to let you go." He studied her. "Saddle your horse, señorita. The time has come for me to escort you home."

"*Gracias.* My name is Marianne."

"A pretty name for a pretty *solidat.*"

She turned to finish preparing Diablo for the ride home and saw Emilio bringing the dun gelding to Armando.

"We are ready to leave," Armando said to his friend. "I'll be back late this night or mañana."

"Be careful, Armando. Señor Phillips's men could be waiting for you."

"I will. I realize this marks the beginning of more trouble. Felipe has not taken my decision lightly."

Emilio nodded. "I will pray."

"We will leave for the mission at San José as soon as I return. Keep men posted in case of attack."

Marianne mounted Diablo unassisted while the two men conversed. She knew Papa would not give up pursuing ownership of their valley. He might use her abduction as an excuse to take revenge upon Armando and his people. Greed ruled her father's motives. Nothing more. If only Papa would look beyond her gender and see how much she needed him.

Marianne and Armando rode up the worn path away from La Flor. Freedom awaited her, and she praised God for His deliverance and for touching her life with His spirit.

Armando stopped his horse at the top of the winding path and took a long look back at the valley. She too turned and studied La Flor, perplexed at her mixed feelings of what had happened over the past three days. How could life change so quickly in so short a time? A part of her wanted to stay. A part of her wished she'd never met Armando Garcia and witnessed his devotion to his people.

If you were a man, I'd ask you to join us. She had earned the respect of her father's enemy.

"*Que bonito.* La Flor is lovely," she said. "I too would not want to leave a home as delightful as this."

"The beauty of the valley and the people living here are the same. Apart, the land would become overgrown and useless. And without our homes, we have no purpose." The sunlight glistened on his black hair and framed his face and shoulders. To Marianne, he appeared noble, a true leader.

She turned to gaze at a small flock of sheep in the distance. "I will do everything I can to persuade Papa." She remembered her betrothal to Don Lorenzo and wondered if she possessed bargaining power for the valley in her upcoming marriage. The thought of spending the rest of her life with the Spanish aristocrat left her feeling empty and longing for a sweeter life. She could only hope the marriage offered a blessing.

"I am sure Señor Phillips does not appreciate his daughter taking sides against him."

"This is not the only matter that he and I have disagreed on." She paused before saying more. "Juan Torres has been more of a papa to me than my own."

"I know. He came to the village yesterday."

Her eyes widened. "Juan? But his leg—"

"You are like one of his children."

She swallowed her tears.

They reined their horses toward the east. Diablo tossed his head, anxious to run, but Marianne soothed him. "Hush, my prince. It's too soon to race."

"How did you tame him?" Armando cast an admiring glance at the white stallion.

She patted the animal's neck. "My father caught him with a herd of mustangs. When he refused the bridle and saddle, Papa labeled him crazy, a *diablo*. His independent spirit intrigued me, and when no one was around, I made my way to the stables to see him. He responded well to my voice and touch, and I simply used kindness until he trusted me. For some reason Diablo has never let anyone but Juan or me near him. It has always frustrated Papa."

"I see. You have a special way with wild stallions?"

"No." She smiled. "I prefer to think Diablo wanted someone to love and who would return his affections."

"The stallion is no different from many men."

Her cheeks warmed. Had he referred to himself?

The horses picked their way over the hilltop until the flat plain stretched out before them. Both animals pulled to run, but Armando and Marianne preferred them to walk.

Against the slow clop of the horses stepping around the rock, Armando turned to her. "Señorita, I wish our paths had crossed under better circumstances. I regret the differences separating us."

"And I do as well," she said, amazed at her boldness. "The valley . . . if only Papa could perceive how much it means to your people."

He drew a heavy breath. "La Flor is not the only problem. I am your father's enemy. He has already sworn to kill me."

"But I will tell him how you set me free," Marianne said. "Perhaps he will listen."

Armando laughed. "Señorita, have you forgotten who broke into your home, abducted you, and stole horses and weapons? Felipe may have been the one to seize his daughter and his property, but I am the leader. I have no intentions of returning any of those things but you. Señor Phillips will not rest until I'm dead. Be certain of that."

The gravity of his words stunned her. Even so, he spoke the truth. She felt naïve, simple-minded. "I'm sorry. I hadn't considered everything."

Distress etched his brow, and his dark eyes narrowed. "I don't blame you. It's the ruthless Spanish and men like your father who are greedy."

Marianne glanced away. "I know what Papa is, Armando. There's no need to remind me."

"Have I angered you?"

"No. Papa's ways grieve me. I wish he were different." Marianne shrugged. "He wanted *un hijo*, not a daughter.

And he's always been disappointed. You see, Papa would never have bargained with you for La Flor."

"He does not realize his treasure." He halted his horse and looked across the sparsely grassed land dotted with junipers and mesquite. He wiped the perspiration from his face with his bandanna and glanced up at the sun slowly moving toward the west.

In one breath he was humiliated that a mere girl had deceived him, almost angry that she'd been privy to all his babbling. In the next breath he realized, for her sake, he should not say more. The idea of becoming more acquainted with her, even the mere chance of seeing her again, warred against his logic and reasoning. The mestizo and the elite. The fugitive and the innocent. Diablo and the *ángel.*

For the first time in his twenty-five years, Armando had an inkling of how his parents might have felt. He realized that if he had stared into the depths of Marianne's blue-gray eyes a moment longer, he would be tempted to see her again. Perhaps his father had done all he could for Armando's mother and lost. Armando remembered the man had been affectionate and giving, and had treated his mother with love, but still he had abandoned them and never returned.

"Marianne, forgive me for tearing you from your home and exposing you to danger. Spur on your magnificent stallion and ride back to your life at the Phillips Hacienda."

"Armando, I will pray for you." She smiled, an image he would seal in his memory.

"And will you go to the missions and light candles for me?" Melancholia tore through him. "I'm afraid the padres do not think highly of me and my *hombres*."

She shook her head. "I'm not Catholic, although I know my father had to declare an allegiance to your faith in order to acquire his land. But my pleas will go to the same *Dios y Salvidor*. I'll pray for your safety and for the people of La Flor."

"Very well. My people need prayers for what lies ahead." *May life be good to you, Señorita Marianne.* "Do not linger. Who knows what evil men may be lurking."

"I shall be careful. *Adios*." She dug her heels into the side of the stallion that carried her away from him forever.

Chapter 11

Armando watched Marianne and Diablo vanish into the distance. As fleetingly as she had stepped into his life, she had left him, leaving a bittersweet agony in his heart. He stood alone, hearing nothing but the call of a distant crow and the echo of their parting words that she would pray for him and his people. Must he be destined to live his life in solitude?

A warm breeze swept across his face, and for a moment its coolness refreshed him. How long before his memory of Marianne faded into obscurity, until she became a fond passing of a sweet señorita who had touched his life? Armando clenched his jaw. He could not cast her aside as casually as she had tossed her burned gown from the fire. His heart would not allow it.

He resented the pain and discomfort he'd knowingly inflicted upon her. She should loathe him, vow to have him punished for subjecting her to his ill treatment. Yet Marianne's first words to him in his native Spanish spoke of her respect for his cause. Did she truly possess such a spirit of forgiveness? He remembered the softness in her eyes and the smooth flow of her voice.

If his life had not been wrenched from him by his commitment to his people, he would have begged her to stay. But the insurmountable walls dividing them had prohibited such folly. He had nothing to offer such a woman—no title, no vast estate, not even a firm belief in anything except the toil of his hands.

He rode toward the valley. Felipe and his followers, who advocated violence, were frustrated over Marianne's release and were certain to spread dissension. Those same men questioned Armando's leadership and looked to Felipe for guidance. If Armando's position was challenged, who would stand with him, and who would stand with Felipe? Would civil unrest divide the people of La For?

Armando had agreed to appeal to the padres at the San José Mission, but he felt the endeavor was foolish. The padres possessed less power than they once did with the Spanish aristocrats, though the dark-robed men were still highly respected. A Spanish gentleman always listened to the wisdom of the padres, for they knew *Dios'* laws and the mandates of Spain. However, Armando believed the padres would soon be mere administrators of the sacraments and teachers.

In the last few years, the missions had slowly deteriorated. The farming and ranching around the fortress, which had kept them alive in the past, now dwindled. Most of the mestizos had been converted, and many of them wanted land of their own, despite the advantages of living behind stone walls that protected them from marauding Comanches and Apaches. Armando sympathized with the mission inhabitants as well as he understood the people of La Flor. If the mestizos must subject themselves to Spanish rule, then those in control should allow the poor to live on their own land.

Stealing, kidnapping, and threatening murder fell under the jurisdiction of the Spanish, and for Armando to plead the dire circumstances of La Flor to the padres sounded useless, but he had promised to try. Yet seeking help for his people might get him hung.

Armando took a labored breath and focused his attention on the problems before him. Could he delude the padres about his lack of faith and convince them to act favorably toward La Flor? If he'd truly dedicated himself to his people, then why did he hesitate to lie to the padres about his relationship with *Dios*?

Even Armando Garcia had his limitations.

Shortly after dusk, he reached the top of the ridge overlooking the valley and stopped to gaze out over its twilight beauty. The placid scene never ceased to inspire and swell his heart with pride. He believed its splendor held the meaning of his life. Without this cause, a home for his beloved people, he possessed nothing.

His thoughts kept returning to Marianne. Willing the sadness to flee his mind, Armando began the winding descent to the village. Tonight he needed to hear Emilio's convictions about approaching the padres at the San José Mission.

He waved at Pepe stationed with a torch at a point above him. "Everything quiet, *mi amigo?*"

"Nothing to report but grazing cattle."

"*Bueno,* cows do not carry weapons." Armando chuckled. "Do you know where I might find Emilio?"

"On the far ridge." Pepe stood and pointed.

"*Gracias.* We'll ride at daybreak." Armando reined his horse to the northern lookout and hoped Emilio guarded the post alone. As he rode closer, a light from a small fire revealed his friend's position.

"Emilio, are you asleep?" Armando suppressed a laugh.

"I was until a wild vaquero woke me."

Laughter rose from deep within Armando, the first today, and he felt its release from all his burdens. He dismounted and led his horse toward the flickering light.

"I didn't expect you back this soon," Emilio said. "But I'm glad you're here."

The sound of the crackling fire lulled Armando into low spirits. "I saw no use in tarrying with the señorita." He shrugged. "What are a few days? I will forget her."

"Will she forget you?"

Armando tossed a dry stick into the fire. "Of course. I'm sure she has many suitors. Certainly none who held her against her will—threatening to kill her."

"None like Armando Garcia," Emilio peered into his face. "I know you would like to see her again."

He shook his head in an effort to deny his heart. "She told me *adios*. We have our own worlds."

"Wise. But it still saddens me for you."

A coyote cried out on the next hill, and Armando acknowledged its solitary wail with a grim look in the animal's direction. "He knows how I feel. But I didn't come here to grieve. I need to discuss plans for tomorrow."

Emilio nodded. "Who is the best choice to sympathize with us?"

"I have been thinking about that. San Antonio de Valero may be dangerous with the presidio located nearby. We're not well liked by the Spanish *solidats*, and if Governor Juan Bautistade Elguezábel has learned of the kidnapping, we could be arrested."

"I too have considered arrest."

"Or shot . . . or hung." Armando studied the face of his friend, expecting him to flinch, but Emilio remained calm. "Padre Bernardino Vallyo has been kind to our people. I believe he would try to help. The padres usually side with us in matters of dispute."

Emilio took a swallow of water from a canteen. "You have been educated to speak properly. Perhaps you can word what happened with Señor Phillips and his daughter in a convincing manner."

Armando considered the request. "I'll prepare an accounting of our *problema*."

"How early do you wish to leave?"

"At daybreak. With you and Pepe. The rest need to stay here and protect the valley."

"We have to trust *Dios* to protect those we love."

"For you that is good."

Armando talked with Emilio late into the night, forming the entreaty to the Padre Vallyo. When the wording was finished, they turned to reminiscing about their younger days, teasing and reminding each other of boyhood pranks.

"Remember when Felipe put a frog in the padre's chalice?" Emilio laughed.

"And how angry the padre became when none of us would confess?"

"I will never forget the expression on his face when he reached for the chalice during Mass. The whipping was worth seeing the padre angry."

After their laughter subsided, Armando glanced up into his friend's face. "I missed you after our schooling."

"The valley was empty without you. Someday our sons will create the same kind of mischief." Emilio paused. "I've forgotten. How many years did you spend at the mission under the padre?"

"To train for the priesthood," Armando whispered. "Far too long—four years."

His friend leaned into the fire. "And you've been gone from there for seven. What happened? One day you were full of love for our *Dios,* then it disappeared."

"I had no reason to continue. My father deserted us, and my mother died."

"So you blamed *Dios*?"

"No. I cannot cast the guilt on something I do not believe in. I woke one morning at the mission and realized a *Dios* did not exist. My veil of love for all men didn't encompass my Spanish father or the wealthy landowners. So I gathered my belongings and came home to Rosa and Manuel."

Emilio stared into the firelight then lifted his gaze to Armando. "I've always prayed for you, whether you desired it or not, and I will continue. I believe in *Dios*, and He alone can quench the restless spirit."

"I should be grateful."

Emilio smiled into the firelight. "You are honest, *mi amigo*. One day you will see the truth."

Armando sought to change the conversation and chose to stand and stretch. His body ached, even if his mind refused to rest. Too many nights robbed of sleep had begun to take his strength. In the starless night, he spotted a man carrying a torch up to the ridge. "Your relief is here. We can walk back together and get some rest before mañana."

"And you, *mi amigo*. Will you sleep this night, or will you roam the hills with the problems before us?"

Armando chuckled. "I am glad you are not my enemy, for you know me too well."

Chapter 12

Mounted on Diablo, Marianne galloped across the plains of her father's vast estate. Familiar landmarks and the joy of returning home should have elated her, but instead she grappled with the plight of the people in La Flor and her strange reaction to their leader.

Marianne had seen this man become transparent with his feelings. She'd sensed his pain for the circumstances plaguing his people, and she'd witnessed his devotion to those destined to lose their homes unless her father abandoned his selfish desires.

Oh, Lord, I feel so wretched. I am grateful for deliverance, but shall I never see Armando or the people of La Flor again?

Digging her heels into Diablo's flanks, Marianne fretted that her father might send soldiers to crush the rebels of La Flor. She must arrive before he took such action. Even so, she knew her return would not quell his desire to have the fertile valley. Papa would still wage his own war against Armando, just as he'd done in the past.

Too many burdens fought for priority in her mind. Marianne recognized the need to see her mother and have her comforting arms soothe the perils of the past few days. More importantly, Marianne longed to tell her about her own renewed faith in the midst of the turmoil, the times that God whispered to her of His love and His presence. She felt certain her mother had prayed for her liberation, and so had Juan and Carmita. They must be properly thanked. But she dared not disclose all the happenings to Mama without admitting her understanding of Spanish and her sympathies for her abductors. So much must be kept hidden, even from Juan and Carmita. She could not involve any of her precious family. Most of all, no one could ever learn of her reaction to Papa's enemy.

The thought of spending the rest of her life with Don Lorenzo, a man she did not love, now seemed more distasteful than ever before. Marianne swiped at a tear trickling over her cheek. But she had given Mama her word.

Hope gave rise to another possibility. Perhaps with the trauma of her kidnapping, all plans for the wedding might be postponed. But extending the date didn't stop the inevitable.

In the far distance, the faint outlines of the casa and barns came into view. A mixture of apprehension and dread took form: the unpredictable nature of her father. Until now, she hadn't wanted to consider that he might prefer her gone from his life . . . except that he would lose a share in the elderly Don Lorenzo's estate.

Evening had settled about her by the time she rode alongside the stable. She spied Thomas, Juan and Carmita's eldest son. He shouted a greeting, then quickly disappeared inside the stable. Her heart swelled that her first welcome came from her adopted family.

Moments later, Juan pushed open the stable door. "Señorita Marianne." His voice rose as he limped toward her.

She wished she could see his face in the twilight, but the sound of his voice was enough to fill her with joy. "*Tio* Juan." Marianne jumped from Diablo and ran into his outstretched arms.

"You're not hurt?" he asked in English, his words filled with emotion.

"I'm fine. Armando let me go," she said as he released his embrace. "I feared I would never see you and Carmita again."

"We prayed for you." Juan swiped at his cheeks.

"I know you did." She lowered her voice. "And I know you came to La Flor to plead for me."

"Armando told you?" Bewilderment soared from his words. "I may have been wrong about him." He cocked his head. "You spoke Spanish to your captor?"

Marianne held her breath. "Not until I knew for certain he planned to release me. I told him this afternoon."

"Ah, my sweet child. He could have hurt you with that knowledge."

"I felt at least one Phillips should be straightforward with him," she said. "Are you angry?"

In the shadows, she could see his smile. "How could I be angry? You are home. Our prayers are answered."

Marianne glanced at the house. "Is *mi madre* all right?"

Juan grasped her hands, and she felt the strength of his spirit sustaining her. "The señora is very sad. She needs to see you at once. Go to her now, and I will take care of Diablo."

Marianne's heart quickened. "Yes, I have missed her. Tell Carmita and the others *gracias* for their prayers. Tomorrow I will come and thank them properly."

She turned around and peered at the impressive adobe house in the ever-increasing darkness. Her home should have represented security and familiarity, instead of the mixed emotions that rippled through her.

Most likely nothing had changed with Papa, but how wonderful to think he might have worried about her.

She made her way up the tiled entryway, brushing past the thick-leafed palms and envisioning spring's fragrant display of colorful flowers. She pushed open the door. The thought of announcing her arrival crossed her mind, but instead she walked through the candlelit reception room and down the hallway to her mother's bedroom. The sights and smells were the same, but something different seized her. Lifting her chin, she realized she'd been the one to change—in her relationship with Jesus and in the awakening of the world around her. No longer could she consider herself a girl. Her experience had made her a woman.

Out of respect, she paused in the doorway of her mother's room and did not rush inside. The sight of Mama's beloved face moved her to a fresh onslaught of tears. She looked so frail beneath the blanket covering her weakened body, her pale face matching the bed linens.

Her mother's eyelids fluttered, and she reached out to Marianne. "Am I dreaming? Are you standing before me?"

"Mama." Marianne hurried to her and slipped into her mother's outstretched arms. "I'm home. I've been set free unharmed."

Her mother stroked Marianne's head. The soft scent of rose surrounded her and the bed clothes.

Marianne had forgotten the solace the fragrance invoked upon her.

"I feared you were gone from me forever," her mother whispered. "I could not bear to spend another day without you. What caused that wretched man to let you go?"

"I'm not sure." Guilt riddled Marianne for the half truth. "Maybe he feared what Papa would do." She raised her head to gaze into her mother's face. "I worried so, with no one to care for you."

Her mother wept. "Me? But you were the one in the clutches of an insane rebel. How like you to concern yourself with me. God has answered my prayers."

Marianne sobered and brushed back an errant lock of light brown hair from her mother's forehead. "Mine, too, Mama. He gave me strength when I wanted to give up. He became my hope and strength. He sent me home to you."

Her mother pulled Marianne close to her bosom. "My beautiful child. He's always been with you."

"It took the fear of losing my life to realize His everlasting love. And Jesus kept me safe as though I dwelled in the palm of His hand." Biting her lip to cease another flow of tears, Marianne attempted to sound light. "But I'm not beautiful, Mama. I desperately need a bath."

Her mother laughed and ran her fingers through Marianne's tangled tresses.

"What goes on here?"

Marianne instantly turned to view her father towering in the doorway. "Marianne," he said, and she thought she saw a flicker of tenderness in his blue-gray eyes. With a slight prodding, she would have gladly flown into his arms. A moment later, his glare flashed with cold regard. "Garcia released you?"

She stood up from Mama's bed to offer him her respect. Her legs shook from the old familiar fear of him. "Yes, Papa, he let me go."

"What changed his mind? Did he fear I would track him down like the animal he is?"

"I don't know." Marianne stiffened. She desired to defend Armando and his people. What he had allowed in her abduction was a terrible wrong, nothing changed that. But she understood his reasons. Her mother slipped her clammy hand into Marianne's.

"Your clothes, what happened to the gown you were wearing the night you were taken?" her mother asked, no doubt attempting to soften her father's questioning.

Marianne glanced back at her but faced her father before she replied. "Burned."

"Burned?" His face reddened. "They set fire to your dress?"

She shook her head. "No, Papa. A fire broke out in the village, and I was trapped inside a hut."

Her mother gasped, and Marianne squeezed her hand to reassure her. "I was pulled from the flames, but the house and my clothing were destroyed. The women gave me these to wear."

"So La Flor had a little fire. The whole place should have been burned to the ground with all of those blasted Mexicans in it."

Marianne's cheeks grew hot.

"But our daughter is home safe." Mama lifted her head from the pillow. "We thought our daughter was gone from this world. Let us rejoice in her deliverance."

Oppressive silence followed.

"The matter is not finished. Now that you are here, I will make a trip to the governor and see about ridding La Flor of all those thieving, treacherous Mexicans."

Marianne caught her breath at the thought of tragedy befalling the villagers. "Papa, it's not necessary. I'm home safe."

She saw anger storm across his features. "Are you defending those animals? Makes me wonder what you did to have Garcia return you."

"Weston!" Never had Marianne seen her mother in this temperament. "How could you suggest such a detestable thing from our daughter?"

Marianne sensed the color draining from her own face, first from shock then indignation. "Papa," she said through a ragged breath. Marianne sank onto her mother's bed, dazed by his implications. "I could never . . . No, Papa, please don't think I'd ever do such a thing. I simply meant there are innocent women and children in the village."

"Slaughter them all." He rubbed his chest, a mannerism she'd seen of late when he was angry. "I meant to have their valley before Garcia ordered his men to break into my home, and I still intend to have it. And him dead along with it."

"Remember our guest," her mother said.

Marianne gazed questioningly at her mother.

"Don Lorenzo is here." Mama glared at Papa. "He was kind enough to ride back with your father when they received word of your kidnapping."

Papa shook his fist at Marianne. "And you'd better not have done anything to jeopardize your marriage to the don."

Marianne tried to swallow the rising fury coursing through her body. She clenched her fists and dug her fingernails into her palms. "Of course not, Papa. I know how important your land is to you, and acquiring more of it is your greatest love."

He lifted his hand, and for a moment she feared he would strike her. Never had she openly defied him with such intensity.

"Weston, Marianne is exhausted from this ordeal," her mother said.

His eyes narrowed before he turned from the room. His footsteps thundered down the hall, shaking the candle by Mama's bedside.

All he cares about is himself. Land and power. No matter what the cost. I'm afraid he'll soon have his wish.

"Please calm yourself." Mama seemed to read her thoughts. "He doesn't mean what he says."

Marianne could not bring herself to look into her mother's face. "Yes, he does. You know it's true." She closed her eyes and took a deep breath. Remorse washed over her fury. "I'm sorry, Mama. God forgive me for what I'm thinking about Papa."

"God understands our trials and pain."

"I know, but it hurts to realize Papa does not love you or me. Some days I think I would do anything to gain his approval, and other days I don't care any longer."

"Oh, but he loves you." Her mother lay back onto the pillow. "Your father simply doesn't know how to express his feelings." In the candlelight, Mama's blue eyes were warm and gentle.

How can she defend Papa? How can she love him? "He surely has no problem in demonstrating his disapproval or anger." She stared at her mother's hand still encircling hers.

"Those are the easy emotions," her mother said. "Admitting love means giving of yourself with no assurance of receiving anything in return."

"But that is the way Jesus instructed us," Marianne said. "I believe my death would have grieved him only because he could not add more land from the don."

"You must love your papa unconditionally no matter what happens. This is the true test of love for our Lord."

Marianne leaned into the shelter of her mother's embrace. "I will pray for Papa and try to be more obedient."

"Good," her mother said. "You are much like him. It frustrates your papa to see an image of himself in you."

"Me?" She shuddered.

"Where do you think you get your independent mind? Or your love for horses? When I see you two battle wits, I see the same fire in your blue-gray eyes and the same stubborn stance. Yes, you are your father's daughter. I firmly believe it will be you who brings him to the Lord, not me."

"I think not, Mama. Perhaps you merely want it to be so, but I'll pray for him no matter how difficult it may be."

Her mother planted a kiss on her cheek. "We shall see. Right now, you need to recover from the turmoil over the past three days. It needs to be forgotten. Go on to bed now and bathe in the morning."

Marianne wearily agreed. Much had occurred, and her mind spun with all the events. Armando. The people of La Flor. Don Lorenzo. Mama's unconditional love for Papa. And her new attempts to understand Papa. Tomorrow things had to be better. She could sort through it all then with better understanding.

Chapter 13

After tossing all night like a man plagued with fever, Armando rose and packed what few items he would need for the journey to the San José Mission. Seven years had passed since he'd walked along those stone walls. The Spanish referred to its structure as impregnable, beautiful, and a model for other missions. In days gone by, when hostile Indians successfully raided the horses and cattle, none were able to scale the walls to get inside. The inhabitants fired guns through the holes in the thick, stone confines to defend their family and homes.

The people worked hard tending the herds of livestock and utilizing the fertile soil to grow fruits and vegetables through the help of the extensive aqueduct systems. Some of the mestizos were craftsmen—weavers of cloth, carpenters, blacksmiths, stonecutters, and other unique occupations.

And the mission itself, the place of worship and learning. . . . Sometimes he thought he could still hear the peal of the three-bell tower and the deep resonant voice of the padre reciting Mass in Latin or offering prayers to the almighty *Dios*. Back then, Armando had memorized the missal, the book containing all the rites necessary for Mass. He even knew the procedures for how to set up a mission, for once this had been his deep desire. Under the tutelage of Padre José Mariano de Cardenas and Padre Bernardino Vallyo, Armando grew to love the church, only to abandon it after his mother's death and before taking his vows. With a heavy heart, he remembered the pride in his mother's eyes when she spoke of her son who studied to be a padre.

Armando drew a restless breath. He needed to sleep. The next few days would be difficult. In fact, he'd rather face Phillips and his foreman Clay Wharton alone without a weapon than the padres at San José.

Hours later, as the sun broke through the horizon in slivers of orange and purple, Emilio, Pepe, and Armando rode from the valley. The three were armed with guns and daggers made in La Flor, in case they ran into marauding Indians or gringos. The vaqueros working for Phillips had family members living in La

Flor, and Armando doubted they would attack the valley or the three men.

Felipe had wanted to come with them this morning, but Armando had put him in charge of the rebuilding. Felipe looked forward to avenging his family's honor since Wharton had brutally abused his sister. Another good reason for Felipe to stay behind.

Frustrated, Armando wished he had given more thought to their arrival. They'd reach the mission near sundown tomorrow—after Saturday night Mass. Sundays were strictly observed as a day of worship, which meant he would not have an opportunity to speak with Padre Vallyo until Monday. A nudging in his spirit warned him that Phillips may have already gained an audience with the governor.

"Tell me what troubles you," Pepe asked, when the sun was suspended directly over them.

Armando considered the man's boyish features. If not for the tiny lines around his eyes, Pepe could pass for a much younger man. "I'm afraid Señor Phillips might have already talked to the presidio at San Antonio de Bejar and alerted the padres to us. We could be walking into a trap."

Pepe pressed his lips together. "We'll have to be careful, but I think it's too soon for us to worry ourselves about the *solidats*."

"I hope your thoughts do not come from being too trusting," Armando said. "The gringo is a clever man. What we've done will not sit lightly. He will want us punished, more so me than you."

"I think Pepe and I should approach the padre while you remain outside the mission, until we see how we are received," Emilio said.

"I think not," Armando said. "Your lives will not be risked for this endeavor. I am the man Phillips wants, not you."

Pepe chuckled. "Perhaps we should tie up this *hombre* until we return."

"Excellent idea," Emilio said. "But seriously, Armando, no one knows us. We'll be cautious in our dealings."

"I don't like the idea." Armando shook his head. "What if something should happen to you? How would I explain your deaths to your families?"

"We'll conceal weapons and be alert for any signs of trouble," Emilio said. "I have learned much from you."

"I don't think so, amigos. I would not send you into a snake pit without me."

Marianne awoke the following morning with heaviness curtaining her eyelids. She tried to recall everything from the evening before, but weariness lured her back into a deep sleep. Hours later she opened her eyes and attempted to muddle through the haziness enveloping her. She found it difficult to distinguish between what had happened when she returned to the hacienda and the peacefulness of her sleep.

In her dreams, she envisioned Armando dressed as a fine caballero, a fine horseman, his black trousers and colorfully beaded jacket enhancing his lightly tanned skin. He held his head high and flashed a beguiling smile. In a voice deep and rich, he beckoned her to meet him at La Flor. She ran to him, and he reached out to draw her into his arms. He told her she didn't have to marry Don Lorenzo. He loved her more than any man Papa could arrange for her to marry.

Foolish notions. Marianne scolded herself behind closed eyes. *Armando has his choice of any woman living in the valley and beyond.* She recalled the seductive dance of Isabella, and the ardent glow in her large, veiled eyes. Marianne saw her love for Armando, and the remembrance ignited a spark of jealousy.

I am acting like a girl instead of a woman. Armando must lead his life in La Flor, and I have mine here. Nothing can alter Papa's plans for me. Everything remains the same. Yet, I have the memories. I must forget him.

Marianne forced her eyes open, and her gaze drifted upward. Red and gold silk damask trimmed with gold and black tassels draped the tall, intricately carved pillars of her rosewood bed. A gold and black coverlet, similar in pattern to the tester, covered her lightly. How she'd longed for her bed during those nights in captivity.

With a sigh, she noted the brilliant light streaming through the lofty recessed windows to her right. The sun's position in the sky announced the noon hour, and Marianne always woke shortly after dawn. Glancing about, she wondered why someone had moved the walnut and brass brazier from the foot of her bed to a corner near the window. Curious, she looked to the opposite side of the room for any other changes. Her mother, dressed in a brown and white morning dress, sat in an armchair. Her hands folded primly in her lap.

"Mama, how long have you been here?"

Her mother smiled, her face pale but blissful. She tilted her head thoughtfully. "Since sunrise."

"Oh, you shouldn't have denied yourself rest."

"This was such great pleasure for me. I could watch you sleep and know that you were home safe." She stood and walked to Marianne's side.

Pulling herself to a sitting position, Marianne noted soreness throughout her body. She nodded at the sunlight. "I did sleep for a long time."

"You needed the morning to recover from your horrible encounter with those evil men." She touched a wayward lock of Marianne's hair and rolled it between her fingertips. "You look rested. I would imagine you're hungry, too. Carmita put aside fruit, eggs, and tortillas from breakfast."

"Thank you." Marianne detected something not so pleasant. "I need to bathe first."

Her mother's fingers slipped from Marianne's hair to her cheek. "I thought as much, and Carmita has heated water."

"Wonderful. I hope this hasn't been too much work for her." Marianne reveled in the comforts of home and those she loved who loved her in return. Without warning, a sadness swept over her. "Are Papa and Don Lorenzo in the house?"

"No, your father took him riding across the estate. They should return by the mid-afternoon meal. The don is concerned about you. He wants to hasten the wedding."

Marianne hid her disappointment in light of the sadness in her mother's face. "I will thank him for accompanying Papa to see about me."

Her mother moved to the window and stood for several moments before turning to Marianne. With her hands folded below her waist, she sighed deeply. "Do you wish to talk about what happened during your abduction?"

Marianne longed to reveal her innermost secrets, the terror and later the bewilderment of being released. But she reminded herself that she could not reveal her knowledge of Spanish or her strange attraction to Armando. She gasped. If she relayed the truth, her dreams would be shattered, and she couldn't bear to send them away—not just yet.

"Mama, I know God protected me, especially when surrounded by such grave danger. Please forgive me, but I'd rather not discuss my captivity. It's best forgotten, as you stated last evening."

A wave of compassion swept over her mother's face and softened her features. "Of course. How could I be so thoughtless to cause you undue pain?"

Her mother focused on Marianne's face, and for a moment, she feared her mother knew those wandering reflections about Armando.

"Do you need to be resting, now that I have wakened?" Marianne asked.

"Soon. Truthfully, I'm exhausted and should lie down. Would you like to spend time with me in the garden this afternoon?"

"What a splendid idea." Marianne took a quick breath. "Could we read the Bible together?"

Her mother's eyes moistened. "I've prayed so long for your true commitment to the Lord. And yes, we shall read anything you desire."

After her mother left her to bathe, Marianne settled into the warm water. She shut her eyes and allowed secret thoughts to drift across her mind. All her life she'd dreamed of a comely man who would make her heart soar. Now that those dreams had begun to take form in a man who was her father's enemy, she felt empty, as though cheated out of a glorious fulfillment. Perhaps she'd lost something to Armando she never really possessed.

But I have gained the Lord. My relationship with Him is worth any price. It's selfish to view the past three days in any other way.

She firmly pushed aside the advancing reminiscences of Armando. God held a plan for her life, a plan far better than she could ever envision. As Mama had always said, "You are a daughter of the King. Conduct yourself in obedience and humility."

Following those words usually sounded simple, unless it involved dealing with Papa. Last night she'd lost her temper, and she should apologize. No matter that Papa cared only for himself and spoke so harshly. Regret crept through her. A surrender of her life to God meant obeying His commands.

Heavenly Father, how can You ask this of me? Please, I cannot go to Papa. He can be so cruel. Marianne glanced at her hands and saw dirt still embedded beneath her fingernails. She remembered the panic when Felipe kidnapped her. God comforted and delivered her then, and He would be with her when she apologized to Papa.

In the early afternoon, Marianne and her mother sat under a stone courtyard archway where a light breeze played among the variegated shades of green bushes and small, ornamental trees. The sun warmed the flourishing plants, coaxing the palms, cacti, aloe, and trailing ivy to rise upward. Yellow-orange blossoms from the prickly pear, winsome daisies, and vibrant verbena seemed to nod at her.

Mama looked much better than she had earlier, for now there was a faint trace of pink in her cheeks.

"What can I read to you?" her mother asked.

Marianne touched her finger to her chin. "I think Daniel in the lion's den." She laughed. "We have something in common."

"My dear daughter, how brave of you to make light of your abduction. I do despise your ordeal."

"But Mama, it happened just as the Bible says. They meant to harm me, but God meant their plans for good. I am forever a changed woman. I have faced death and can no longer fear its sting."

Her mother failed to respond but the tears in her eyes spoke volumes. Marianne placed her hand over the cracked, black leather binding of the Bible resting in her mother's lap. "Here, I will read, and you enjoy this beautiful afternoon."

Mama relinquished the Bible, and Marianne thumbed through the well-worn pages. Her mother's handwriting and dates beside Scripture passages caught her eye. She wanted to study them. "Do you mind if I read your notes?"

"No, of course not."

"I plan to study God's Word every day. Will you help me when I don't understand the passages?"

A contented sigh escaped her mother's lips. "Oh, yes. But there are confusing parts for me, too. Perhaps we can help each other."

Marianne gathered up her mother's hand. "A wonderful idea, but I'll be the student and you the teacher for a long time." She gazed into her mother's lovely features. "I pray God makes you strong again."

"And I will do all I can to ensure this happens."

"I know, Mama. We need each other for strength and comfort when the days are difficult. I don't want to think of another day without you. If my words are selfish then I'm sorry. And I've decided that when Papa returns, I'll apologize for being disrespectful last evening."

"I hoped you would come to that conclusion. You please me, Marianne." She glanced beyond the courtyard to the distant hills. "Do you feel better about your marriage to Don Lorenzo?"

Marianne refused to lie. "I'm not looking forward to the marriage. This is a difficult adjustment for me."

She avoided her mother's gaze and took a deep breath. How could she consider sharing her life with this man, a stranger, after Armando awakened her heart? He touched her life with his passion for living and opened her eyes to the hope of a divine love between two people. If she ever did see him again, she'd beg to never leave his side.

Her mother studied her closely. "This morning you spoke in your sleep."

"That's strange. Perhaps I was having a nightmare from my captivity"

"You called out a name."

While outwardly Marianne guarded her response, inwardly she knew her dreams betrayed her. "Mama, did I call out for you?"

"You called out for Armando." Mama glanced around nervously as though speaking his name ushered the man into their presence.

A chill trickled through Marianne's body. "He threatened to kill me if Papa refused to meet his demands."

"The manner in which you repeated his name did not indicate your dislike for him." Her mother trembled. "I must ask this, my daughter, although I believe you have not lied to me or your papa. Did he seek your affections . . . and steal your innocence?"

Marianne rushed to reply, feeling repulsion for the mere thought of such an ignoble act. "He did not in any way abuse me," she said. "Your fears are unfounded."

"There you are, Elthia, Marianne," a familiar voice called from inside the house.

Her father waved as he and Don Lorenzo approached. Marianne's heart sank. Papa always acted as if he loved her and Mama when guests were present.

"Good afternoon, Weston, Don Lorenzo." Mama's words were spoken tenderly.

Papa translated his wife's greeting to the don, and the elderly gentleman responded. Marianne often questioned why Papa didn't want her or Mama to learn Spanish when he spoke the language fluently. Perhaps his refusal had to do with power over her and Mama and Marianne's relationship with Juan and Carmita, though it seemed strange to think Papa might feel envious of her affections for the Torres family. She'd gladly bestow her love to him, too.

"Please offer a welcome to the don for me," Marianne requested of her father. "And thank him for accompanying you in light of our family's misfortune." She prayed for strength. "Papa, I apologize for my disrespect last evening."

His mustache twitched, indicating his agitation with her. "You could appear happier in the presence of your future husband," he said with a pleasant demeanor.

She managed a pleasant smile and nodded at the don while her father interpreted her words of welcome and gratefulness. Summoning her wits about her, she focused her attention upon the don. He looked distinguished, and in a fatherly way, polite and attentive. In the few times she'd been in his presence, Marianne had appreciated his hearty laugh and the merriment in his brown eyes, the same color as the sherry Papa served him. His hair and beard were a glimmering white, although he did not have the etchings of age in his face. Marriage to him might have interested her if not for Armando.

"Marianne, the don and I spent the morning riding over the hacienda and discussing your future," her father said. "He desires for you to learn Spanish and to study Catholicism. I assured him of your agreement to this, and I will make immediate arrangements at the Mission San Antonio de Valero for a tutor."

"Yes, Papa." Her stomach twisted. She wanted to declare she already spoke Spanish and didn't incline herself to learn about Catholicism. Rebellion engulfed her, and stubborn pride battled with obedience to Papa. With an inward sigh, she yielded to the desire to bridle her tongue and leave her feelings behind. At the first opportunity, she would confess to the don her Spanish-speaking ability and ask him to refrain from informing Papa. As for the Catholic instruction, she needed to learn the differences between her own beliefs and those of her future husband. Marianne saw no other alternative.

The don cleared his throat. "The señorita looks most charming dressed in blue and white. May I take her for a stroll? Even though we do not speak the same language, it is a way to become more comfortable in each other's presence. Perhaps you and the señora might join us?"

Her father gave his approval and announced to Marianne the plans. She stood and the Spanish nobleman offered his arm with a charming smile.

Marianne fought the churning inside her again, not for linking arms with the don but for what it represented: the beginning of a future she could not change.

Chapter 14

Armando, Emilio, and Pepe arrived Saturday afternoon outside the Mission San José y San de Miguel de Aguayo, known as the Queen of Missions. As suspected, they could do nothing until Monday morning. Padre Bernardino Vallyo did not receive callers unless a critical situation arose. He said High Mass on Saturday mornings and promptly oversaw cleaning of the church and sacristy. Then all the women came for a portion of soap so they could wash clothes for their families. To the padres, cleanliness ranked at the top of important matters.

As the sun began to set and steal the view of overhanging trees bent with moss, Armando and his friends heard the brief ringing of the bells summoning all Mexicans to gather. They were instructed to pray the

Rosary and finish with singing. From what Armando remembered, the padre spent the evening in prayer and in preparation for Sunday. The thought of wasting an entire day disgruntled him.

Emilio and Pepe believed the padre would require confession before hearing about their plight. The two did not mind; in fact they looked forward to it. For Armando, feigning faith in *Dios* bothered him more than having to wait another day to see the padre. Surely there must be another way.

"We could hide here among the trees during the evening services," Emilio said, and Pepe agreed. "And we could attend Mass in the morning."

"That choice may not be wise," Armando said. "What if someone alerts the *solidats* in San Antonio de Bejar? We could be tortured or hung before we have an opportunity to approach the padre. We'd be accepting defeat."

"You're right. We can make camp close by and stay in hiding until Monday." Pepe's boyish face wore a serious look.

The three men settled down for the night. Soon Armando heard their even breathing as Emilio's and Pepe's bodies relaxed. Why must sleep elude him? The wretched unrest. Always his thoughts raced and could not be subdued.

He didn't feel comfortable entering the mission. Although San José had no fetters or stocks, Spanish *solidats* could be out and about. They were easily spotted, wearing short blue jackets with red cuffs, a red collar, and knee-length blue pants. They reminded Armando of strutting roosters marching about carrying muskets and swords at their sides.

The questions and probing sure to come from Padre Bernardino Vallyo proved troubling. Armando remembered well his manner of advising one to seek *Dios* resolutely and not to waiver. And Armando had not seen the man since he left the mission seven years ago. The padre had wept at Armando's declaration of unbelief.

Dread plodded through his veins. He didn't welcome the meeting, but the padre loved his flock and had helped them in the past. Unlike so many missionaries who imposed heavy tasks upon the mestizos, Bernadino Vallyo worked to lessen their burdens. He was La Flor's only hope, and for his people, Armando must comply with his friends' wishes.

Just as sleep began to soothe him, a vision of Marianne danced across his mind. To see her again and hear her say his name, he'd consider walking to the gallows. He dreamed of her and refused to push her memory away. So many times he had been tempted to give his heart to Isabella. She loved him and would make a good wife, but Armando didn't desire her. Just like his *madre*, he yearned for forbidden love.

The next morning, Armando noticed the Mission San José y San Miguel de Aguayo had changed little since his departure. Its massive stone walls were well maintained, with each inhabitant responsible for an area of work. As Armando and his friends walked toward the church, he recognized faces changed by age and hard work. The men still wore the white cotton shirts and pants, and the women dressed in loose-fitting shifts. All the clothing was issued by the padres. Every detail of their lives came under the authority of the mission. As before, a few appeared happy, especially the children, while others trudged through their daily assignments. He imagined the men and boys heading out to the fields, orchards, and quarries, while others stayed behind to work at various tasks. Some of the men tended sheep, cattle, and goats in surrounding fields outside the mission walls. The women and girls worked at cooking, sewing, gardening, and making soap, candles, and pottery. Their only reprieve came with Mass on feast days.

Armando ached with the thought of his people subjecting themselves to such a miserable life. To him, it meant enslavement to the Crown of Spain, and he despised it. His *tio* and *tia* had come from this mission.

They seldom complained of life back then, for their needs were met, but they much preferred the freedom of La Flor.

Whatever happened today, the welfare of his people came above all things, even if it meant sacrificing himself.

"I don't see any *solidats*," Emilio said while they walked the circular stone path around the mission to the church. "And I didn't see any of them earlier when Pepe and I observed the activities inside the mission."

Armando merely nodded. Each wood and mortar dwelling they passed looked the same, one after another, and all symbolic of Spain. The doors were hand-carved cedar, and each had an iron lock and key. Various craftsmen worked on the opposite side of the mission: weavers of cloth, those who constructed saddles and bridles, leather workers, carpenters, a blacksmith, and whatever else the padre deemed necessary according to the time of the year. To Armando, it seemed depressing—the inhabitants were forced to worship *Dios* and give of the fruits of their toil for the betterment of the mission.

Pepe loved his son enough to consider living here if necessary, and Mexicans were always needed to perform tasks and skilled crafts. For a brief moment, Armando wondered about a child of his own, a delight he would most likely never enjoy. Could that affection be even stronger than his love for the people of La Flor? Would he, like Pepe, give up his whole life's work for the sake of a child? Armando lifted his head proudly. He'd already committed his life for all the children of La Flor and their parents.

Armando couldn't help but think of his own father, the Spaniard Joseph Garcia, the man who'd deserted his illegitimate son and the woman who had loved him. But Armando refused to dwell on such things when he needed to concentrate on his purpose.

The old familiar despondency settled about him. When he lived at the mission, he couldn't put his feelings into words, but now he acknowledged the problem. His body and spirit had craved peace. Padre Bernardino Vallyo had sensed his need and urged him to pray and fast, but those sacrifices never helped. Always the restlessness. Always the desire for something deep within the core of his soul. Would he ever find a release?

He glanced up at the Rose Window, its richly detailed stone frame resembling the petals of a perfect rose. *Si*, the mission was beautiful. He could not deny the excellent workmanship done by those who initially constructed the church and the fortress shielding it.

Too soon for his liking, the three men stood at the walnut double doors. Armando had forgotten the richly carved stonework framing the doorway. The awe he once felt for the beauty of the mission resurfaced again.

Respectfully, they removed their sombreros, and Emilio and Pepe crossed themselves before entering the church. At the sight of the crucifix, Armando stopped and studied the image of the suffering *Salvador*. He crossed himself and remembered the days when his whole life centered on the cross and all it meant. Did faith in *Dios* really mean nothing? He swallowed hard and glanced about him. The ornate figure of *Madre Maria* stood more beautiful than he remembered, especially in contrast to the bleakness of life around them. He did not remember the statues affecting him like this in the past. Denying the pull on his spirit, he decided his confusion must come from his trepidation over speaking with the padre.

The brown-robed figure of Padre Bernardino Vallyo entered the small chapel to the right of the altar. He stopped, knelt, and crossed himself before turning and making his way down the center aisle.

Armando's heart drummed against his chest. What manner of fear overwhelmed him? Not even when he faced the tumultuous undertaking of leading his people had he experienced such cowardly reactions. It angered him, and he resolved to conquer his fainthearted response.

The padre stopped in front of Armando. The years had etched more lines into his leathered face, and his once dark hair now held many strands of gray. His eyes, the color of pecans, shone with kindness and compassion. Hard work had kept him lean and muscular, reminding Armando of how the man had toiled alongside the Mexicans, often teaching them how to perform a task. Tears filled the older man's eyes, and Armando sensed emotion on the verge of consuming him, too.

"*Mi hijo*," Padre Bernardino Vallyo reached to pull Armando close. "How very good to see you."

Armando almost refused the padre's embrace, but he reconsidered, for it might hinder the chances of getting his help. But no sooner had the deliberations plagued his mind than he realized the padre's friendship had been greatly missed. The calming voice and the smell of his robe, a mixture of earth and soap, filled Armando's nostrils and returned him to another time. This man had been a teacher and a true father to him when his whole world collapsed.

But Armando, on the brink of manhood, had refused the love and kindness. He associated it with a trickery of *Dios* to enslave him within the walls of the mission.

The two men parted and Armando contained himself enough to speak. "You look well, Padre. It's good to see you."

"Too many years have passed between us, and not a day has gone by that I have not prayed for you." Tears flowed unashamedly down his cheeks. "*Dios* has answered my prayers."

"I think not." Armando refused to give the padre any false illusions. He gazed deeply into his eyes. "My presence today is to discuss a grave matter."

"Do you desire confession?"

Armando forced a light smile. "No, this is about La Flor."

The padre nodded and extended his hand in the direction of the rear door. "Let us walk in the garden and talk about your valley. Will Emilio and Pepe accompany us?"

"Padre, we'll wait here and pray." Emilio's wide-set eyes revealed his great love for the padre. "I would like you to hear my confession before we leave."

"Of course," Bernadino said. "You also, Pepe?"

"*Si.* It's been a long time."

"*Dios* is always ready to hear the confession of a man's heart." The padre placed his hand on Pepe's shoulder. "I see the grief in your eyes for Dorothea. *Dios* will help you. And Rico? Is he well and growing?"

"*Si, Padre, mi hijo* is my life. I would like for you to see him one day." Pepe's words were gentle and affirming while his hand clutched blue-and-white rosary beads.

"I've been in prayer about visiting La Flor." The padre's gaze rested on Armando. "It's not good for a shepherd to leave his flock unattended." He nodded at Armando. "Come, let's discuss the problem in the valley. I pray I can help."

As the two men strolled outside the church to the garden Armando had once tended, pleasant memories washed over him. He remembered the satisfaction of watching young, tender shoots burst from the fertile soil and eagerly anticipating their growth. Knowing he'd assisted in the process had always filled him with satisfaction. The morning sun warmed his back, and the songs of birds rang melodious in his ears, just like the ones in his treasured La Flor.

"Padre." Armando's rehearsed words had left him. "You know how I love the valley and the people living there."

"It is your home, Armando."

"As it is for so many others . . . but our happiness is threatened. Señor Weston Phillips wants our valley to graze his cattle."

The padre stared at the ground where the grass had been trodden until it refused to grow. "He's a rich man with much power. It must be that *agua* is the *problema*.

I know the Phillips Hacienda borders on the Medina River. Could he irrigate as we have done at the missions?"

"Possibly, but Señor Phillips is a greedy man, and La Flor is kept fertile by underground springs. Grazing his cattle in our valley means he doesn't have any worries about *agua*."

"I understand." Bernardino Vallyo took a labored breath and placed his arms behind him. He continued to walk in silence. "Tell me more." He glanced up at Armando and smiled. "With you, there's always more to tell."

Armando knew his former actions invited reproof, but in order for the padre to speak with the governor in San Antonio de Bejar on their behalf, the religious man must hear the truth. "When we refused to leave, he said he would force us out."

"Has anything else happened?"

Armando hesitated. "He or his foreman have visited the valley twice a week since then. Each time, Señor Phillips becomes more forceful. Once he shot one of our horses and another time his foreman, Clay Wharton, destroyed some of our gardens. The villagers were frightened and wanted someone to lead them."

The padre sighed. "And they elected you."

"*Si, Padre.* Several months ago I rode to see Governor Juan Bautistade Elguezábel, but the *solidats* would not permit me entrance into his palace." Armando stopped along the path and faced the padre squarely. "I stole cattle from the Phillips Hacienda to feed my people and a few horses to breed our own."

Bernardino Vallyo frowned, his brows knitted together.

"I know stealing is wrong," Armando said, determined to finish his speech. "But I have more to tell you. When he threatened to kill me and anyone else who opposed his taking over the valley, I gathered men together to unite against his efforts. We were and are prepared to fight for our land. It is all we have. In my plan to bargain with Señor Phillips, I did nothing while a few of my men broke into his casa and kidnapped his daughter. They also stole horses, muskets, swords, and daggers."

The padre's eyes grew wide. "No, Armando. Surely you didn't do such a terrible thing. Did you harm the señorita?"

Armando shook his head. "No, I could not. Killing her meant we were no better than the enemy. She has been returned to her home. But we kept the other things."

"*Bueno.*" They walked a little further. "Surely Señor Phillips has reported this to the governor. He will have the *solidats* after you. Weston Phillips will demand justice."

"I know, and if a man took my daughter, I would want him dead too. I'm not afraid for me, but for the fate of my people and their valley."

"How can I possibly help you?"

Armando felt courage surge through him. "Take my appeal to the governor so the people can live in La Flor."

"I can talk to him, but what of the crimes you've committed?"

Armando nodded. "I've thought of little else since yesterday. I can return the stolen weapons, the cattle, and the horses, but Phillips will want revenge for my kidnapping his daughter."

"I know this man," the padre said, "Like you, I'm afraid he'll want you dead."

Armando paused. Memories of Marianne tore at his heart. "I believe he would trade me for La Flor."

Bernardino Vallyo grabbed Armando's shoulders. "You don't need to die for your crimes. There must be another way." His voice rippled with emotion. "A trial, perhaps. One that revealed to Governor Elguezábel why you did these things."

"My people cannot lose their homes," Armando said. "I see no other way to appease Phillips or the governor."

The padre stared at him while the sounds of nature echoed around them. Armando stared up at the moss-covered trees, hoping Bernardino understood.

"Do Emilio and Pepe know what you are proposing?"

"No, they would attempt to dissuade me."

"I want to fast and pray about this. The ways of *Dios* are not as ours, and He may have a different solution. *Por favor*, stay here for the night while I seek His will. Even if the *solidats* come looking for you, they'll not find you here."

Armando considered the request. "One night," he said.

Padre Bernardino Vallyo placed his hands on Armando's shoulders. "To die for a worthy cause is good, but I pray *Dios* can solve our *problema* without your death."

Chapter 15

After Bernardino and Armando made their way back inside the church, the padre offered a morning meal. Although Bernardino refrained from eating due to beginning his fast, he did ask questions about their families and friends.

"I must plan to visit La Flor. I know there are baptisms, marriages, and religious instruction to be done there. God forgive me for neglecting your valley."

"We will greet you with open arms," Emilio said.

Emilio and Pepe talked freely and inquired about the activities in and around the mission. Armando listened but offered little to the conversation. Discussing church life and kindred affairs held little appeal for him. Instead, his mind spun with questions of how the padre might be able to help the village. Without his old friend's help,

La Flor might be lost. The villagers would be forced to live at the mission or at a hacienda where the owner would demand payment or work in exchange.

When Bernardino excused himself for the remainder of the day to pray about the dilemma with Señor Phillips, Emilio and Pepe decided to spend the morning in prayerful observance of what lay ahead. Armando left them and stepped outside. With the burden of his destiny weighing upon his shoulders, he walked to the north gate and examined the grape arbor. As he expected, it looked well cultivated, and the granary was in good repair with plenty of corn available until harvest. Under Bernardino's frugal leadership, Armando did not expect anything less.

Armando paced the perimeter of the mission and stopped in front of the church. A sculpture of Saint Anne holding the infant Mary, Jesus' mother, captured his eye. He recalled when the mission and church served his every need, or rather when he *thought* the church met his needs. He didn't like being here. The constant reminder of the *Dios* he'd forsaken seemed to needle at his heart and mind. Had he realized that there was no God when he'd left the mission or had he just been rebellious? The unrest in his spirit added to his troubles.

Glancing about, he saw that the palmed roof of an abandoned hut needed repair. It surprised him, considering Bernardino's meticulous care. With a shrug, he went to work. As the morning wore on, the heat intensified, and he wiped the sweat from his brow with his sleeve. Still, the toil did not relieve his worries wavering between La Flor and Marianne, neither of which he could do anything about.

Marianne he must forget. And for La Flor, he was ready to give his life.

During the late afternoon, Emilio and Pepe approached him.

"You've been busy," Emilio said. "Now someone can use the hut."

"Maybe me," Pepe said, "if our valley goes to Señor Phillips."

Armando shook his head. "I will not let that happen."

"I know *Dios* is on our side, but—."

"Hush, Pepe," Emilio said. "We will not lose our valley."

Their voices rang with desperation, and Armando despised it all. "I should like to leave at daybreak."

"We will be ready," Emilio said.

"No doubt Felipe attempts to turn the others against us," Armando said. "We must keep our peoples' spirits high."

"*Si, amigo.* You can depend on us." Emilio lifted his chin. "For now, we will continue in prayer. For everyone involved."

If the people of La Flor were forced from their valley, they would have to choose between living at the mission and scraping by in an existence constantly threatened by Comanche Indians.

Armando wished he knew what Padre Bernardino planned to do. In one sense, he respected the padre's dedication to fasting and prayer, but in truth he felt it useless. The waiting simply prolonged the reality of life as dictated by the Spanish. They didn't care about the injustices suffered by the poor, only that their empire be extended and protected from the French and the Americans.

The padre would have to use Armando as bargaining power to secure La Flor.

That evening, typical of most nights, Armando lay awake until he finally rose and walked outside under the faint light of a half moon. Tomorrow seemed like an eternity away.

When the first hints of dawn in pink and purple crested the horizon, Armando entered the church in search of Bernardino. The padre knelt in front of the statue of Jesus, his head nearly touching the floor. No doubt he'd been there most of the night.

The robed figure rose and crossed himself. In the pale light, he turned to Armando and called from the back of the church. "You did not sleep," he said and made his way down the aisle.

"No, Padre."

"Some things never change. I saw you walk the mission, just as you used to do when matters worried you."

Armando smiled. "Old habits are hard to break."

"And did *Dios* tell you anything?"

"No." Armando understood the padre wanted him to renew his faith, even above all the pertinent matters before them.

Bernardino sighed. "I hoped and prayed you would return to take your vows, but *Dios* has not yet answered my prayers."

Armando stepped closer. He didn't seek to criticize but to convey his heart. "I no longer believe," he said. "You know my misgivings, Padre."

Bernardino nodded in the shadows. "*Si*, but people do renew their faith in times of turmoil."

"I see no purpose in trying to please a *Dios* who does what He wishes to a man. One can never be good enough, work hard enough, or say enough prayers to equal Him, so why try?"

"Because He is *Dios*. We believe in His deity, and we obey."

The familiar surge of irritation simmered in Armando's spirit. He bit back caustic words. "I cannot accept your faith, Padre. *Por favor,* let us talk of more urgent matters—the villagers of La Flor."

"Of course. You and your amigos are anxious to hear if I can help." He paused. "I believe *Dios* would want me to speak to the governor. And I believe it's wrong for Señor Phillips to take land that does not belong to him. I grieve for those who have been threatened and fear what he could do. I will make the journey tomorrow."

"Gracias."

"But I wonder why you did not come to me sooner, before the situation grew so serious."

Armando stared into the padre's face, outlined in the early morning light. He must be truthful. "I feared Señor Phillips's influence with the Spanish. He's rich and powerful. And, Padre, because of our past relationship, I thought you might refuse to assist us."

"Mi hijo, it is not I who chose a different path. I've committed my life to the people of Tejas, and I will never stop praying and fighting for them." Bernardino spoke his words softly, yet with conviction.

Remorse tore at Armando's heart. "I apologize for not trusting you with La Flor's well-being. Now I know if we'd come to you in the beginning, the situation might have been resolved more easily. As their leader, I'm the one to blame for breaking the laws.

In the future, I'll encourage my people always to seek your counsel. But what of my crimes?"

"When I visit Governor Elguezábel, I'll describe you as a man who loves his people so much that he made foolish decisions. I'll tell him of your desire to return all of the possessions belonging to Señor Phillips and your confession of doing nothing when others in desperation kidnapped Señor Phillips's daughter." He folded his hands at his waist. "I plan to testify of the years you spent with me in the mission and your devotion to the matters of *Dios*. My prayer is the governor will have mercy on your plight and release you to me in full pardon."

Armando wet his lips. "And what does that mean for you?"

"Simply said, if you break any more laws, I will be held responsible."

Never had he expected Padre Bernardino Vallyo's generosity. "Why, Padre? I don't deserve your risking your excellent reputation, and I'm ready to take any punishment Governor Elguezábel issues."

A smile spread across Bernardino's face. "These are the things the *Dios santo* has revealed to me. Perhaps He desires you to understand His unmerited mercy."

Armando felt a yearning in his spirit, and he began to wonder if he'd been wrong in his evaluation of *Dios*.

Then, as quickly as the thoughts entered his mind, they disappeared. In its place came the doubt and guilt so dominant in his mind. "I will never forget all you've done for me and my people," he said. "I swear I will not dishonor your name or cause you to regret your decision."

"I can do no less for those I love," Bernardino said, and placed a hand on Armando's shoulder.

Armando knew of only a few times when speech escaped him, but he could not bring himself to express his gratitude to the padre in the proper words. "I'd like to stay until you receive word from the governor, but Emilio and Pepe need to ride back to their families."

A smile played on the padre's lips. "I welcome your company."

As soon as he spoke, the bells rang out summoning the people to morning Mass. Armando attended the services, knowing his presence pleased Bernardino. This time he didn't mind the religious atmosphere, for elation filled his spirit at the thought of his people's safety. Hope replaced the fear of his people suffering injustice at the hands of the gringo or the Spanish, and Armando drank in the rare peace.

Shortly after a morning meal of cornmeal mush, Emilio and Pepe left for La Flor. Meanwhile, Bernardino prepared himself to journey the nearly ten miles to San Antonio de Bejar by wagon. Armando planned to go with him disguised as a peasant.

"This may be foolish, *mi hijo*." The padre frowned. He stared at Armando dressed in the typical white shirt, pants, and sandals common to the mission people. "Why not wait here until I return in the late afternoon?"

Armando grinned. "Look at me, Padre. I belong with you." He climbed up onto the wagon and took the reins of a sway-backed horse hitched to the wooden structure. He patted the palm hat pulled down over his eyes. "I'm your driver, and I can keep you from wild *hombres*."

Bernardino climbed up beside Armando. "You always were a stubborn one." He chuckled. "But I am glad for your company."

Armando urged the horse forward. It had been a long time since he and the padre had discussed books, history, and life. Without the dreaded topic of *Dios*, it would be an enjoyable trip.

"Padre." Armando sensed a lightheartedness not often prevalent in his life. "Did you ever discover who put the frog in the chalice during Mass?"

Bernardino chuckled. "Ah, it was not Felipe, but the rascal sitting beside him that morning."

"*Si.*" He laughed. "The other boys believed Felipe had done the mischief, and he enjoyed the glory."

As the men talked of the old days, the trip progressed quickly. Yet finally, Armando felt compelled to ask. "Do you believe the governor will reach a decision today?"

Bernardino swatted a hungry mosquito resting on his hand. "I don't know, but I pray he will. It all depends on how he interprets what I tell him, and if Señor Phillips has already been to see him. I've been thinking you may need to go into hiding."

"Not unless I am assured the valley is safe," Armando said.

"Perhaps I shall have an answer today."

"Then I shall wait near the wagon."

"But not patiently. Armando Garcia never waits patiently."

The sun had not reached its peak when Armando drove the rickety wagon into San Antonio de Bejar's market place. Excitement buzzed like honeybees, and the shouts of those wishing to sell or barter their goods echoed across the plaza. Creaking two-wheeled ox-drawn *carros* bringing poultry, colorful *serapes*, pottery, and various other goods ambled through the dirt street, while owners drove their cattle to the center of activity. Children scurried about in play, and lovely señoritas stole moments with the young men. *Madres* laughed and scolded as they prepared to serve food later in the day, now and then taking a long look at the colorful blankets and pottery. This was the capital of the Spanish province of Tejas.

Armando drove on past the busy people intermingled with the despised blue-coated soldiers and on to the governor's palace. Stopping in front of the heavy, carved walnut door, he watched the padre step down from the wagon.

"Where will you be?" Bernardino's forehead lined with concern.

"In the marketplace. I'll not be far."

"*Dios* be with you," the padre said, as though by habit, but Armando saw the anxiousness in his brown eyes.

"Don't worry. I'll not get into trouble, and no one will recognize me today." With those words, Armando tilted his palm hat farther down over his eyes and gathered up the reins to continue on his way.

Armando refused to think of what might happen if Governor Elguezábel refused the padre's request. For now, Armando must tuck himself away in the marketplace and watch the people carry on their business.

Lingering among the merchants past the midday meal and siesta, he ignored the hunger gnawing at him. He really had no mind to eat, for impatience had begun to take its toll. Just when he believed the padre must be begging for La Flor and Armando's life, the brown-robed figure appeared.

"We need to leave immediately," the padre said with no visible trace of emotion. "We can talk later."

Armando accepted the request without question, and soon the two men were on the road south toward Mission San José.

"It went well," Bernardino finally said. "I don't know if we were followed, which is why I wanted to leave the city before we talked."

Feeling his muscles relax, Armando swallowed hard as he waited for the padre to explain what occurred with the governor.

"*Dios* was with us," he began. "Just before I arrived, one of the *solidats* had visited Governor Elguezábel with a complaint. It seems an American who holds an important position at the Phillips Hacienda has dishonored a señorita and refuses to take her in marriage."

Armando lifted a brow. He well knew the gringo, Clay Wharton . . . and remembered what he'd done to Felipe's sister. "I know the man," he said, "a bad *hombre*."

"The governor is highly displeased—and angry with all Americans. The French have sold Louisiana to the Americans, and their occupation threatens Tejas borders." He turned his attention to Armando, and a wave of sadness seemed to pass over him. "Forgive me, *Dios*, for I am rejoicing over another man's sin and a señorita's dishonor." Bernardino's gaze met Armando's. "Governor Elguezábel will not allow Señor Phillips to take La Flor. I am responsible for your actions now, which means I will be journeying to La Flor soon."

For a moment he thought he might break down and weep like a child. His people would be able to remain in their homes.

"And he will not bring charges against you for kidnapping the señorita. At least not today," the padre said. "He expects you to return the weapons and half of the livestock."

All the hatred Armando held for the Spanish suddenly dissipated, if only for the moment. "How am I to return the weapons? Señor Phillips will have me shot if I am within miles of his hacienda."

Bernardino nodded. "The governor will dispatch an envoy to La Flor in three days' time to gather the stolen items and return them to Señor Phillips. At that time, he'll learn of the governor's decision about La Flor and his demands regarding Señor Wharton."

"I want to select thirty additional heads of cattle for them," Armando said, "and horses that I know came from his herds." He wanted to owe the gringo nothing.

The padre touched Armando's shoulder. "*Dios* has saved La Flor and your life. He must have something extraordinary planned for you." His voice faded to barely a whisper. "Turn back to Him, *mi hijo*. Turn back to Him. *Dios* loves you more than you can imagine."

Chapter 16

Armando knew what Bernardino wanted to hear, but pleasing this dear man meant lying. He had too much respect for the humble padre to resort to such low means.

Finally Armando spoke. "If only to console the heaviness in your heart, I would gladly come to confession, even take my vows. But I cannot live in deceit." He peered into the clear, compassionate eyes of his amigo. "I owe you my life, the work of my hands, but not my soul."

"Stating that you don't owe me your soul says you believe in *Dios*," the padre said. "I will continue to pray." His face held an ethereal glow, and Armando saw the visible peace that he sorely desired for himself.

Armando studied the ruts in the road. Could Bernardino not see he didn't need *Dios*? With an inward sigh, he forced himself to examine the truth. When anger did not override his senses, he wanted to believe *Dios* existed for all of mankind.

"I see the worried frown on your face," Bernardino said. "We don't need to talk of such things now. I have a matter of great concern to discuss with you, not of La Flor or Señor Phillips, but of your father, Joseph Garcia. I wanted to settle things with the governor before I shared with you that Joseph contacted me."

Armando immediately focused his attention on what the padre had to say. Each time he believed his father didn't matter to him, something nudged him and a host of old memories, both good and bad, crowded his thoughts. Masking his turmoil, he turned to Bernardino. "And what about this man do you wish to relay?"

"After you left the mission, I received a letter from him to give to you. Since that time, you haven't returned for me to place it in your hands. And those few times I visited La Flor, you were absent."

"What does it say?" Armando kept his gaze on the dirt road ahead, attempting not to sound overly anxious or even to care about the letter's contents.

"I haven't read it, only the portion addressed to me." Bernardino pulled a leather drawstring bag from inside the folds of his robe. "I placed it in here to protect it." He held out the bag to Armando. "It's yours. Perhaps it will ease the bitterness of his departure. I feared," he sighed, "if the *solidats* arrested you, you might never know his words for you."

Armando took the pouch, deeply touched that his friend cared so much to keep the letter. He fingered the yellowed paper and mentally calculated when he'd be alone to read its contents. Placing it inside his shirt, he wondered if the words would feel as soft and supple as the leather against his skin.

"Your father was a good man," Bernardino said. "He went to his grave loving you and your *madre*."

Armando clenched his jaw to keep from firing the words coursing through his mind. "Enough to leave us?" he asked. "Enough to send *mi madre* to an early grave?"

"Sometimes a man chooses to do things out of love and duty when no one understands but *Dios*."

Suddenly Armando remembered Marianne. He'd sent her away with tears in her eyes. "I will read the letter with an open heart." No pretense laced his words. Heaven forbid if his sweet señorita ever felt indignant toward him when all he wanted rested in her happiness and safety.

Later in the evening, after he'd bid Bernardino good-bye, Armando sat by his campfire and allowed himself to linger upon the memory of Marianne. He'd been a fool not to hold her just once. If he had expressed his emotions then, he might not feel this ache now. For certain, if ever their paths should cross again, he'd kiss her lips and draw her to him until he heard her heart beat next to his.

The news of the governor siding with the villagers still stunned him. Throughout the ride back, Armando had contemplated La Flor's good fortune. A part of him wanted to ride night and day to his village, and the other desired to savor the report like droplets of honey. Whether the favorable news was attributed to luck or *Dios*, Señor Phillips would not have the grazing lands of La Flor.

Armando added another log to the spitting fire. He stared into the yellow flames as though the answers to all his problems were buried beneath the embers. The time had come to open his father's letter.

He pulled the letter from the leather pouch and studied the Garcia seal on it. With no one around but the singing insects and the coyotes calling in the distance, he sought the reason for Joseph Garcia's abandonment.

My dear *hijo*, Armando,
    Over two years have passed since I last saw you and your *madre*, and I long to be in your presence. I despise myself for leaving both of you—even more to learn of my Lucita's death. Perhaps you hate me too but no more than I detest myself.

I was a coward to leave and sail home to the comforts of Spain, but my family feared my health would deteriorate in the new land. Here in my homeland, under the care of good doctors, perhaps the pain in my chest would subside. How unwise of me. I am wallowing in self-pity for things I cannot change and dying slowly day by day. Oh, how I miss you and your *madre*. I should have spent these lonely two years with my Lucita and my son.

Armando, my earnest desire was to return to you and your *madre* as a whole man, healthy, strong, and breathing without pain. I wanted to marry your *madre* and be a true father. I wanted so much for you . . . to tell you of many things and watch you grow into a man. Instead I listened to my family's urgings to leave you and your *madre* behind and seek good health. *Dios* have mercy on my weak soul.

This letter has not said all that I intended. It cannot bring you peace or joy, or even fill the emptiness from losing your parents. But above all things, please know this: I loved your *madre* and I love you.

Learn from my mistakes, *mi hijo*. Do not be easily swayed from your convictions. Search for truth and love. Uphold the integrity of the Garcia name. May *Dios* give you the courage to forgive me.

Joseph Garcia de la Menendez y Lopez

Armando covered his face with his hands and wept. All these years he'd hated his father, loathed his name, and wished his *madre* had not allowed the name Garcia to be entered in the mission birth records. Now Armando knew the truth. Joseph Garcia, frail and weak as addressed in the letter, had fallen prey to his family's wishes and the demands of nobility. At the time, Armando's father had done what he believed would ultimately be the best for the woman and son he loved.

Shaking his head to rid his mind of the guilt and regret, Armando tucked his father's letter inside the leather bag and slid it inside his shirt. Moments later, he lay on the hard ground and slept. And for a precious few hours, his mind ceased to race.

The following morning, Armando returned to La Flor. Emilio waved to him from the lookout.

Armando lifted his rifle into the air. "Assemble the men. We have much to celebrate."

"So the news is good?"

Armando laughed. "The padre spoke in our behalf to Governor Elguezábel. We will keep our homes."

The news spread throughout the village. Once more, the evening rang with laughter and song, and the people called Armando *un héroe*. For the first time in a long while, he felt like joining them. Even so, he wondered how he should spend his days now that his mission had been accomplished. He relished the thought of raising his own cattle and horses.

"It is a miracle that the governor sided with us," Emilio said. "The padre is a good man."

Armando smiled. "I believe so." He refrained from revealing the information about Señor Wharton. One of the residents of La Flor might know the girl's family and be humiliated.

In the days that followed, Armando's joy in seeing the valley prosper in the hands of his people subsided, replaced by the old restlessness. He worked hard with the other vaqueros to keep the cattle and horses together. They branded their stock as the missions had done for years and kept close watch so as not to lose them to the open range or the warring Comanches. All unmarked livestock became the property of the Crown, not the villagers, and they were mindful to secure their own herds. Armando had to admit, some of the mission's ways were good.

For now, all was well in La Flor, with no more visits from Señor Phillips and his foreman. Armando hadn't heard what happened with the gringo Wharton, but by now a wedding had been scheduled, or the *hombre* had been shot. He preferred the latter.

As in days gone by, Armando's *Tia* Rosa lived only to please him, and señoritas flashed their eyes in his direction at every opportunity. He should have felt flattered, but not so. Always his mind turned to two matters—his unrest and Marianne. The turmoil in his spirit had always been there, but the yearning for Marianne was another matter. At times he believed if she stood beside him, he could conquer the darkness of his moods. But what if the quest proved impossible? Dare he submit any woman to the torment plaguing his soul?

Marianne led Diablo from his stall and quickly saddled and bridled him. She had to flee from the house. Mama's excitement over Marianne's upcoming marriage had left her with a pounding headache. She was tempted simply to give in to the overwhelming depression threatening to engulf her and ride Diablo to the ends of the earth. But those actions would not glorify God. Gown fittings, Spanish lessons, Catholic instruction, all prepared her for marriage to Don Lorenzo. Even Mama, with all the goings-on, found time to drill her in Spanish culture. She didn't want to think of such things a moment longer.

Glancing about to make certain no one lurked in the barn, she breathed a sigh of relief. In her present temperament, she sensed an urgency to be with God and allow Him to be her solace.

"I see you're going riding." Clay Wharton's voice jarred her senses and filled her with dread. "Since this is my last day as a single man, I think you should allow me to accompany you." He spoke in a dangerously low tone, and a stab of fear caused her to tremble. Carmita had told her about his involvement with a young Spanish girl in San Antonio de Bejar and how the governor had ordered him to marry.

"No, thank you, Mr. Wharton." Marianne refused to glance his way. Gratefully, Diablo wouldn't permit Clay to step any closer. "I prefer my solitude today."

An awkward silence followed while she led Diablo toward the front of the stable where Clay leaned against the door. She felt his deep piercing gaze bore through her, and her stomach knotted. Silently she prayed for the young girl who was to be his wife. She would need strength to soften Clay's demeanor.

"Miss High and Mighty, you were almost my wife." Clay cocked his hat. "So don't act like you're better than me."

Marianne thought it wise not to speak her mind. She still had vivid memories of the time when he had attempted to abuse Juan's daughter. Lifting the latch, she turned to him. "I hope you will be happy in your marriage."

"If I had my druthers, I would have preferred being married to you." His half-smile sickened her.

"You speak rather boldly, Mr. Wharton. Have you forgotten both of us are betrothed to those not privy to this conversation?"

"Does it matter?" He stepped closer. Diablo snorted. The stallion's ears laid back flat against his head.

Marianne reached under the stallion's muzzle to soothe him. "Your bad manners may not affect you, but they offend me." She lifted her chin. This time she made sure her chiding stare captured his. With more confidence than she truly felt, Marianne slid open the door and allowed morning sunlight to cast its glow inside. "Miss Phillips," he said. "At the risk of being accused of, ah, let me say, behaving like less than a gentleman, I would like to ask you a question."

"Yes, Mr. Wharton." Reluctantly, she faced him.

"What exactly did you do for Armando Garcia that he let you go free?" He pushed back his wide-brimmed hat. "Especially after he said he'd kill you."

She dug her fingernails into her palms and glared at him. Clay chuckled and stepped away from the door. How had this uncouth man become her father's foreman? Oh, how she longed to disparage him. "Your question doesn't deserve an answer. My father or Don Lorenzo would not appreciate the way you have elected to address me."

"But you'll not reveal a word of this, because you know I'm right." His mouth twisted in a triumphant sneer. "Your father may have his weapons, his daughter, and his cattle back, but he still thirsts for revenge, just as I do. Neither of us will rest until that dirty Mexican is lying in a pool of blood."

Marianne gasped at Clay's words. A pitchfork rested against the side of a stall, and she wrestled with the thought of using it on him. Shaking so much she feared she might fall, Marianne led Diablo from the stable and hoisted herself onto the saddle. Without looking behind, she rode away from Clay Wharton and his wicked tongue.

She swallowed her temper and focused her attention on God's grace, His provision for her during the kidnapping, and in the life to come. Juan had told her about the governor's ruling in the matter of La Flor. Marianne had rejoiced with him, knowing the people in the village must be overjoyed. Yet she kept her praise sealed inside when in the presence of Mama and Papa, for both suspected her of inappropriate behavior during the time of the kidnapping and that Armando had released her because she sided with the people of La Flor.

Marianne repeatedly pushed away the tender feelings for Armando. But she was losing the battle. She did care for him, and the realization frightened her. How she longed to tell her mother and to ask for help in understanding this invasion of her heart, but to reveal her innermost yearnings invited trouble. Papa had arranged for her to wed Don Lorenzo, and nothing could change the course of events. In time, she prayed she would love the respected Don Lorenzo. She admired his gentle ways, and he lavished her with attention. He ordered many fine gowns and expensive gifts for his bride-to-be. He seemed to look forward to the wedding and sharing his vast home with her. How wicked of her to think of Armando while betrothed to a kindly man.

Always, when burdens raged through her mind, she raced Diablo across the plains of her father's land. With the wind blowing through her hair, she felt liberated from all of the demands. It was the only time she felt somewhat free.

I know God will see me through this. He has a plan for my life—a wonderful plan.

Up ahead, where the spring-fed Medina River lent itself to bald cypress trees, she decided to stop and allow Diablo to drink of the cool water. The white stallion heaved from running, and she walked him for several minutes before leading him to the river's edge. She smiled as three white-tailed deer skirted the opposite side and disappeared in one fluid, graceful movement.

Sitting on a shady bank, she watched her beloved horse nibble at the grass. Diablo lifted his noble head as though guarding her safety. My *solidat*, she thought fondly. The stallion snorted.

"I'm fine," she called to him, laughing. "My prince, do not worry so."

A while later, he snorted again and raised his head to stare upstream. Alarmed, Marianne hurried to his side and swung up on the saddle. She trusted her stallion's instincts and made ready to leave. She focused her sights on the Medina's upward flow, but saw nothing. Uneasiness crept over her. How many times had Juan and Mama warned her of this? Had she not learned her lesson weeks ago?

Before giving Diablo full rein to carry her safely back to the stables, she took one last glimpse up the river. A dun-colored horse seized her attention, and she lingered beneath the trailing branches of a tree to see the rider.

Her heart pounded. She wanted to believe the lone horse carried Armando, but if wrong, she must not tarry a moment longer. She heard the splashing of water and the steady steps of the dun. Slowly, the horse emerged from the growth of trees and brush to the banks of the river.

A surge of joy swept over her as Armando rode into view.

Chapter 17

"Armando." Marianne urged Diablo into Armando's path.

Clearly startled, he allowed a slow smile to spread over his handsome face. "What are you doing here?" He turned in his saddle to scrutinize their surroundings.

She felt her spirit suddenly take flight. Seeing him real before her and not a vapory figure from her dreams warmed her heart and sent chills up and down her bare arms. At once she regretted not wearing more acceptable clothing, although her manner of dress was common to him.

"I stopped Diablo to rest in the shade and drink from the cool river."

"You are alone?" He leaned on the saddle horn.

"*Si*," she said. "I left without permission." She studied the man before her, dressed in brown *calzoneras* and a white shirt open at the neck. "I despise staying confined in the *casa* on such a beautiful day."

Armando tilted his head and gave her a stern look. "It's not safe, Marianne. Comanches lurk about, and no one would ever find you. We must keep constant watch at La Flor for raiding Indians." He paused. "Do you know what they would do to a lovely señorita?"

The softness in his tone swept over her. "*Por favor,* don't scold me," she said. "I know you're right, but I'd rather risk the danger than deny myself happiness."

Armando dismounted, and without hesitation she followed his lead. "Dangerous as it may be, I am glad to see you." A smile curved at his full lips. "But perhaps the next time Juan or one of the vaqueros should accompany you."

"Having someone ride with me is not the same. I crave quiet beauty."

He stood by his gelding with nearly twenty feet between them. She felt uncertain about approaching him, afraid of her own unbridled emotions and still bound to Don Lorenzo by her father's pledge.

An awkward silence settled like a cloud of dust. Many times in her musings she'd spoken openly to him without reservation, but now she merely stared, speechless. She remembered his parting words from their last meeting. He'd asked her to forget him, an impossible task when her waking and sleeping hours were consumed with Armando Garcia. She knew her eyes revealed the carefully guarded secret.

"I'm happy for La Flor," she said. "At last your people can live in peace."

"*Gracias*, señorita. We have great joy in the village." A chuckle escaped his lips. "Much singing and dancing. La Flor's people love to celebrate."

Marianne recalled Isabella and her enticing body. "And little Rico? Is he well?"

"*Si*. And what of you?"

Regret swirled inside her until she managed to swallow her tears. "I'm well, Armando."

He took a step forward. "Why do I not believe you? Your angelic face tells me of sadness."

She moistened her lips. "You must be mistaken."

Armando glanced about the trees before turning his attention back to her. "Emilio tells me you are to marry Lorenzo Sanchez de la Diaz y Franco."

Marianne smoothed her pale blue riding skirt. She dreaded her reply. "It's true. *Mi padre* arranged the marriage for me."

"A bride should be radiant, glowing. I hear Señor Sanchez is a good man."

Was it her imagination, or did she detect a note of sorrow in his features?

"He appears to be very kind." She listened to the birds call to each other. If only they could talk of more pleasant things.

"Then why are you unhappy?"

Marianne could not bring herself to answer. She attempted to pray, but for what? Permission to lie or strength to tell Armando the truth?

She no longer could keep silent. "I fear my heart belongs to another."

He started toward her and stopped. "And does the man who has stolen your heart know of this?"

"No. I don't believe he fathoms how deep my feelings are."

Diablo snorted in protest at the advancing man, and she soothed the stallion.

"Why haven't you told him?" Armando's gentle questioning seared her soul. He brushed back his sombrero and raked his fingers through raven hair.

She willed her heart to cease its incessant pounding. Her words must sound strong. Instead they tumbled from her lips like a baby's babble. "The man I love doesn't believe we could ever be together. We come from different worlds."

"And you love each other?"

She shook her head and felt her cheeks flush. "I'm not certain if he cares for me . . . in that way."

An eternity followed.

"He's afraid of his feelings for the señorita. He cannot give her the fine things she deserves." He walked toward her again, and she commanded Diablo to keep his stance. Releasing hold of her horse, she watched Armando step closer. "*Mi ángel*," he whispered. "Let me hold you."

Marianne fairly flew into Armando's arms. The moment he grasped her waist, she wrapped her arms around his neck. Her world spun in the dizziness of twisting emotions. The scent of him, a mixture of leather and the freshness of the forest, the touch of his strong hands encircling her, never had she imagined such fervor.

"*Mi ángel*," he repeated, and pulled her so tightly that she could feel his heart racing as rapidly as her own.

Marianne felt a tear slip from her eye, then another. Caught up in his embrace, she wept tears of joy and sadness. How could their love be forbidden?

Armando buried his head into her hair, and he quaked ever so slightly. Slowly, he swept his fingers across the soft curve of her shoulder and pressed her away to arm's length. With the thumb of his free hand, he gently brushed away the wetness gracing her cheeks. Marianne forced a smile, not wanting him to see her tears.

"I'm so sorry," he said. "I shouldn't have reached for you, and I have no excuse except the need to hold you. Now, I have made you cry."

She took a breath to gain composure. "I'm crying because I thought I would never feel your arms around me. Even at this moment, standing before you, I feel I'm in another world."

A disconcerted look swept over his face. "How can two people find love in so short a time? We should be enemies. Instead we are here, like this."

Marianne shook her head, and another errant tear trickled down her cheek. "I don't want to marry Don Lorenzo."

"Hush." His sable gaze searched her face. "You have no choice. Your padre has decided this. I cannot give you the wealth or title the don has to offer. With me, your soft hands," and he brought her fingers to his lips and kissed them, "would soon become rough and calloused. The work is hard and relentless."

"It doesn't matter." She touched his cheek. "I've never felt this way before, and I never will again."

"You're young." He grasped her fingers upon his face. "One day you'll look back on this, and it will all be a young woman's fond memory."

"No, Armando. I shall never forget you, and I can learn to work and take care of you."

"But what of the danger?"

Her eyes widened with his question.

"Señor Phillips would not rest until I was dead for stealing his daughter. And Señor Sanchez, is he not an honorable man? Do you expect him to merely step aside while his betrothed chooses a desperado over him?"

Armando's words pierced her heart. He spoke the reality of their hopeless situation, even if she didn't want to hear it.

"But it's so unfair for me to spend my life with the don when I don't love him."

His dark gaze bore into hers. "Do you love me, Marianne?"

"I do with all my heart."

"And I love you, more than I thought possible." He paused and kissed her hand again. "Then do this for me. Return to your home as I asked you before. Take your position with the don as his wife." He sighed deeply. "If you truly love me, *mi ángel,* this will make me most happy. I want to remember you as the beautiful señorita—not watch you grow old too soon from living as a fugitive's wife."

This time Marianne could not stop the flow of emotion. "*Por favor,* Armando. Must I live my life without you?"

"Indeed you must," he said. "I beg of you. Ride Diablo from here and back into the arms of the one you should marry. I have nothing to offer you but unhappiness.

My comfort will be in knowing you are taken care of without want." Armando moved beyond her grasp. His eyes held his sorrow no matter how incessant his words. "Someday you will have children, and you will want those children to have the best of everything."

She struggled to contain her emotion, desiring him to see her smile. Marianne knew he spoke out of love for her, but she couldn't bring herself to believe marrying Don Lorenzo was the answer.

"My heart will always be with you," she said. "I don't need wealth to make me content, but neither do I want you hunted down by my father or the don. I'll continue to ask *Dios* for a way." She turned and walked toward Diablo, then whirled around to face him. "Whatever *Dios* asks of me, I will do. For your life, I will do anything."

She took one last glimpse of her beloved Armando and sealed it to memory—the way he stood proudly, the light of love in his dark eyes, and the faint smile upon his lips. "I beg of you to forgive me for so selfishly wanting you," she said. "I will never forget you—never." Grasping the stallion's reins in her shaking hands, she pulled herself onto the saddle and allowed Diablo to carry her home. The home she did not want.

Armando and Emilio rode the open range from that morning until sunset looking for mustangs. Having rounded up five mares, they added them to the valley's herd.

In the shadows, the two leaned against the corral admiring the increasing sturdy stock of horses. "Armando," Emilio said, then wiped the accumulation of dirt from his round face, "you have been quiet all day. Is something wrong?"

Armando breathed deeply of the night air, noticeably cooler than the steamy temperatures of earlier today. Or perhaps his chance meeting with Marianne had caused his discomfort. "Early this morning, I took a long ride along the banks of the Medina River, a long way from La Flor." He paused. "I saw Marianne with Diablo."

"Did she see you?" Emilio asked.

Armando stared out over the horses and fixed his sights on a prized red roan that had been captured earlier. "We talked for a while. If I ever wondered about her feelings for me, I learned of them today. She admitted she had feelings similar to my own, strange as the circumstances may be."

"Isn't the news good?"

In the shadows, Armando glanced at the man's face. His earnest questioning slashed into Armando's soul. "You know she is betrothed to Señor Sanchez, and a life with me promises heartache and sorrow."

"Her father might forgive."

Armando chuckled to keep from weeping like a small boy. "He'd see me dead first. Marianne and I would spend our lives on the run. Even if the gringo chose not to track me down, La Flor is not a rich hacienda."

"I understand." Emilio nodded his head. "I'm so sad for you."

"I'll work, and I'll forget." Armando felt ashamed of his friend seeing him despondent. Instead he vowed to cover his wounded heart. "Ah, I hear rumors of you and Isabella." He attempted a smile. "And did I see her with you keeping watch last night? Perhaps a kiss in the dark?"

"*Sí,*" Emilio said with a broad grin. "I like her."

"Like her?" Armando laughed. "Like is what we felt as boys. Love is for a man."

Emilio shrugged. "She cared for you a long time, but now it may be my turn."

"I hope so, *mi amigo,*" Armando said. "I want to see you happy with many sons and daughters. You'll make a good husband and father."

Armando turned and braced himself against the back of the fence. The restlessness snapped at his heels like a hungry dog. How he longed to find peace in his life. At one time, he wanted to think Marianne could ease the need. But he was a loner, haunted by an anxiousness for which he knew no cure.

Chapter 18

Marianne rode Diablo until late morning. For more than an hour she'd wept, willing the tears to cease and her mind to ponder Armando's request. A part of her wished they hadn't met today, that she hadn't been forced to face the impossibility and the frivolousness of their sharing a future together. She hurt beyond any pain caused by her father's rejection.

Armando. She shivered at the thought of his nearness, and an image of him caused her head to spin as if she possessed a perpetual fever. As her tears dried, she permanently engraved his every feature in her mind, like a fine line of gold framing a priceless portrait. She would need his memory during the lonely days and nights certain to come. Granted, his undeniably handsome face sent her senses reeling, but she loved his heart more. How could such a good man be misunderstood by so many?

If she'd learned anything at all from her mother's diligent instructions, it was the importance of judging a man by his character, not his comely or uncomely looks. Pondering these things, Marianne well recalled Armando's love for the people of La Flor and his dedication to their happiness. He could have committed any number of atrocities against her while she remained his captive. For a moment she dwelled on the times he had been alone with her. He could have easily used her naïveté to steal her innocence. Instead, he saved her life in a raging fire, released her when others wanted her killed, and today urged her to marry Don Lorenzo despite his admittance of love. Those things proved him an honorable man, one worthy of any woman's heart.

She reluctantly admitted that Armando's manner of forcing Papa's hand in the matter of the village showed a high disregard for the law, but she understood why. Not that Armando's tactics were excusable. No, not by any means. He'd done wrong. Praise God, Governor Elguezábel had ruled with leniency. In the deep recesses of her heart, Marianne knew her father still plotted Armando's death, just as Clay had said.

So Marianne rode and prayed, desiring God to reveal His purpose in her life. His word stated He had a wonderful plan, and she must simply trust in His provision.

Gazing up into a cerulean sky, she watched the billowing clouds roll away like dreams floating aimlessly by. She shook her head and looked to the plains where the outlines of the house and stables rose like monuments to her father's power. Home. Duties. Responsibilities. She must come to terms with her feelings for Armando—not tomorrow, or on the day of her wedding to Don Lorenzo, but now. Whisking away the wetness flooding her eyes, she sat straighter in the saddle and prayed for strength to keep her resolve. Patting Diablo, she galloped toward the hacienda. Marianne needed to talk to her mother.

After relinquishing her stallion to Juan and changing clothes, she sought the company of her mother in the shade of the courtyard. Mama's pallor appeared somewhat brighter lately, obviously due to her enthusiasm for the upcoming wedding.

"Mama, I'm so pleased to see you in the fresh air." Marianne bent to place a light kiss on her cheek. "You have such a radiant glow about you. God is making you stronger every day." Her mother held her Bible open to the book of Psalms.

"Thank you. I'm really trying to regain my health. Since we're studying together, I want to memorize Scripture as I used to do."

Marianne smiled. "What are you reading?"

"Psalm 61." Her mother peered up into Marianne's face. She wore a lavender morning dress, and seated amidst the greenery and flowers, she looked as young as a girl. "Daughter, did you ride Diablo without a companion this morning?"

Knowing she had willfully disobeyed, Marianne chose her words carefully. "Yes, Mama. Please accept my apologies, for I know it worries you." She kneeled at her mother's side. "I promise you I will never take Diablo out again without a proper escort."

Her mother's eyes widened. "What has happened that you have decided this?"

She sighed and took a deep breath. If anyone deserved to know the truth, it was her mother. "I thought about many things today, and I wish to speak about them with you."

Her mother tilted her head slightly, allowing a lock of light brown hair to curl down the side of her face. "Could it be you have realized your mama and papa do know what is best for you?" A smile curved her lips.

"Perhaps so." Marianne relived the heaviness of the morning. "Are you strong enough for a stroll?"

Her mother nodded and rose to her feet. Linking arms, they walked through the stone archway and away from the main house.

"Mama," she began, "I have some things I want to tell you—some of which will not be pleasant. But I beg you to listen until I have finished."

"Does this have anything to do with your aloofness? Since the dreadful incident . . . when you were taken away, you have been so distant."

"Yes, Mama, it does, and with you I cannot mask my feelings any longer." She stopped and seized the courage to speak her heart. "Today, I had a chance meeting with Armando Garcia."

Her mother gasped and paled, but Marianne continued. "I want you to know that Armando has done nothing to compromise my innocence. He is far more of a gentleman than you may believe. I don't condone the things he has done. None of us will ever forget the horror of fearing for our lives when Felipe entered our home and abducted me. Yes, I have forgiven all of them. In place of revulsion for Armando, I found something I never expected." She glanced into her mother's troubled face. "I love Armando Garcia. I am as certain of it as I am of this moment with you. Today he spoke from his heart, and I must abide by his wishes."

"Oh, Marianne." Her mother broke into sobs.

"No, Mama, there is no need to fret any longer. He loves me as I do him, but he has asked me to fulfill my obligation to Don Lorenzo as his wife. Armando believes my place is with him."

She felt her mother's stiffened body relax.

"I have wept until I can weep no more, and I have no choice but to obey Papa. To refuse is to break the commandment to honor my mother and my father. I will marry the don without argument, and I'll do my best to be a good wife." Marianne swallowed the tears she thought had vanished. "I wanted to be truthful with you, and I could no longer keep it all pent up inside me."

Her mother's silence weighed on Marianne's mind, but she waited as they walked on. She prayed the news did not send Mama back to bed.

"I married your Papa because I loved him. However, my father objected." Mama took a labored breath. "He had heard rumors of Weston's temper and didn't approve of his family. I refused to listen and followed my heart." Her mother smiled. "As much as I despise Armando Garcia, I understand how you feel. And I appreciate what he has asked of you. You have always shown wisdom in judging character, so perhaps you see a good side of him not evident to me."

"Thank you, Mama. One more thing." She hesitated and ordered her racing heart to cease its thunderous roar. "I have another confession to make, and I fear you will be upset with me."

"Daughter, I love you. Granted I may be uncomfortable with what you have to say, but my love will never change."

Several long moments passed while Marianne formed her words. "The truth is I speak Spanish, and I have done so for some time."

"What you did was against your papa's wishes."

Marianne nodded. "I know I disobeyed."

"I suspected your knowledge the evening of your abduction. You were too quick with Carmita's translation. But I believe I know why. Juan and Carmita are dear to you."

"Yes, Mama."

Her mother sighed. "While we are being truthful with each other, I have something to tell you too. What I need to say as your mother is this. I have never regretted my life with your papa, for he has given me you. But my father loved me, and he was a wise man. He did know best. Now, I understand his insistence, and many times I wished I had obeyed his wishes. One thing I have realized over the years is," her mother paused, "if God had not blessed me with you, I would still have Jesus. I am telling you this because the only advice I can give you is to pray for God's leading and do not ignore His voice. Sometimes—"

"Mama, what else?" Marianne searched her mother's face. "I know you want to tell me more."

Her mother nodded and glanced at the path before them. "Sometimes it's hard to understand life, but God always answers prayers, and He is perfect and just."

"Yes, Mama." Marianne silently prodded her mother to say what seemed to plague her.

"I am with child," her mother said.

Marianne covered her mouth. "Your health. Oh, Mama, I will be living with the don then. Who will help you?"

"I have Carmita. This child is part of God's plan. I . . . I am pleased, and you know how I have prayed for another baby. Share in my joy, Marianne, for God has blessed me with another opportunity to give Weston what he so desperately wants."

Marianne drew her mother close. "We have both shared our hearts today. Mama, you are truly my treasure. I will pray for you and the baby every day."

"I'll tell your papa this evening. He has been working long past sundown, but tonight I plan to tell him the good news."

"He will be happy," Marianne said, but a twinge of fear caused her to shiver. She wished Mama had grown stronger before conceiving again.

Long after dark and near to bedtime, Papa arrived home. Marianne heard him enter through the front door. His heavy boots resounded down the hallway toward them.

"Shall I go to my room now?" Marianne asked. She saw the glow upon her mother's face. Mama's happiness gave Marianne strength to endure the months ahead.

"Perhaps after you bid your papa good night."

Marianne maintained a pleasant demeanor despite her reluctance to see Papa. Usually he came in late in a fitful mood. She'd become accustomed to his familiar scowl.

"Good evening, Weston." Her mother glanced up from her needlepoint.

"Hello, Papa."

He muttered something, but it didn't stop her mother. "Is there anything I can get for you?"

"No," he said with more than a generous supply of gruffness.

Marianne wondered why he even bothered to step into her mother's room. "I'm going to bed now." She gave her a kiss goodnight. "Sleep well. Good night, Papa."

"Did you complete your studies today?" He tugged his gray, horseshoe-shaped mustache.

"Yes, sir." The Spanish books on Catholicism were difficult to understand, but she felt bound by her commitment to learn the material.

"Don Lorenzo expects you to learn quickly." He glared at her, as though he expected her to refute his statement.

"I'll not disappoint him or you." She faced him squarely. "May I go to my room?"

He nodded and clenched his jaw.

Marianne wanted so much to see affection in his eyes, but she had nearly given up. "Sleep well, Papa." With an inward sigh, she brushed past him.

Once in her room, Marianne succumbed to the exhaustion from the day. She shed her gown and petticoats for her chemise and crawled into bed. A light breeze blew gently through her window, and she turned her face to let it cool her. She tried to pray, except her mind kept wondering how her mother fared in telling Papa about the baby. In her previous confinement, Papa had treated Mama kindly, which had been a blessing for everyone.

She allowed her thoughts to float back to this morning and dwelled longer than she intended upon Armando. They had said their good-byes, and her dreams lay shattered. Up until now, she had comforted herself in a childish belief that the two of them could somehow be together. That was now in the past.

Again, she tried to pray, but from deep within her sorrow wrenched through her body. *Oh, God, help me through this. I can't face another day without You to steady me. I want to be pleasing in Your eyes, but I am so miserable. Must I live my life without Armando? How can anything else, except for You, compare to the joy of his embrace?*

God would be enough . . . God would be enough.

Chapter 19

The month of July brought sweltering temperatures, including long afternoons when Marianne and her mother indulged in siestas during the heat of the day. Everyone looked expectantly to cooler evenings, when temperaments became more pleasant. Papa grumbled and complained of everything and everyone, but to her mother he softened. Marianne appreciated his attentiveness to Mama, although it stemmed from the prospect of a new heir. Why couldn't he be kind without thought of himself?

Mama stayed in bed most of the mornings until her sickness with the child subsided. Despite her fatigue and lagging health, she smiled more. Her joy seemed to bounce from Marianne's upcoming wedding to the new baby. Neither Mama nor Marianne ever mentioned again the afternoon they confessed the truth of their souls. And, for Marianne, the silence suited her wounded heart.

Armando floated in and out of her thoughts, but she remained steadfast to her resolve and pushed him from her mind. But late at night when sleep overcame her, dreams of the sable-eyed man comforted her. *God is my strength*, she often told herself. *He will sustain me through whatever lies ahead.*

Don Lorenzo often visited the Phillips Hacienda. He and Papa spent a good deal of time riding across the expanse of the land and discussing matters behind the closed doors of Papa's study. She often wondered what they talked about at such great length, mostly because she feared Papa plotted revenge against Armando and the people of La Flor.

"What do you suppose they do late into the night?" Marianne asked of her mother one evening as the two women made ready for bed.

Mama offered a reassuring smile. "Men always speak of things we women aren't of a mind to hear—political matters and business affairs. It's boring, and often the topics are distasteful for a woman's delicate ears."

Marianne wanted to trust her mother's judgment, but the reply failed to erase her suspicions. She didn't trust her father and believed he hadn't abandoned his desire to secure the fertile valley and destroy Armando and his followers. The thought of such evil intentions needled her and caused her to pray even more fervently for Armando and Papa. God forbid if Papa had enlisted the help of Don Lorenzo in it all. Marianne understood how the don could be persuaded to her father's way of thinking, especially when Armando was held responsible for the kidnapping. Oh, the matter never ceased to frighten her. If she thought advancing the wedding day might help dissuade Don Lorenzo from assisting Papa, she'd gladly do so. But there were so many things she didn't know.

During the don's stay, he had Papa translate requests for her to accompany him on walks or sit with him in the courtyard. One evening, Papa enlisted the vaqueros on the hacienda to stage a bullfight for the don, an amusing affair when the supposedly ferocious bull preferred eating to charging the matadors. Clay Wharton participated in the festivities with his pretty young wife, who observed the activities with eyes only for her husband. The hacienda's foreman looked happy. Marianne smiled at his bride and prayed Clay would love and treasure her.

Marianne assessed the don as a gentle man, and she felt assured of his good heart. Daily she prayed his charm and manners were sincere and would not disappear, as Papa had done with Mama.

Papa questioned her constantly about her studies of Roman Catholicism and Spanish. Her tutor, Antonio de Valero, who studied for the priesthood in San Antonio, praised her quick mind, but her father simply demanded she work harder. He always wanted more than she could give.

Marianne finally decided she could no longer deceive Don Lorenzo about her knowledge of Spanish. She must tell him and hope he kept the secret from Papa. After viewing her parents' relationship, she felt a marriage should be based on honesty, not deceit.

One morning, during one of his visits, she asked Papa if the don would like to go riding. The older gentleman pleasantly agreed, and Marianne excused herself to change into proper riding attire, a loose skirt rather than one of her frocks. The idea of riding Diablo sidesaddle did not settle well, but she'd done so before, and Mama insisted she conduct herself as a proper lady.

Juan bridled and saddled Diablo and one of Papa's finest mares for Don Lorenzo while she and the Spanish nobleman waited.

"You wish for me to ride the white stallion?" he asked in Spanish at the sight of the high-spirited horse.

"No, Señor Sanchez." Juan limped from the stables, leading Diablo. "The señorita always rides him."

Don Lorenzo's gaze peered curiously at Marianne. "But her father said no one could ride this horse. He insists the stallion is loco."

Juan smiled and handed Diablo's reins to Marianne. The stallion pawed at the dust, anxious for a run. "She is the only one who has been able to tame him. Fortunately, the stallion allows me to groom him, but even then sometimes he gives me trouble."

Marianne regretted feigning ignorance of their conversation, but soon she could apologize. She felt proud of Diablo and wanted to show the don how well he responded to her commands. The don stepped toward Diablo, but he snorted menacingly and lifted his front legs in defiance.

"Hush," Marianne said in English and coaxed the horse to calm. "I'm here. No need to fear."

Shaking his white head in disbelief, Don Lorenzo laughed heartily and took the mare's reins from Juan. "I will have to learn the señorita's secret."

Once the pair had galloped beyond the stables, Marianne slowed Diablo to a walk and the don did likewise. With a deep breath, she prayed for courage with her confession. If Don Lorenzo revealed her secret to Papa, Juan might lose his position. Granted, he could take his family to La Flor, but Marianne preferred the move be his choice, not her father's command.

Marianne had to admit, Don Lorenzo made a dashing figure dressed in dark blue *calzoneras* trimmed in fawn-colored leather and silver studs. A matching vest and a bright red scarf tied around his neck gave him a distinguished look. Beneath a dark blue, wide-brimmed hat, hair as thick and white as clouds framed his face. He carried himself proudly with his hand resting at his waist within inches of a magnificent, gold-handled sword.

"Don Lorenzo, may we talk?" she asked in Spanish

He lifted a questioning brow. "*Si*, of course. You are learning my language well."

She forced her gaze to meet his. "I have a confession to make. I learned the Spanish language before you requested a tutor."

Startled, he pulled the mare to a halt. "Your padre didn't tell me this."

She reined in Diablo. "He doesn't know, and I hope you'll not disclose this information to him."

"Why?" he asked with a frown. "I fail to understand. Shouldn't he be proud of your accomplishments?"

Marianne carefully formed her words. "I asked Juan and Carmita Torres to teach me without obtaining Papa's permission. The family is dear to me, and I wanted to talk with them in their own language."

"Ah, I see." He nodded as though he already anticipated her father's reaction. Papa hadn't attempted to cover how he felt about the part Indian, part Spanish people.

"I pray this can be our secret?" she asked and released a sigh. "And I do want to continue with the young priest who tutors me. I fear my reading and writing skills are lacking."

He smiled warmly and reached for her hand. "*Gracias.*"

"For what?"

"Now I know you will be a good wife. Not only are you lovely, but you value truth between a man and a woman. I'm honored and blessed by *Dios* to have found you before I reach my fiftieth year."

Marianne fought the tears welling her eyes. If she could not give her life to Armando, then she accepted the role of Don Lorenzo's wife. Never let it be said that she denied him the delight of a devoted woman. She could marry him and give him happiness.

"Marianne," he said a few moments later. "May I ask you a question? It is concerning a rather unpleasant topic."

Considering what little she knew of the man, Marianne hesitated before replying. "Most certainly."

"When you were kidnapped, did it help to understand your captors?" He set his jaw firmly. "I apologize if you don't wish to discuss this. The whole incident still angers me."

Marianne offered a prayer of understanding. "Let me begin by saying, my abductors spoke freely among themselves. They wouldn't have been so open if they had known of my ability. *Si,* it actually made the entire ordeal easier to bear. I knew exactly what my fate was to be. It also provided me insight into their plight."

He stared into her face as though searching for something, and she wondered what thoughts occupied his mind.

"What is it?" she asked. "Has my answer offended you?"

"No, not at all." He shook his head. "I believe you are a strong young woman. Most señoritas would have resigned themselves to solitude after undergoing such an ordeal. I admire your strength, and the sympathy you obviously have for the people of La Flor."

Marianne smiled and relaxed. "It's my turn to thank you. I've never been prone to fainting or avoiding uncomfortable situations. Those three days brought me closer to *Dios,* for He truly delivered me, and gave me a clearer understanding of the people living there."

"Why is it you don't despise them?" He leaned closer on his saddle horn.

"They were a desperate people, and I feared for my life. But given the same circumstances, I might have made serious errors too."

He stiffened and narrowed his dark eyes. "How can you excuse their barbaric treatment of you?"

Marianne caught her breath. "You are mistaken. I refuse to condone their behavior, but I have compassion for them and choose to forgive."

"Are you being naïve, my dear?" His question was not the least condescending.

She glanced away briefly in the direction of La Flor, then found his gaze again. "I prefer to think I'm trying to be like Jesus." She brushed a loose strand of hair from her face, wishing she could explain her position about the valley.

"Your faith is commendable, but Armando Garcia cannot be trusted." He urged his mare to walk, and Marianne did the same with Diablo. "And to think his padre and I were amigos. We grew up together."

Marianne could only stare, bewildered with the Don's information. "Where is his padre?"

"He died some years ago. His family sent him to Spain in hopes the doctors there could cure an illness with his lungs, but they were unable to help him."

"So his *madre* lives in Spain?"

"No, she died here shortly after Joseph sailed back." Don Lorenzo hesitated. "Armando's parents never married. She lived in La Flor."

Marianne more clearly saw the shaping of Armando's life—he, the product of a Spanish nobleman and a villager. No wonder he fought for the valley. No wonder he despised the wealthy.

Don Lorenzo shrugged and stroked his long, bushy sideburn. "Armando spent many years at the Mission

San José y San Miguel de Aguayo studying for the priesthood."

Her heart fluttered like a butterfly's wings. "A priest," she said, more calmly than she truly felt. "From a priest to a rebel?"

"I'm afraid so," he said. "First his father left, and prior to his taking his priestly vows, his *madre* died. Soon afterwards, he deserted the mission. Armando has been causing trouble ever since, and always it's about some unrest with the people of La Flor. He renounced his commitment to *Dios* for his people."

Marianne studied the don. He'd opened her mind about Armando. No doubt his private crusade for La Flor stemmed from the circumstances with his parents. Who else would fight for the rights of the villagers?

But Armando had never been overly cruel, even in the beginning. Certainly not like Felipe. She shuddered at the memory of the man's viciousness. In contrast, Marianne remembered Armando's words when he didn't know she spoke Spanish. His heart lay with his people, their needs and their happiness. He'd returned her to the hacienda, and later he resigned her to Don Lorenzo's care. She wondered how the Spanish gentleman might feel about that gesture. Armando had most assuredly made a few unlawful decisions, but he did subject himself to the authority of Governor Juan Bautistade Elguezábel.

She'd overheard Papa and Clay talking about the guns, swords, and daggers that the governor ordered Armando to return. The weapons were cleaned and in excellent condition.

Governor Elguezábel hadn't ordered compensation for all of Papa's stolen cattle, but Armando selected several from La Flor's stock and had the soldiers herd them onto his land. Much to Papa's surprise, the stock appeared healthy and of good quality.

"I don't believe Armando Garcia is an evil man," she said. "Perhaps misguided best describes him."

"A man who nearly took his vows to administer the holy sacraments has no excuse for breaking the laws of the Crown," Don Lorenzo said.

She nodded. Caught in the middle with her sympathies falling on both sides, Marianne fought the urge to sink into despair. Later, when she had time to mull over this new information, she'd ask God to help her understand the strange happenings in this beautiful land.

Armando a priest . . . still the thought of him committing his life to God's work startled her. Did he have a relationship with Jesus Christ, or had he only been caught up in the duties and responsibilities of representing the church for Spain?

Chapter 20

The days of summer passed aimlessly, and each one brought Marianne closer to her September wedding date. She spent hours under the guidance of Antonio de Valero, memorizing the catechism and perfecting her Spanish reading, writing, and speaking abilities. At other times, her mother instructed her in how to supervise a household of servants and how a wife should conduct herself. Don Lorenzo sent a seamstress to fit her for several more new dresses, one of which would be her wedding gown. The seamstress brought samples of fabric, most of which were of Spanish designs in vivid colors.

In mid-August, Don Lorenzo arrived with three huge leather trunks full of the new gowns and many gifts for Marianne and some for her mother. In his generosity, Marianne secretly likened him to her Heavenly Father: He showered her with things that she didn't deserve. The don hadn't demanded affection or made her feel uncomfortable with physical expressions of love. Instead, he stood back and appeared to take great pleasure in presenting her with exquisite treasures.

Sometimes she wondered if he guessed her heart, but upon further contemplation, she realized no one knew her inner turmoil but God and Mama. And both understood her desire to obey in His will and to follow Him. If only she could capture the same love for Don Lorenzo as she possessed for Armando. Perhaps then she wouldn't feel the guilt and shame.

Alone in her bedroom with Mama, Marianne opened the trunks with the anticipation of the new gowns. "Oh, Mama, look at these." She caught her breath and covered her mouth in surprise and delight.

Gingerly, she lifted the first one from the top, a bright green day dress trimmed in gold. Clasping it to her body, she viewed the effect in front of a full-length mirror. Indeed, it looked lovely. Not an item of ladies' apparel had missed the don's consideration, and Marianne blushed with the intimate undergarments: dainty chemises and petticoats embellished in delicate embroidery and yards of lace. He included beaded fans, exquisite lace mantillas—as many as her gowns—elbow-length gloves, some that freed her fingers for riding; and always, jewelry from his family in fine gold and precious gems. How could she ever wear such finery, especially when she preferred the comfort of Mexican dress?

"Mama, I'll look strange in these beautiful clothes," Marianne said. "And how will I ever be able to sneak away to ride Diablo in the plain clothes that Carmita gave me?"

Her mother smiled and helped her fold the green dress. "You will have to address the matter with the don." She laughed. "And are you sure your father will allow you to take Diablo to the don's hacienda?"

"Of course. Papa has no use for him. I'm sure he'll be glad to be rid of my Diablo." She stole a moment to imagine herself riding her stallion freely without criticism at her new home. She had yet to see his estate. She glanced at her mother. "This is all so new, and it frightens me."

Her mother's gaze clouded. "My dear, I thought little alarmed you, at least little that you are inclined to reveal."

"Am I strange?"

"No." Her mother laughed again, and touched her hand to the side of Marianne's cheek. "You are simply like your father."

She chose not to comment on her likeness to Papa. The thought left her feeling confused. If the truth seeped through, he'd be glad to see her gone. And she simply felt numb with the idea of starting a new life as a señora.

Together, Marianne and her mother sorted through the lovely dresses, each one more beautiful than the one before. At the bottom of the third trunk lay a white lace and silk gown. "How can I wear this?" she whispered. She lifted it to examine the lovely, detailed design. Tiny beads dotted across the bodice, up and down the sleeves, and around the lace of the wrists.

"I don't understand?" Her mother assisted her to press the delicate dress against her body.

"It is far more elegant than I should wear." Marianne handled the gown as though it were woven with pure gold. "This should be worn by a fine Spanish lady."

Her mother lifted her chin. "You are a fine, noble lady, and you are far more beautiful than any of this finery. Foremost you're a Virginia woman, well bred and proud. Soon you'll take your place as a *doña*, the wife of Lorenzo Sanchez de la Diaz y Franco. His hacienda expands far greater than ours, and I'm told his home is a mansion fit for a queen. You will be happy there, and your reputation as a perfect wife for the don will be known to all."

"I won't disgrace you." Marianne had slowly begun to realize what her new life involved. "You will be pleased with the reports."

Her mother smiled through heavily veiled lashes. "Nothing you could do would disappoint me, for you have placed God first in your life."

"You know my heart, Mama. I will always strive to be worthy of the don's name, despite . . ." Her reply choked in her throat.

Her mother took the white gown from her and draped it across the bed. She gathered Marianne into her arms and kissed the top of her head as though she were a little girl again. The closeness brought tears to both of them.

"Go ahead and cry," Mama said. "All of this is so new. And even without the excitement and expectations of the future before you, your heart breaks for another."

"Mama, I have prayed to forget him," she said. "And just when I think I've triumphed, a word or a thought brings back his memory. I try. I really try."

"I understand, for I remember attempting to forget Weston when my papa forbade me to see him."

"But this is so difficult."

"You're stronger than I am," Mama added. "For I did not listen to the wisdom of my father. We've talked of this before. Fight the tug of your heart, my dear. Don Lorenzo is the better choice. A life with Armando Garcia invites misery and suffering. You, my daughter, deserve the best God can give you."

"I know you're right." She whisked away the traces of tears. "I must try harder. The don is a good man, and I have looked for signs that he might not be so."

"I too have searched for those indiscretions and have found nothing that indicates he is anything but an honorable man who adores you."

Later, during the afternoon meal, Marianne thanked the don in meticulously worded Spanish for his generosity.

His white mustache turned up with pleasure. "I am delighted that you have examined the contents of the trunks and are satisfied with them."

Marianne nodded. "More than satisfied, I am overwhelmed with your kindness."

He smiled and she saw a sparkle in his clear brown eyes. "Your Spanish is excellent, and your tutor writes glowing reports about your progress." He turned his attention to her father. "Weston, you are blessed with a beautiful, intelligent daughter. I have no doubt that when I'm gone, she will manage my hacienda proficiently. At my age, I cannot guarantee a male heir. In fact, I plan to begin instructing her about how to manage my estate as soon as we are married."

For a brief moment, her father looked startled with the don's declaration, but it soon passed to one of pleasantness. Marianne fought the urge to laugh. The only reason Papa had arranged the marriage was to expand the Phillips Hacienda. Papa had gambled on all the land being transferred to him upon the don's death. The thought of the wealthy holdings remaining with Marianne must fill him with rage. Papa and Marianne quarreled enough for him to realize she'd never allow him to possess one tenth of the don's land.

In essence, Papa had lost all he desired to gain in arranging for his daughter to wed the owner of a baronial estate.

"I'm not so sure you would want to entrust your land to a woman who has no experience with business," Papa said.

Don Lorenzo lifted his glass of wine to his lips. He paused, no doubt allowing the liquid to settle on his palate before replying. "I have no reservations about my future wife's ability. Although it is not a common practice, I've given the matter considerable thought. Besides, who else could accomplish such a feat? All of my family is in Spain." He raised a questioning brow as if silently challenging Papa.

He comprehends Papa's mind. Don Lorenzo will not be fooled by one man's greed. God has provided well for me.

The next morning, Don Lorenzo left the Phillips Hacienda with the understanding he would return in eight weeks' time for the wedding. On his way home, he planned to visit the Mission San Antonio de Valero to speak with Padre Garvino Valdes to finalize the arrangements. Don Lorenzo wanted the ceremony at the San Fernando Church and urged her father to escort Marianne and her mother there to visit the padre and the site of the wedding. Papa protested. He didn't have time to leave his work, and he expected old friends from Virginia any day.

"I insist." Don Lorenzo's insistence was more than a match for Papa's stubborn will. "The priest will want to meet with Señorita Marianne and question her about our faith."

Papa agreed with the spirit of an enraged bull. Marianne understood his compliance lay with his desire still to please the Spanish nobleman. She felt sure Papa hadn't given up hope of one day gaining control of the don's vast land.

While bidding Don Lorenzo good-bye, she wished she could speak with him about Papa and his friends from Virginia. She remembered the morning months ago when he told Clay about his friends from Virginia going to help him gain possession of La Flor. But Don Lorenzo already knew Papa's heart. That had become evident during yesterday's meal. She prayed her suspicions were wrong, that she was mistaken about Papa's motives, and Papa's friends were to just visit. The governor could make life very difficult for Papa. Surely he wouldn't risk all he had gained for vengeance.

She shuddered with the revelation of the Virginian guests. She remembered Papa stating he'd sent for men to help him secure La Flor and drive out Armando and his people from the valley. She thought Papa had abandoned his thirst for their land when Governor Juan Bautistade Elguezábel ruled on the matter. The thought sickened her. Nothing had changed, even with the governor's edict. She resolved to pray more fervently for the people of La Flor, Papa's hard heart, and Armando.

Late in the morning, Marianne decided to visit Clay's bride and welcome her to the hacienda. They had married at the San Juan Mission, and she had yet to visit the young bride.

The newly married couple lived in a small, thatched-roof hut set apart from where the other servants and the vaqueros lived. Marianne had learned her name was Angelina, a pretty name for a pretty young woman. Although Angelina's father had forced Clay to marry his daughter when it became clear she carried his child, the couple appeared to be happy the evening when Don Lorenzo visited, and Clay competed with the vaqueros.

Gathering a bouquet of red flowers from the courtyard, Marianne walked toward the small hut where Clay and Angelina lived. She hesitated for a moment and wondered if she should have selected some food items from the kitchen as well, but fresh vegetables or bread could be brought on another occasion.

Chastising herself for not making the effort to call on Angelina sooner, Marianne suddenly realized how lonely the young woman must feel. She came to the hacienda not knowing anyone, and with the other servants busy with their duties, she most likely did not have much activity to fill her hours.

This is the type of pleasantry I shall need to do for the don.

As she neared the home, Marianne considered Clay. He normally left with the vaqueros at dawn, and she hoped his habit had not changed. Meeting up with him shook her resolve to be polite, and thinking about their last encounter made her shiver in disgust. Marianne still found Clay despicable. She prayed the marriage to Angelina and the prospect of fatherhood had changed him permanently.

She inwardly sighed when she saw no visible signs of Clay. She knocked on the wooden door and waited for Angelina to answer. When the girl did not appear, Marianne thought she must be resting or possibly enjoying a walk. Marianne studied the flat, dry land around her for the Spanish girl and saw nothing. Everything looked deserted.

I'll simply come by another time. Glancing at the fresh flowers in her hand, Marianne contemplated what to do. She really wanted to leave them as a gesture of friendship, but not in the hot sun for them to wither and die.

"Angelina, are you there?" Marianne asked in Spanish. A peculiar sound reached her ears, as though a kitten had mewed in response to her question. "Angelina?" She leaned her ear against the door.

Silence met her ears and just when Marianne decided to leave, a slight whimper came from inside the Wharton hut. Curious, and feeling a twinge of apprehension, Marianne grasped the latch and lifted it. Slowly the door swung open, and her gaze swept across the dimly lit room. She blinked then gasped in horror at the sight before her.

Angelina lay in a heap on the bed; her body twisted and distorted atop a blood-soaked blanket. The young woman could not open her eyes, for they were swollen shut in a hideous mass of black, blue, and dried blood. A faint moan escaped her lips—what Marianne had originally thought was the sound of a kitten. Angelina's face appeared to be one bruise upon another, and her upper lip seeped blood.

Instantly Marianne kneeled at her side. Compassion, then anger tore through her for the young girl.

"Angelina, can you talk?" She wanted to touch the young woman but was afraid of hurting her more. She saw huge, purplish-blue marks from her wrists to her shoulders, and one arm lay crooked across the bed, most likely broken. If all had not sickened Marianne before, the finger indentations across her throat gave a clue to what her assailant had attempted.

She instantly recoiled at the sight of blood caked through Angelina's black, tangled tresses. At least she still breathed life. "I'll get help," Marianne uttered in Spanish then added, "And I must find Clay."

Angelina stiffened at the words. With a limp hand she gripped Marianne's arm and shook her head. Why wouldn't she want Clay? Surely he hadn't done this to her? Would he beat his pregnant wife and leave her alone to suffer? She bent close to the young woman's ear. "Don't be afraid. I'll return shortly with someone to tend to you."

Angelina tried to move her lips, but she was too weak. "Do not speak," Marianne said and stood above her. The thought of leaving her seemed cruel, but Carmita would know how to treat her. And Papa . . . He hadn't left the house today. Surely he would help with this tragedy.

With her hand on the door, she turned to gaze once more at Angelina. "Holy *Dios*, I pray for Your healing for this young woman."

Marianne lifted her skirts and raced back to the house. Her chest ached, and perspiration dripped down her face by the time she arrived home. She entered through the double front doors and hurried down the hallway to her father's study. Without knocking, she turned the latch and burst inside.

"Angelina has been hurt," she managed in between breaths. "I just came from there. She's been beaten, bruises, blood everywhere, and I think her arm is broken."

Her father's eyes narrowed. He pounded his fist on the walnut desk. "Is Clay there?"

She shook her head and took another quick breath to keep from accusing the foreman. "She couldn't talk," Marianne said. Later, when Angelina recovered sufficiently, she could relay who attacked her.

"Is the girl alive?"

"Yes, but I fear for her life."

He stood from his desk and cursed. "I warned him. Her father will slice him in two for this." He lifted his stormy gaze to her. "Go get Carmita, and I'll go after Clay."

So Papa suspected Clay too. *God have mercy on a man who would do such a thing.*

By the time Marianne and Carmita reached Angelina, the young woman lay still.

Chapter 21

Carmita stepped past Marianne and bent over the limp form of Angelina Wharton. The woman turned her ear to the young woman's chest. "She's alive," Carmita said in English. "I hear her heart."

"Thank You, God." Marianne clasped her hand to her chest and fought the urge to cry with the wrenching sight of Angelina's battered body. "What can I do to help?"

Already Carmita had stripped back the bloodstained blanket to see the extent of her injuries. "I have to see how badly she's hurt before we can do anything." She gently examined the loosely clad young woman.

With the movement, Angelina moaned, and Marianne sickened. Clay should be whipped for this. The upper part of her body bore the results of the hideous beating, but luckily her stomach area held no marks.

"She must have protected the baby," Carmita said.

Some areas held faded bruises. Angelina must have received other beatings. Had Clay beaten her even before they were married?

Carmita turned to Marianne. "I need water, clean cloths, and one of my medicine plants. Josefa knows where to find everything. Ask her to come too."

She once again ran back to the big house where Josefa had taken over Carmita's duties in the kitchen. While Marianne fetched a wooden pail of water and gathered up clean cloths to bathe and bandage Angelina, Josefa hurried to the courtyard for a large pot containing an aloe plant.

"Mama says this will cure almost anything," Josefa said as the two girls struggled with their burdens toward the Wharton hut.

Marianne merely nodded. She remembered when she'd fallen in the stable and scraped her hand on a pitchfork. Carmita had broken off one of the thick stalks of the plant, sliced it lengthwise, and coated the wound with the thick, clear liquid. Shortly afterward, her hand felt better and soon healed without infection.

When Marianne and Josefa reached the hut, Angelina cried out pitifully with the obvious pain raging through her body. Not since her mother suffered through child-birth had Marianne witnessed such agony.

"Who could do such a terrible thing?" the dark-eyed Josefa whispered to Marianne. She held her breath at the grotesque sight of the young woman. "Did you say Señor Phillips rode after her husband?"

"Yes, I'm sure Papa will find him soon." Marianne didn't want to say that Clay had most likely done this to his wife. Papa's words had rooted her suspicions.

Marianne set the water and cloths at Angelina's bedside. She questioned how the young woman had endured the beating. She looked more dead than alive.

Carmita cleansed Angelina's cuts and bruises while the young woman sobbed pitifully with the torment searing through her. She couldn't bear Carmita's touch and repeatedly cried out, as though she relived each excruciating moment of the beating.

The older woman began to sing a familiar song about the love of a mother for her child. As Carmita sang, she lightly dabbed the injuries with a damp cloth before applying the aloe. While the clear, low voice of Carmita echoed in sweet whispers around the room, Angelina bit her lower lip until the sores began to bleed again.

A feeling of helplessness swept over Marianne, and she prayed God would ease Angelina's suffering and heal her body. Glancing at Josefa, Marianne saw her young friend had tears streaming down her brown cheeks.

"Josefa," Carmita said. Her gaze never left Angelina. "Hurry back to our hut and bring back my pouch of herbs. And Marianne, start up the cooking fire to boil water. We need to make Angelina a tea with the herbs to lesson the pain." She turned to the girls. "I will need pieces of wood to splint her arm."

Marianne and Josefa did as Carmita instructed, leaving the older woman to resume her work and continue her soothing song. Neither of the pair spoke as they rushed to their destinations, but they both exchanged worried glances.

Mama must have discovered the house was empty, for she found Josefa with the herb pouch. When Josefa explained what happened to Angelina, Mama accompanied her to the Wharton hut. Together Mama and Carmita applied medicine, bandages, and set the broken arm. Marianne marveled at how Mama put aside her own need for rest to tend to the injured young woman.

Hours later, while Angelina rested in the late afternoon, Papa returned—without Clay. He strode into the open doorway of the Wharton hut in a dour mood.

His gaze fixed on the injured young woman. "Clay's gone. Must have left sometime last night."

"He did this," Mama said. Never had Marianne heard such bitterness from her mother. "I'm sure of it." She rose from a bench near the bed and stared at Papa.

Several long moments passed. "Looks that way to me. Is she going to live?"

Her mother used a cloth to dab her sweat-bathed face. In the hut, the temperatures soared. "Carmita has done all she can do."

"Can she speak?" Papa asked.

"No, only moans like a hurt animal." Mama touched his arm. "What are you going to do?"

He sputtered a curse. "Clay is going to bring down trouble on us for this. The governor is already unhappy with me, and Angelina's father is a close friend of his. I need to send a rider after her father."

Marianne swallowed an angry retort. Papa didn't feel any compassion for Angelina. Instead he worried about upsetting the Spanish . . . and possibly losing his land.

"She should not stay alone," Mama said.

"She can have my bed," Marianne said, "and I'll sit with her."

Papa rubbed his whiskered jaw. His eyes narrowed revealing his irritation. "I suppose her father would appreciate knowing we were doing all we could. The governor would appreciate it too." He expelled a curse so vile that Mama gasped.

The familiar uneasiness twisted in Marianne's stomach. Why did Papa always have to think only of himself? *Please, God, help me with him. I want to love him like You do, but it's so difficult.*

"We need to get her to the main house," Mama said.

Papa took off his hat and wiped the sweat dripping from his forehead. His pants and shirt were coated in yesterday's dirt. "I can carry her," he said after a long pause.

Carmita immediately stood where she'd been kneeling at the bedside. "Moving Angelina will cause her much pain. Let me hold her arm where I've splinted it."

Papa frowned and allowed Carmita to assist him. Angelina moaned and sobbed. The word "Papa" escaped her lips.

Papa's lips pressed firmly together. General Enrique Guerra, an officer in the Spanish army, worked directly with the governor, and Papa no doubt feared what he might do. Once the news of what Clay had done spread among the Spanish nobles, Papa's name could be ruined. Some of the influential noblemen already distrusted him and voiced their disapproval of Americans settling on their land.

Another thought occurred to Marianne. If Papa had given permission for Clay to marry her, she would be the one beaten. Had Papa considered this at all?

Flickers of sunrise filtered through a deep blue sky the next morning before Angelina stirred and her eyelids fluttered. Her once large, doe-like eyes had been reduced to mere slits surrounded by a swollen mound of black and purplish-blue. Carmita and Marianne had sat on opposite sides of her bed the entire night, praying and watching her by candlelight. The older woman feared the trauma to Angelina's body threatened the life of her unborn child, but the baby seemed to have remained safe. At times when the pain reduced the young woman to feeble cries. Carmita sang. Her low voice seemed to comfort the young woman. Marianne's heart filled with compassion. Angelina didn't look much more than fourteen years old.

"When will we know if she's going to be all right?" Marianne asked as dawn threaded its way across the sky.

"Soon, I think," Carmita replied. "She survived the beating and the night. We must pray and be here when she awakens."

Marianne sighed and studied Angelina's face. "I never liked Clay, but I didn't think him capable of such brutality."

Carmita nodded. "He drinks too much, and it makes him loco and mean. We should ask *Dios* to heal Angelina's body and soften Clay's heart." In the candlelight,

Marianne believed the older woman looked like an angel, one with black hair and smooth brown skin. When she bowed her head to pray, her entire face glowed in the certainty of God. Surely her friend had been God's messenger to Angelina.

"El Dios santo, many times I have asked You to mend this poor girl and to protect her unborn child. Now I also ask You to stop this demon in Clay. Help me to nurse this dear girl who is in so much pain . . . and quickly bring her padre."

Marianne raised her head. Heavy thoughts pressed against her mind. "Why are some men born wicked and cruel, while others are good and God-fearing?" She peered into the dear face of Carmita.

"If we knew the answers to that, the world would be a better place to live," Carmita said. "I hope," and she paused as her voice rang with emotion, "Angelina's mind does not suffer from this. She is so young and with a little one to care for."

Marianne studied the young woman who barely held onto life and recalled her beauty before the beating. Carmita had said that ever since Angelina had come to the hacienda, she had laughed and smiled all the time. Now everything had changed, and only God could heal her.

"Madre Santa," Angelina moaned in Spanish. "Help me."

Carmita stroked the young woman's head. "*La Madre Santa* hears your prayers, little one, and we are here to take care of you. Rest and let your body heal."

"I hurt," she said through a ragged breath. "Leave me alone. I want to die."

"You must fight for your *bebé*," Carmita said.

"I . . . I don't care." A tear slipped from Angelina's eye. She attempted to raise herself slightly from the bed, only to fall back on the pillow.

"*El Dios* loves you," Carmita continued, "and so do we."

Angelina stiffened with the pain. "Not Clay," she finally said.

"Did he do this to you?" Marianne asked. All the while fury caused her to tremble, but she had to be sure.

"*Sí*. He doesn't love me. *Mi padre* . . . he spoke the truth . . . Clay is evil."

"Save your strength." Marianne hoped her voice relayed comfort. "Sleep if you can." Angelina closed her eyes. "Papa warned me. I should have listened."

"Hush," Carmita said. She lifted a mug of lukewarm tea to the young woman's lips. "Here, little one, try to drink this. It will make you feel better."

Marianne watched Carmita coax Angelina into taking a few sips of the herbal brew. The tea would make her sleep and allow her body time to heal without the unrelenting pain.

Glancing at the ascending light creeping across the sky, Marianne recalled Papa had sent a rider for Angelina's father at daybreak. If anyone had doubted Clay's hand in Angelina's beating, they would no longer. Suddenly she felt Papa needed to know the young girl had revealed her attacker.

"I will tell my father about Angelina's condition, and who did this," Marianne said to Carmita. "I know the rider may have already left, but I believe Papa should be informed of everything."

Carmita wordlessly agreed and continued to administer the herbed potion. Marianne slipped from the room toward Papa's study. She met him in the hall and relayed the news about Angelina.

"So she shall live." He stroked his long, gray-streaked mustache. "Good. The situation is bad enough without her dying."

"No word from Clay?" Marianne knew full well Papa disapproved of women questioning the affairs of men.

He frowned. "He's gone, and if he's smart he'll keep riding until he's out of Texas."

Marianne chose not to reply, although she wanted to know if Papa had encouraged Clay to leave. The two men had been friends for as long as Marianne could remember. Papa treated Clay like a son and overlooked his crude mannerisms. How did he feel about Clay now?

"Aren't there things you should be doing?" he asked in a manner clearly indicating his dismissal of her. He set his sights on the door leading to the courtyard. "I have work to do." He left her standing in the reception room hallway.

Alone, Marianne peered around the study. Its familiar surroundings in the shadows of early morning looked foreign. Heavy, ornate wooden chairs with leather seats and backs, a small shelf of books written in English and Spanish, a display of Spanish swords and daggers given to him by Don Lorenzo. Those things represented home. But this was Papa's house, not really Mama's or hers, and the contents reflected his life.

Marianne's gaze traced back down the hallway to her room where Angelina labored for every breath. She prayed the young woman's papa loved and cared for her. Marianne understood the turmoil of needing a father's love and not receiving it. She didn't wish those feelings on anyone.

Chapter 22

Toward sunset, Angelina's father, General Enrique Guerra, arrived at the Phillips Hacienda. Alone. No soldiers. Marianne heard Papa step outside to meet him. She waited with Angelina, hoping neither the general nor Papa would taunt the other into an argument. Moments later, he and Papa entered the house. The sound of their boots trudging down the hallway echoed like an army brigade. She hated that sound. She'd go to her grave detesting it.

"What do you mean my daughter has been injured?" the general asked, as though barking orders to his men.

"Right this way," Papa said. "She's in the back bedroom."

Staring into the troubled, sleeping face of Angelina, Marianne hoped the Spanish officer had pity on his daughter. She exchanged a quick glance with Carmita and her mother before the three women stood in respect for the Spanish officer.

"How badly is *mi hija* hurt?" the general asked. He and Papa neared Marianne's bedroom. "What happened? Where is her husband?"

Angelina's father, a tall, thin man dressed impeccably in his soldier's blue and red uniform, gasped at the sight of his daughter. Stunned, he clasped the polished brass handle of his sword. A moment later he kneeled at her side. He reached out to stroke her hair, then drew back. A mournful wail from deep inside him surfaced. Grief, like none Marianne had ever witnessed, poured from the man's soul. General Enrique Guerra's tears fell unashamedly onto his daughter's face.

"Angelina," he said after several moments of struggling for control, "can you tell me who did this to you?"

At the sound of the general's voice, the young woman stirred. "Papa," she whispered. "You came."

He bent closer to her swollen and slashed mouth and lifted his weather-beaten hand as if to touch her, but clenched his fist instead. "Nothing could keep me from you, my little one. Your mother will be here tomorrow. Your *tio* is bringing her."

"I'm sorry." Angelina licked her blood-stained lips. "You . . . you were right about Clay."

General Guerra arched his back. "He did this, this wicked thing?"

"*Si,* Papa." Her voice was barely audible. "He despises me and our *bebé.* He wishes us dead."

The general's huge hand lightly patted the top of Angelina's head where dried blood still caked her dark tresses. "Hush now and rest. I'll not leave your side. Your mother and I will stay with you until you are strong enough to journey home."

"Oh, Papa," Angelina whispered. She took a breath and then another. "You and Mother will take care of me?"

The man's sobs reverberated around the room. "I love you, Angelina." And he kissed her bruised cheek.

When she closed her eyes, General Guerra stood from the bed and with a heavy sigh turned to Mama. "I owe you my life for what you have done for my Angelina." He swallowed hard. Emotion seared his words. "Without you to care for her, *mi hija* would have surely died."

Carmita softly translated, and Mama responded in English. "We're so sorry for Angelina and her intense suffering. Our daughter," and she pointed to Marianne, "found her. However, Carmita has nursed her."

Carmita translated Mama's words, and the general thanked the brown-skinned woman. His attention reverted to Papa. "I want Clay Wharton." His hand once more clutched his sword. "We need to talk away from the women."

Papa nodded and the two men left the room. In the hallway, Angelina's father voiced his anguish and sorrow. "Tell me, Señor Phillips, what would you do if that were your *hija* near death?"

"I would tear the man apart with my bare hands."

Her father's words sent chills through Marianne's body. For an instant, she allowed herself the joy of believing Papa loved her. Then she remembered her abduction at La Flor. Papa's words were for General Guerra's benefit.

Angelina slept through the night with her father seated beside her. Exhausted, Marianne spent the wee hours of the morning in her mother's room, but Carmita made a pallet on the floor so she could administer the herbal tea and help the general nurse his daughter. The injured young woman still lay in grave danger. Mama and Marianne prayed relentlessly, and General Guerra appeared to be in a constant state of turmoil.

Marianne viewed the man with awe and curiosity. She heard him pace the floor, sob in unfathomable distress, and curse Clay Wharton with an oath of retribution for what he had done to his beloved daughter.

Surprisingly enough, the next morning, when General Guerra offered Papa's vaqueros a substantial sum for the return of Clay Wharton, Papa doubled the amount. The vaqueros disliked Clay and clamored for the reward. Papa helped them comb the land in search, but Clay had vanished.

Marianne wondered if her father's generosity and willingness to help stemmed from his fear of the general's relationship to the governor, or if he truly abhorred what Clay had done. No sooner had the suspicions about Papa entered her mind than she immediately asked for forgiveness. Her father did have commendable traits despite his harsh mannerisms, and she knew he must be upset with what Clay had done to Angelina. Mama loved him . . . and she did too.

General Guerra's wife arrived near sundown, and the two kept a constant vigil at their daughter's bedside. They slept little, both refusing to leave the room except for brief moments. On the fourth day, Angelina showed a marked improvement. She talked and sipped a bit of broth, but begged not to be left alone, often becoming hysterical.

"We'll take Angelina home in five days," the general said, "providing she's strong enough to travel. She's safe at our hacienda, and that animal, Wharton, will never harm her again."

Marianne spoke to Angelina on the eve of the family's departure. She gathered up Angelina's hand and lightly touched her cheek. "I'm so glad you're feeling better," she said in Spanish. "I pray *Dios* will guard your heart and continue to heal your body."

Angelina smiled and took a quick breath. "It hurts to speak, but I must talk to you. If . . . if you hadn't found me, I would have died. *Gracias*, señorita. I'll never forget what you, Carmita, and your family have done for me."

"Carmita, with the help of *Dios* guiding her hands, brought you back to the living," Marianne said. "He is the One we must thank."

"You're right." Angelina grimaced and bit her lip with the pain that tormented her body.

"Please, don't talk. I can't bear to see you in distress."

Angelina shook her head. "I know everything will be fine, and I will recover. *Mi bebé* may not have a father, but my child will have loving grandparents and a devoted mother." She tilted her head slightly on the pillow. "Oh, how I regret not listening to my parents when they tried to warn me about Clay. I thought I knew better and believed his lies. He said I was beautiful, and he loved me. Instead, I had to learn a most difficult lesson."

Marianne remembered the horror in finding Angelina near death. The result of a foolish decision.

The swelling had begun to fade on her face, and some of the bruises were changing to a green color; the first signs of healing. She had one scar on her forehead, which her hair would hide, and perhaps another on her lower lip. But Marianne worried about the wounds inflicted upon her heart and mind. The ones only God could heal.

"I hope we can visit each other after I'm married to Don Lorenzo." Marianne forced cheerfulness into her voice. "I believe his hacienda is not far from your casa."

"*Por favor,* do come to see me. I want us to be amigas." The young woman's eyes moistened. "May I talk to you? My mind is so burdened with the sadness that I've given *mi madre* and *mi padre.*"

"Of course, Angelina, you can tell me anything. I will tell no one."

The young woman looked beyond Marianne to make sure they were alone. She relaxed slightly. "I do need to tell someone this. Perhaps then I will feel better." She closed her eyes as though garnering strength. "Several months ago, I first saw Clay when I accompanied my parents to San Antonio de Bejar. He introduced himself to my family, and I found him handsome and charming. His smile thrilled me like no man ever had before. Sometime later, he asked permission to call on me, but my father refused. He felt I should seek the company of a man of Spanish descent. I was so upset. I cried and begged, but it did no good. Then Clay contacted me through one of the servants, and we began to meet secretly."

She paused and took several deep breaths. Marianne thought Angelina might weep again.

"He swore he loved me. He said he would do anything for me. His kisses were sweet, and I desired to prove my love for him." She paused, and whisked away the dampness beneath her eyes.

"When I discovered I carried his child, he became angry and said I should have been more careful. He told me he never wanted to see me again, that the baby could not possibly be his. His accusations broke my heart. So out of desperation, I told my father, who went to Governor Juan Bautistade Elguezábel. The governor ordered Clay to marry me. I believed I could change him, make him remember his love for me and want our baby. But he never forgave me for going to *mi padre*. I never saw Clay happy again, unless he'd been drinking. When he drank heavily, he became mean . . . and cruel. He beat me many times in the short while we were married. I couldn't seem to please him no matter what I did."

Marianne peered down at Angelina's tear-stained cheeks. "During the last beating he said he wanted to kill me and our child. He'd come home drunk, more drunk than usual, and soon became angry because I didn't feel well. I went outside with the sickness, and when I returned he accused me of being with one of the vaqueros. The more I denied his charges, the more he hit me. I pleaded with Clay to stop and covered my stomach, but he kept hitting me until I could not say anything for the pain." Angelina lifted her head and rose slightly on her elbows. "How I grieve for hurting my parents. Telling them I'm sorry doesn't remove how horrible I feel."

Marianne listened to every word, wanting just one opportunity to tell Clay what an evil man he was. "Your parents love you. They will take good care of you."

Angelina shrugged and eased back onto the pillow. "They say all is forgiven and forgotten. But why do I feel so soiled? I want to bathe and scrub myself until I have no skin left. Maybe it is like Clay said. I am no good, and the only reason he said he loved me was because he felt sorry for my lack of beauty." She began to sob and brought her bruised hand to her mouth to stifle the sounds.

Sympathy welled in Marianne. She remembered her kidnapping and how the peace of God sustained her, and she longed for the distraught young woman to know the same assurance. "No, Angelina, Clay lied to you. You are beautiful, and he's the one who is ugly and wicked. *Dios* can remove your bad feelings. He will forgive you if you ask."

Angelina turned away from Marianne. "I don't deserve anything from *Dios*."

"But *Dios* loves you and wants you to come to Him. That is why He sent *Jesús* to die for our sins, so we can all be His children."

The young woman continued to sob. Finally she gained control. "I want to confess, but where do I begin? I'm too ashamed to speak with a padre. I don't want anyone to know my horrible sin."

Marianne prayed Angelina would understand that true peace came from her relationship with Jesus Christ. "Let me help you return to *Dios*." When Angelina hesitantly nodded in affirmation, Marianne breathed a quick prayer. "I know you will want to confess to a padre, but you can pray now for forgiveness." She took Angelina's hand. "Right now, you can thank our *Dios Santo* for sending *Jesús* to save you from your sins. Without the gift of life from His Son, we all would perish. Ask Him to live in your heart forever and to rule your every thought and word. This is the only way to peace and forgiveness."

A few moments later, Angelina smiled. "*Madre Santa*," she said. "My heart is at rest. *Dios* has filled my soul with His forgiveness and love."

Marianne bent and placed a kiss on her cheek. "I will pray for you every day. We shall be like sisters, you and I. Tomorrow will not be good-bye; only a short time will pass until we see each other again."

"I would like that."

"We will laugh and have a most splendid time."

Both young women blinked back their tears and managed to laugh at their show of emotion. Marianne thanked God for using her to help Angelina. Now her new friend could start over by trusting in her Heavenly Father. And Marianne desperately needed a friend who trusted in God, for now she feared her new life with the don. What if he changed and became like Papa or Clay?

That evening, while waiting for sleep to overcome her, Marianne once more pondered Angelina's horrible ordeal with Clay. Admittedly so, the young woman regretted not listening to her parents about him. She realized they were right and wanted the best for her. Mama wished too that she had been obedient to her father's wishes and stopped seeing Papa. Both women had been blinded by love and chose their hearts over submission to those who loved them. Marianne considered the comparison of Angelina's life and Mama's to her own. God must want Marianne to learn from those two marriages so she would not consider doing something foolish with Armando.

But Armando didn't have the traits of Clay Wharton or Papa. Did he? Had Mama and Angelina felt the same pull on their hearts, believing in the men they loved as good and kind?

Why am I torturing myself with thoughts of Armando? I will marry Don Lorenzo as Mama and Papa have planned. Nothing can change. Even Armando realized my place is with the don.

Trust Me, a voice whispered. *Trust not your heart, neither the advice of others, nor the workings of your thoughts.*

What do you mean, Lord? She startled in her bed. *Have You not instructed us to seek wise counsel from those who love You?*

Seek ye the Kingdom of God, and all these things shall be added unto you.

Heavenly Father, am I not following You with my whole heart? Marianne peered into the darkness. Confusion rested heavily upon her. Twice she had viewed the consequences of women marrying men their parents objected to. Loving God meant that she abided by Mama and Papa's instructions, just as the commandment stated. God's Word assured her of blessings for adhering to His commands. Why then did she feel such unrest with her future?

Chapter 23

Armando waved to his friends as they circled around a rocky hill and rode toward him. While he waited in a clearing, they splashed across a creek lined with white-faced rock.

From a nearby hilltop, he had spotted a herd of longhorns days ago, and now they planned to drive the cattle back to their own herds. For some time now, the men from La Flor had rounded up the wild longhorns to increase their own stock. The villagers risked their lives each time they ventured farther from the valley in search of cattle or mustangs. Raiding Comanches roamed the desolate land and left mutilated corpses of their victims behind—a warning to those who strayed far from safety. Armando and his men took their chances with the marauding Indians. Their people needed the cattle and horses, and his spirit cried out for adventure.

Armando regretted compensating Weston Phillips for the stolen cattle, but he felt a sense of satisfaction in hand-selecting the best from their small herd. His pride had a great deal to do with the decision. He wanted the governor to know Armando Garcia as a man of honor, and he needed Marianne to remember him as a man of his word.

"The longhorns are grazing near that winding stream, over there." Armando pointed. Just beyond a deep arroyo and a sprinkling of mesquite and brush, the cattle fed and drank freely. Emilio, Pepe, and Felipe followed his gesture. "I counted about fifty head."

"Any sign of Comanches?" Emilio's worried gaze searched the sparsely dotted land around them.

"I saw pony tracks yesterday, but not today." Armando sensed the danger of the remote area, but he refused to comment on it.

"They could be here and waiting." Pepe glanced about. "Let's round up the cattle and drive them back now."

"*Sí*, we don't need the remains of our bodies laid out for wild animals to devour," Armando said in an attempt to make light.

Felipe said nothing. He appeared to be scrutinizing the cloudless blue sky to the west of them. "Vultures," he said, and they viewed the hovering birds.

"We're like women," Armando said. "Do we get the cattle or not?"

Felipe jerked his horse toward the longhorns. "I haven't ridden all this way for nothing. Already I have a hungry belly, and being called a woman from the likes of you makes me mad."

Armando understood Felipe's impatience in the heat as well as Emilio and Pepe's natural fear of Comanches. "I'll see what the vultures are feeding on while you get behind the cattle," he said. A dead animal would set their worries at rest.

His path took him down a gully and around a rocky ridge, his senses acute to everything around him. Apprehension settled like a dust cloud. He saw nothing, but victims of Comanches seldom saw their aggressors before they struck. Armando's instincts usually swayed him in the right direction. Perhaps he should turn back. He pulled his gelding to a halt and stopped to peer around him and then on to where the vultures feasted.

Armando spotted a body. Sprawled out on the rocky earth, a man or the remains of a man lay prey to nature's method of eliminating the dead. He rode closer, his rifle ready. Armando choked back the stench filling his nostrils and covered his mouth and nose with his bandanna. After a moment's hesitation, he dismounted and walked toward the body, wondering who could have met up with the Comanches and hoping it wasn't anyone he knew. He used his weapon to turn over the tortured body. Although a spider scurried about his eyes and nose, he still could recognize Clay Wharton. The Indians had used him as an example of their hatred for those invading their land. For a moment, he stared at the body before turning to mount his horse and head toward the others.

"Did you find a dead animal?" Emilio pulled his horse to a halt.

Armando took a deep breath. The sight and smell would have affected the strongest of men, and it distressed him greatly. "It wasn't an animal." He captured his friend's attention. "I found Clay Wharton's body."

Emilio's face paled. "Comanches?"

"*Si.*"

"Out here? What could have driven him so far from the Phillips Hacienda?"

Armando shook his head. "He's been there a while."

"Should we take him to Señor Phillips for burial?" Emilio glanced nervously around him, as though expecting Indians to leap from nowhere.

"We can't. It's impossible."

"Armando, I must bury the dead. Take me to him."

"My friend, the Comanches tortured and killed him. The sight is gruesome. Let us—"

The sound of Pepe and Felipe's approaching horses ended Armando's words.

"Tell them what you found," Emilio said.

"Clay Wharton's body."

"*Bueno*," Felipe said. "He deserved whatever happened to him for the things he did to my sister."

"No man should die such a brutal death," Emilio said. "No matter what he has done. Again, I ask, show me his body, and I'll bury him."

Felipe started to protest, but Pepe interrupted. "I'll help you, but let's not argue. We still have cattle to move."

Not wanting to watch his men engage in a futile debate, Armando silently rode in the direction of Clay's body. A short while later, the four men stood over the lifeless form.

"You're right." Emilio held his bandanna over his mouth and nose. "We can do nothing for him but pray for his soul." He studied the terrain about them. "Pepe, would you help me pile rocks on him?"

Armando joined Pepe in silently covering the body to keep the wild animals from eating Clay's flesh.

Felipe watched, no doubt believing vengeance had been administered for the injustices done to his sister. Finally, hot and dripping in sweat, the men retrieved their mounts and rode toward the longhorns.

"Should we reveal this information to Señor Phillips?" Pepe asked, his boyish face earnest.

Armando felt the weight of Pepe and Emilio's faith guiding their words. "I cannot be seen near the hacienda. Perhaps you and Emilio could ride there after we return."

"He has a wife," Emilio said. "My brother told me Wharton married a short time ago, and she's with child."

"Then do what you feel is right." Armando was eager to be on his way to La Flor. "For now, we have cattle to drive."

While they moved the longhorns toward La Flor, Armando's thoughts lingered on the demise of Clay Wharton. Why was he out here? Had he been alone? Granted Armando hated the gringo, but to die at the hands of the Comanche? Certainly not a quick death.

He set his jaw firmly. So Wharton had married. He had no thoughts about the matter, except what Bernardino had revealed to him weeks ago about the governor's displeasure. Armando recalled the stories of how the gringo had abused women and the beatings he'd inflicted upon those who refused him. Nothing mattered now, for he'd left a widow.

Although Armando had no desire to give Wharton's wife or Weston Phillips the tragic news, he did feel a twinge of regret in not seeking an opportunity to see Marianne. It would be the last time before her wedding to Don Lorenzo Sanchez. When would the ache leave him? His memory of her sharpened with each passing day. Sometimes he even felt envious and melancholy over Emilio and Isabella's happiness. Self-pity nudged at him again. He must be destined to live his life alone.

The following evening, Armando paced the floor of Manuel and Rosa's hut awaiting Emilio and Pepe's return. His *tia* and *tio* understood his anxiousness stemmed from concern for his two friends, and Manuel and Rosa gave many excuses for the delay. The two men rode across the vast estate of their enemy, Weston Phillips, in a mission of mercy, and Armando hoped they hadn't stepped into a trap. Without Wharton's body, Señor Phillips might accuse them of murder.

Pushing his fears aside, he dwelled again on the curious state of finding the dead man alone and so far from the Phillips Hacienda. And Marianne . . . would his friends catch a glimpse of the honey-haired señorita

with her sparkling eyes and gentle ways? More priceless than gold, his Marianne. Armando hoped Don
Lorenzo Sanchez treasured his bride.

Leaning against the doorway of the hut, Armando
sipped on cool water and watched the sun begin to set
in fiery shades of red and orange. Within an hour's
time, darkness would cover the village. A slight breeze
floated across the valley, cooling his face; however, it
did nothing to ease his anxiety. He deliberated saddling his horse and riding toward his friends. Pondering the thought one more time, he set his sights on
meeting Emilio and Pepe. He couldn't wait a moment
longer.

All the while he prepared his dun, Armando's mind
swept over the worst of fate for his friends. Then two
men rode toward the corral.

"Armando," Pepe called. "Where are you going,
mi amigo?"

The sound of his friend's voice soothed him like children's laughter. "Looking for you." Armando laughed.
"I thought you two might need to be rescued."

"We would have been here sooner, but Carmita
insisted we stay while she prepared a meal for us." Pepe
patted his stomach.

"My brother's wife is the best cook in all the land,"
Emilio said. "Who could resist?"

"And Señor Phillips did not threaten to shoot you?" Armando knew his voice rang with teasing, but he wanted a full accounting of everything since their absence.

"No," Emilio said. "Pepe and I learned a sad story about the short marriage of the gringo." He dismounted and led his horse to the corral. "We found out Señora Wharton no longer lives at the Phillips Hacienda, and I don't think the foreman has been missed."

Armando lifted a brow. "I want to know what happened. I'll help you rub down your horses while you talk."

In the evening shadows, Armando listened to how Clay Wharton had impregnated a general's daughter, and the governor had forced Clay into marriage, which Armando had learned from Padre Bernardino when he visited the mission. Emilio told him that Clay beat his bride, almost killing her, then rode out in a drunken rage. The young woman's father, General Enrique Guerra, had offered a large reward for any man who could find Señor Wharton, but neither he nor Señor Phillips had any success. As soon as the young señora gained her strength, the general and his wife took their daughter home.

"Whom did you inform about the body?" Armando brushed against Pepe's horse, a fine looking red roan.

"First my brother. When he heard what the Comanches had done, he went in search of Señor Phillips." Emilio paused. "Pepe and I feared the gringo would accuse us of murdering Wharton. He had caused enough trouble in La Flor for us to be accused."

"And he didn't?" Armando asked.

Pepe shook his head. "Our report appeared to satisfy him. But I think if Señor Wharton hadn't beaten his wife so badly, we would be in serious trouble. According to Señor Phillips, the Comanches did the Spanish a favor. General Guerra had vowed to kill him for what he'd done to his daughter."

Armando released a pent-up sigh. "It's over, and we no longer have to deal with anyone from the Phillips Hacienda."

Pepe opened the corral and led his horse inside. "Armando, I'm tired and I want to see *mi hijo*. Mañana we can talk more."

Armando wished Pepe well and watched him walk toward his hut. "I'm glad you took Pepe with you," he said to Emilio. "And I feel better knowing you're here and safe."

Emilio chuckled. "I worried a few times about our venture." Leading his horse inside the corral, he latched the gate. "I saw the señorita."

Armando's pulse quickened. "From a distance?"

"No, *mi amigo*. She came to Juan's casa after hearing about Señor Wharton. I don't think she grieved his death because of what he'd done. She asked Pepe about Rico, and after a while she inquired about you."

Armando refrained from sounding too eager, but his thoughts raced with Marianne. "What did she want to know?"

"If you were well . . . and if you had been with us when we found Wharton. Armando, her eyes told of her love for you. Only a fool would be blind to how much she cares."

"I know how she feels," Armando said.

"I regret that you two must be separated."

Armando felt a hint of anger, but he knew Emilio wanted his happiness. "She has her station in life, and I have mine."

"I understand what you say, and I've been thinking." Emilio paused. "Perhaps *Dios* stopped you from taking your vows as a priest for her."

"I left the mission because of my mother." Armando's voice rose. "No other reason."

"*Dios* guides our path." Emilio's soft voice continued. "He knows what's best, even though we think we are in control of our lives."

"I'm in charge of my own destiny."

"If so, then the señorita would be with you."

Armando said nothing. He respected his friend too highly to argue against the existence of *Dios*. The thought of a God purposely making his life miserable angered him. Once, he might have agreed with Emilio. Those days were gone, just like the moments shared with Marianne.

He'd lost his zeal for *Dios* when his mother died, and in time he would forget Marianne. Armando glanced up into a dark blue sky and noted a pattern of stars framing a half moon. Why deliberate about *Dios* or Marianne. Neither must hold a spot in his heart. He must be logical. He must be strong. He must live for his people.

Chapter 24

"Why were you at Juan and Carmita's hut this afternoon?" Marianne's father asked. Seated behind the heavy wooden desk of his study, Papa drummed his fingers over its walnut top. "It is degrading enough that you choose their company over your mother and me, but those filthy Mexicans from La Flor were there. Have you no sense of fear or pride?"

"Papa, I'm sorry."

His mustache twitched. "Sorry? Why were you there? Paying a social call?" Her father fired questions as though raking over a vaquero who had displeased him.

"Juan . . . Carmita . . . they're almost like family. They're my friends."

"Family? Friends?" Her father paused. "You," and he pointed his finger at her face, "are never to associate with those Mexicans again except to give instructions. They're servants, only a step above the niggers I owned in Virginia."

Marianne had her own opinion about folks owning slaves, but she kept her views to herself. She and Papa argued over too many topics without adding another.

"I enjoy their company." She arched her back in the wooden chair. All the while, mounting anger battled with a strong conviction that she should honor her father.

"And I'm ordering you to stay away from them." He pounded his fist on the top of the desk, sending a carved, brass bowl and a quill pen to the floor.

"You never cared before. Why now?"

"Don Lorenzo would never approve." He glared at her as though she were filth beneath his feet. "Do you have no esteem for the man?" He massaged his left arm.

Marianne choked back a terse remark, but another one fell from her lips. "I have more respect for him than you, Papa. You simply want to remain in the don's good standing so he'll change his mind about leaving me as his heir."

Her father instantly charged to his feet. "You insolent, ungrateful—"

"Maybe so." She rose defiantly from her seated position across from him. "But I am just like you in one regard. When I believe in something, I fight for it. And you're wrong to shamefully treat Juan and Carmita or any of the people from La Flor like animals. Those villagers only did what you would have done."

"How dare you compare them to me?" He stepped around his desk, his face a fiery red.

"Tell me, then. If you risked losing this hacienda and all you worked for, wouldn't you do anything to keep it?" She trembled with the rage exploding inside her, but she couldn't bring herself to stop. "You know the answer, Papa. You would kill any man who tried to steal your land."

"I've heard all that I intend to." He towered over her, and she saw his chest rapidly move up and down in his fury.

"Why? Because it's the truth? I agree those men were wrong to break into our home, take your weapons, and kidnap me. But are they any different from you? They are the same—strong fighters for what they believe. And that's why you despise them." Marianne took a deep breath in an effort to contain her emotions.

"That animal, Garcia, turned you against me." Papa's gray eyes flashed his contemptuous feelings.

"Their leader has nothing to do with this." She fought the desire to say so much more.

Her father pushed the chair Marianne had just occupied crashing to the floor. "He has everything to do with it. He took what was mine and thought that because he returned it, I should forget. Well, it won't happen. I vowed revenge, and I'll not stop until I get it. Truth be known, they are the ones who murdered Clay."

She realized their quarrel heightened with each utterance they threw at each other. Their argument merely added stones to the barrier separating them, and she must cease her deplorable, vicious words. If she didn't leave his study soon, tears would fall and render her helpless against his tyranny.

"Papa, one more time I've lost my temper." Marianne massaged her arms and took a deep breath. *Oh God, what have I done now?* "I'm sorry to upset you. I'm sorry to be disrespectful, but, oh, how I wish your vow for revenge had something to do with affection for me." She walked away, determined to leave him with her statement. With her hand gripping the door, she turned to capture his narrowed gaze.

"Everything I do is for you."

Startled by his words, her lips quivered. "Your love is all I've ever wanted." Without giving Papa an opportunity to reply, she left him. Grasping the sides of her dress, she rushed down the hallway to her room.

Marianne collapsed on the bed in a state of near hysteria. Tears flowed freely from her eyes and over her face. How many times had she and her father exchanged heated words, and how many times had she hated herself afterward? As a child when she stood up to him, he referred to her as rebellious and disciplined her with the back of his hand. As she grew older, he banished her to her room. Now with her wedding day in a month's time, how would he punish her? She didn't fear the consequences; perhaps she deserved whatever came from her outburst of temper. No matter that she'd apologized. This time she'd provoked him by crossing the boundaries of disrespect.

Why did I deliberately provoke him when I should have said nothing? Even with committing my life to the Lord, I cannot control my tongue. What is wrong with me? I am too much like Papa. I'm more like him than Mama . . . dear, sweet Mama who's kind and good. She certainly never has battled with Papa as I do.

Her weeping continued, a mixture of self-pity and desire for the relationship she craved with her father. Her entire life had been spent in seeking approval from him, although most times she tried to tell herself she no longer cared. Too many quarrels, too many hostile feelings.

Armando. She'd nearly said his name in front of Papa, and had bitten her tongue to keep from linking him with her father's degrading remark about the villagers. Papa's accusation about Armando sounded as if he knew what happened in La Flor. Admittedly so, her bitter tears also stemmed from forbidden love. Must life always be so complicated?

Marianne stayed in her room the remainder of the evening. She feigned a headache to her mother, which in part held truth. Any confrontation with Papa left her feeling ill. Once the tears subsided, she proceeded to pray about her uncontrollable temper. Notably so, she spent half of her time quarreling with Papa and the other half making amends.

Darkness surrounded her in a welcoming blanket of quiet. She lay awake, stomach rumbling, realizing she must apologize again to Papa. Except this time she wanted to ask him if he had any time to spend with her before the wedding. They had but a few short weeks remaining, and then all would be lost.

Heavenly Father, forgive me for my impetuous words to Papa. I don't know why I must always challenge him. I'm so sorry to grieve You. Each time this happens, I vow it will be the last, but then I lose my temper again. I cannot curb my tongue, Lord. You have to do it for me.

A soft knock at the door interrupted Marianne's prayer. She knew without asking that her mother stood in the hallway. Earlier, the house had thundered with

Marianne and Papa's argument, and Mama must have heard every word.

"Marianne?" her mother asked.

"Yes, Mama." She quickly blinked back her tears and sat up on the bed. "Come in, please."

Her mother carried a candle and guarded its flame to Marianne's side. "Are you feeling better?"

"Yes. I'm sorry you heard everything."

"The quarrels sadden me, especially when it's between two people I love."

Marianne took a deep breath. "Well, I am on my way to apologize for losing my temper. I believe I was too angry before to say the proper words."

"I knew you would, but I'm here for another reason." She set the candle on a small table beside Marianne's bed. "Your father has guests, and he would like for us to greet them properly."

"It's late for guests. Who has arrived at such a late hour?"

Mama moistened her lips. "This is important to him, and he has requested our presence."

Marianne rose from the bed and smoothed her dress. "I should brush my hair and wash my face. I won't be long."

"Your papa wants you to wear one of the new gowns Don Lorenzo had designed for you."

She gazed at her mother in the faint candlelight. "What an unusual request. I planned to wear them only in the don's presence, but if you feel it's important then I will comply with Papa's wishes."

"Please," her mother said. "I believe it might help your father's grim mood. And I'll help you dress."

"Of course." Marianne stepped to the trunk containing her most elegant gowns.

Selecting a bright blue one, her mother helped her fasten the many buttons. Moments later, they entered the hall for the reception room where the roar of men's voices echoed throughout the house.

Marianne expected to see Spanish noblemen or even soldiers, but not the dirty assortment of characters seated in her father's chairs and filling their glasses with Papa's finest wine.

"There you are." Papa had the telltale smell of wine on his breath and a slight slur of his words. Normally he drank only one or two glasses. He claimed it clouded his judgment, and he prided himself on being in control. Tonight, however, she wondered if he'd partaken of more.

The sordid lot stood as Papa began the introductions.

"Daughter, these men are from Virginia, where we came from. Your mother met these gentlemen earlier.

They've ridden a long way to see our hacienda and deserve our finest welcome."

Marianne forced herself to smile while her heart pounded against her chest. Could these men be the ones Papa had contracted to help him secure La Flor? She counted six bearded, unkempt men who desperately needed a bath. "It's a pleasure to meet you," she said. "I hope you will enjoy your stay here and come to see why we love Texas."

They all removed their hats and nodded politely. Some tripped over their responses and others merely nodded or grinned, revealing missing and yellowed teeth.

"I've asked Carmita to prepare a hot meal for our guests," Papa said.

He poured wine into awaiting glasses, splashing its contents on a heavy wooden table. Marianne noted regretfully that the wine had been a gift from Don Lorenzo.

"We shall see how Carmita is progressing," her mother said, beckoning to Marianne with a nod.

Once in the kitchen, Marianne commented on the foul odor coming from Papa's guests and asked why the men were visiting.

"I'm not sure." Her mother bustled about to assist Carmita. "But we'll make their stay with us pleasant."

Marianne searched through the *trastero*, the huge cupboard, looking for appropriate serving dishes. It proved a difficult task due to the flickering candlelight. Some of the dishes had been broken when Felipe and the others broke into their home, and the dishes hadn't been replaced. From the looks of her father's friends, she doubted if they minded whether their plates were chipped or not.

A short while later, Marianne and her mother served the arrivals from Virginia. Fortunately, the effort didn't require much work as the men appeared to inhale Carmita's beef stew and tortillas. How could they even taste the food? While attending a man who asked for a second plateful, Marianne noticed his gaping shirt across his stomach. Even in the shadows, she could see his hairy stomach protruding like a pig's rump. The sight disgusted her. She'd grown accustomed to poor people but not uncouth ones.

Papa's guests cursed with every breath and displayed no manners to speak of. At last, she and Mama were free to retire to their rooms.

But Marianne could not go to bed yet. She still needed to talk with Papa about earlier in the day, but not until his friends left the house for the night. She guessed they'd sleep with the vaqueros.

Time trickled by. Fully dressed, Marianne fought the urge to sleep until she finally rose from her bed and paced the floor. Shortly after midnight, she heard the outside door close and the sounds of coarse laughter and crude remarks cease. She listened a moment longer, then eased open the door to be certain the house was empty except for Mama and Papa.

Marianne knew her father would be in his study, a habit before retiring to his room. He would sit back in his chair and stare straight ahead. She often wondered what thoughts sped past his mind in the quietness of night, but she never had the courage to ask.

Stepping closer through the reception room, she distinctly heard the low hum of men's voices. Pausing, she curiously inched forward until she saw the light from the study door cast a faint shadow on Papa and one of the men from Virginia.

"So how do you plan to go about this?" the man asked. The chink of his glass against a bottle punctuated his question.

"Here, take a look at this map," Papa said. "I've marked La Flor and the easiest way to drive a herd of cattle into the valley."

Marianne held her breath for fear they might discover her. What was Papa planning to do?

"When do you want it done?" The man cursed and gulped his drink.

"I want to leave mid-morning. That gives us plenty of time to round up about a thousand head of my cattle and hold 'em until way after dark."

"I see," the man said. "Then we stampede those longhorns into the village." He chuckled. "Those huts will be flat by the time we're finished, along with the people sleeping inside."

"Exactly. Armando Garcia and his rebels are going to pay for what they did to me. And as soon as the last steer is through, I want to set fire to those huts. I don't want any evidence left for the Spanish. The governor has given me enough trouble."

Chapter 25

Marianne covered her mouth to keep from crying out. Papa planned to destroy La Flor and everyone living there. Innocent men, women, and children would die at her father's hand. How could he conceive such an evil plot?

"Ain't ya worried the least bit about the Spanish?" the man from Virginia asked.

"No. I have it all worked out. In the morning, I'll announce to the vaqueros that I'm taking all of you north to look for mustangs. We'll ride out, then skirt around west toward La Flor. By the time the Spanish find out about the burned village, you will be long gone to Virginia, and I'll have a perfect alibi."

"You've thought of everything," the man said. "Just like in the old days."

"You can gamble on my words and win a fortune."
Papa's voice rang with confidence, or perhaps the
alcohol spoke for him. "And I have a few mustangs that
Clay and I rounded up before he died. We can drive
them this way on our way back from the valley."

"I was looking forward to a couple of purdy
señoritas."

"I don't care what you do as long as they end up as
charred bones." Papa laughed. An ugly laugh.

Marianne couldn't bear to listen to any more. She
fought her first impulse to confront Papa with his mur-
derous scheme. But he could easily confine her to her
room while they were gone. How could he be stopped?
Even if she alerted Juan or one of the vaqueros to ride
for help from the soldiers in San Antonio de Bejar, they
would not return in time. She crept back to her room
to think and pray.

To do nothing meant abandoning all the villagers to
their deaths. And even if help from San Antonio arrived
in time, Papa would be tried for murder. What choice
did she have? How could she send her own father to the
gallows? How could she send the people of La Flor to
their deaths?

Flinging herself on her bed, Marianne shivered,
but not from any cold. How could Papa plan so many
murders? With dry eyes she pondered her father's
malicious intent. Armando, his aunt and uncle, little

Rico, Emilio, and the others faced death at the hands of her father. How could he live with himself? How could she live with herself if he succeeded, and she did nothing to prevent their deaths?

Marianne sat upright on the bed. In the flickering candlelight, shadows danced on the walls. As she studied their patterns, a thought occurred to her. She shook her head to dispel the lingering notion, but it refused to leave her.

Oh, Lord, are You talking to me? Am I to consider such a dangerous thing? She stood and rubbed her arms to banish the numbness waging war with her senses. *What You are asking frightens me. I can't do this.* She walked to the window and peered outside at the night sky. A myriad of stars greeted her, burning more brightly than the candlelight illuminating her room. A full moon held her spellbound. The heavenly bodies cast an ethereal glow to the earth below.

Whom shall I send? whispered the Voice that challenged her to do His bidding.

I don't know if I'm strong enough. I would have to ride within the hour to reach La Flor by daylight.

Didn't you see the moon and stars lighting your way?

She caught her breath. Had she really a choice in the matter? By doing nothing, she sent many people to their graves. Ignoring Papa's hideous scheme meant she was as guilty as those who drove the cattle to La Flor and lit the torches to their homes. Her stomach churned with the undertaking. Memorized Scripture escaped her while she wrestled with the panic that seized her heart and mind. What if she lost her way? Did Comanches roam the night for unsuspecting prey? What if Armando did not believe her?

She wrapped her arms around her waist and begged for the unrest to leave her. Instead, images of those she knew and loved in La Flor flashed across her mind. She had no choice but to try to warn them and pray God would right Papa's savagery without anyone being killed.

While Marianne waited for Papa's friend to leave the house, doubts again assaulted her. Fighting fear of the unknown, she praised God for using her to warn the people of La Flor. She would not be alone. No matter what happened, He rode with her.

Another hour passed before the big door creaked and closed. From the side of her window, she watched the man swerve and stumble on his way to the bunkhouse. His drunkenness and accompanying sleep would be her clear path to the stables. She changed from her elegant gown back into the dress she'd worn earlier. If she had to ride in her own clothes, she certainly didn't want to soil Don Lorenzo's gift.

Again, Marianne kept her ears poised at the door until Papa's heavy boots plodded down the hallway to his room. Anxious to be on her way, yet fearing discovery, she stood motionless, hearing nothing but the sound of her own heartbeat.

When at last she heard Papa's snores, she stole down the hallway, through the reception room, his study, and on to the kitchen. She slipped outside, grateful the door opened without the familiar creak. Once safely beyond the house, she released a heavy sigh. Another problem presented itself. Could she saddle and bridle Diablo in the dark? She couldn't risk a lantern in the stable. And what of a change of clothing? She needed to ride in the skirt and blouse packed in the trunk near Diablo's stall.

Marianne hurried to the stables and lifted the wooden latch. She doubted if anyone lingered inside, but the threat still played havoc with her mind. Normally, Papa had a vaquero guard the house and barns, but she had yet to see him. After pulling the door to a close, she leaned against it and inwardly breathed a prayer of thanks. Diablo sensed her presence and began to stir in his stall.

"Hush, Diablo," she whispered. The sound of her voice alerted her to how quickly she might be discovered.

Suddenly, she realized she could see the objects about her. Glancing up to a high window, she noted that the moon was set perfectly in the night sky and shone down through the rafters. She smiled despite the circumstances. How wonderful of God to place the silvery light to guide her.

She tiptoed to Diablo and assured the stallion of her presence. In silence and with ease, Marianne prepared her horse before securing her pale riding skirt and blouse. She purposely hung her dress on a peg in the stallion's stall. In the morning when Papa and his friends saddled up to leave, she needed them to find her clothes and to assume she'd taken an early morning ride.

The thought of returning home made Marianne fearful. No. She refused to think of Papa's wrath. God already knew her destiny, and she must trust Him to deliver her. Gathering up Diablo's reins, she led him through the stable and closed the door behind her. Glancing about, she saw no one and in one fluid motion, she stepped into the stirrup and onto the saddle.

"Señorita. Stop," a voice said behind her.

Marianne whirled on Diablo and peered into the barrel of a musket.

Armando woke with a start. Silence. What had drawn him from his few precious hours of sleep?

His *Tio* Manuel snored lightly and outside he heard a few insects, but nothing else. He remembered his dreams . . . Marianne. Lately, she seemed to haunt him rather than bring him a moment of consolation. He tried to comfort himself in knowing she would live a comfortable life as the wife of Don Lorenzo Sanchez, but nothing worked. Even the freedom enjoyed by his people failed to cure the ache. At times he searched the faces of the brown-eyed señoritas of La Flor to find a young woman to take her place, but all he could see was Marianne's blue-gray eyes.

Isabella and Emilio were to be married in two weeks' time. Armando gave all the outward appearances of happiness for the couple, but inside he envied their love and devotion. He despised his own loathing of their promising future.

Shaking his head in the dark, Armando could not deceive himself. He had hoped that in securing the land for his people he might find release for his restless soul. But clearly not even Marianne could fill the void plaguing him. If only he knew how to find lasting peace. Most claimed the hand of *Dios* calmed the wayward soul, yet one must believe to enjoy the blessings. Lately, he wondered if he had been wrong. Ever since Padre Bernardino had told Armando about his father, he'd felt a softening in his spirit and a desire to return to the *Dios* of his youth. A verse from Micah that he had memorized years ago often came to mind. *He hath shewed thee, O man, what is good; and what doth the LORD require of thee, but to do justly, and to love mercy, and to walk humbly with thy God?*

Marianne wished she could stop the incessant hammering of her heart against her chest. The sickness she'd experienced earlier now resurfaced. "*Por favor,* do not summon *mi padre,* I beg of you."

The young vaquero lowered his weapon. Straining to see him in the shadows with his hat pulled over his eyes, she thought she knew his face, a recently hired young man.

"My duty is to serve Señor Phillips," he said.

She held her breath and prayed. "By all that is holy and good, turn away and let me go."

"Señorita—"

"*Por favor,*" she said barely above a whisper. "You did not see me this night."

The young man hesitated and slowly brought the musket to his side. A moment later, he walked away.

Marianne did not waste a moment digging her heels into Diablo's side. She refused the thought of Papa or his friends from Virginia pursuing her. They would have to catch her first, and Diablo had chosen to fly with the wind.

Never had she seen the night sky light up the earth with such clarity, as though God Himself lit the path toward La Flor. *Surely God is with me. Why else this miracle?*

Fear left her as she gave her stallion full rein. Leaning over Diablo's neck, she felt as one with him. They were crusaders, a pair hoisting high a banner of righteousness. She chastised herself. How silly of her to compare herself to a soldier of God. She was but a mere young woman sent on an errand of warning. Nothing more.

"My rebel, my prince," she whispered to Diablo. "You are just like my Armando." A fluttering nudged at her stomach. Yes, before the morning sun broke through a blue-black sky, she would see her beloved. The excitement . . . the mission . . . the notion of touching Armando pushed her on.

Miles were behind her, and La Flor lay ahead. She did not know what the people would do to protect themselves, but she'd help.

A hint of yellow crept across the horizon while Marianne viewed signs of the approaching valley. *Awaken the dawn. Prepare to fight.* Many hours would pass before this site became a battleground. Dare she return home and hide what she'd done? In a twinge of regret, she considered her actions. Papa might be killed as a result of her warning the village. Even so, Armando and all of his people would be murdered if she held her tongue. Her thoughts warred with her spirit. In one breath she believed in her purpose, and in the next she feared this was nothing more than another rebellious act against Papa.

Oh, God, I believe this is Your will. Forgive me if I have been impulsive and sinned against You and my family.

Studying the skyline, Marianne wondered how long it would be before the posted guards stopped her. Slowing Diablo to a walk, she rode cautiously, having no desire to get shot or struck down.

"Halt." A man stepped in front of her path.

Marianne tightened her hold on Diablo. The stallion would stomp the man to the ground if given an opportunity. "I need to talk to Armando Garcia," she said in Spanish. "This is most urgent."

The man lifted his head. Felipe.

Chapter 26

Felipe peered up at Marianne, and his eyes narrowed. Months ago, he'd been furious when Armando released her, and she could only imagine what was going through his mind now. Remembering his harshness and the things he'd said and done during her abduction, she trembled. Nothing stopped him from abusing her. Nothing but Diablo's fierce loyalty.

"Felipe, La Flor is in grave danger. *Mi padre* has arranged for everyone here to be killed."

He turned his head as though casting aside her words. A moment later he stared into her eyes. "How do I know this isn't a trap? Señor Phillips may be behind you."

Marianne shook her head. "I'm alone. Please believe me."

"You rode from the Phillips Hacienda without an escort?" He spat upon the ground.

"Look at the hour. I've rode this distance alone to warn the village."

Felipe said nothing, as though contemplating her words. He stepped toward her, and Diablo snorted. She held the stallion's reins firmly, but she'd not hesitate to allow Diablo to protect her.

"I know the Spanish have insured your valley, but *mi padre* has devised a plan to possess it despite the governor's mandate."

He looked beyond her, as though expecting an army of Papa's men to ride up. "Who else is with you? Juan Torres?"

"No one. I couldn't risk Juan's life or any of the vaqueros."

"But who followed you?"

She thought back over her encounter with the vaquero. Could he, in fact, have trailed her to La Flor? "I don't believe anyone knows I'm here," she said. Felipe knew she feared him, but he needed to see her determination. "Time is short. I must speak with Armando."

"I could kill you and hide your body."

"But you won't." Her words sounded braver than she felt. "You love your people and this valley too much to risk it. If I'm lying, then you have the right to kill me."

He hesitated.

"I have no reason to lie to you."

She waited while the sounds of early morning chorused around her.

"I will have someone take you to Armando." Felipe scrambled to the top of a large rock and waved his musket signaling another guard. "I need to keep my post in case we are attacked."

Marianne didn't care whether Felipe believed her or not. What mattered was warning Armando about Papa's plan. She followed a young man on a burro through the narrow streets of the village. The beginning sounds of a new day caressed her ears and the smells of a morning meal caused her stomach to rumble. At Manuel and Rosa's hut, the young man jumped from his mount and knocked on the door.

The reality of seeing Armando suddenly shook her senses. Would he think she'd devised a scheme to come to him? What if he refused to consider her warning? Her arrival could make him angry, especially if he'd grown fond of a young señorita from the village.

She swung her leg over the saddle and lowered herself to the hard ground. Trepidation raced through her veins. Patting the stallion's neck, she noted he needed food, water, and proper grooming. Surely Armando would not deny care for the stallion.

"Marianne?" Armando called from the doorway, his voice rippling with sensuality.

Holding Diablo's reins, while her heart clung to God, she caught a glimpse of his face. Dawn ushered its shadows across his unforgettable features.

"*Si*. I'm sorry to disturb you, but I have news—news that could not wait." Her voice faltered in his presence, not at all possessing the confidence she desired.

He stepped closer and Diablo protested. "Hush," she said. "Armando will not harm me."

"What has happened?" He ignored the stallion's snorts. "Are you all right?"

She wanted to see if his eyes still held the same warmth and tenderness, but she couldn't permit herself such vulnerability. How she loved him, but she had a matter before her more important than her love. "I learned something horrible last night. Papa plans to destroy La Flor and everyone in it."

"Destroy the village? How?"

"By stampeding a herd of cattle through here late tonight and then setting fire to the huts. I overheard him finalize his plans near midnight."

"Where is your escort?" he asked. "Please do not tell me you rode here alone." Lines deepened across his forehead.

"I couldn't risk the lives of others."

"You traveled all night?" He rubbed the back of his neck. "Were you not afraid?"

"*Sí*, very much. I am a coward when it comes to the night. But I am more afraid for La Flor, and I am afraid for Papa. Some will die this day, and I wish none of it to happen." She calmed Diablo, then walked toward him. "Papa still wants the valley for himself . . . and he plans to kill all of you for it."

Armando reached for her, and she dropped the reins to fall into his embrace. "*Mi ángel,*" he whispered. With one hand against the back of her waist, he guided her quivering body against his chest. His other hand wove his fingers through her tresses. She heard his rapidly beating heart and felt his face brush against the top of her head.

Cautiously, as though she were but a fragile piece of porcelain, his fingers slipped from her hair to her neck and on to her lips in feather-like softness. He touched them lightly, and she lost herself in the dark pools of his eyes, the depth of which seemed to have no end. His head descended and she tilted hers to meet him. Lips parted, Marianne silently begged for his kiss, and Armando did not disappoint her.

At first he tasted her lightly, like a butterfly glides upon a summer breeze and embraces a flower. Then he deepened his fervor, claiming her with his gentle brand.

The intensity of his passion sent a glorious, warm tingling through her veins. How long she had dreamed of this moment. If only time could suspend forever.

Armando lifted his head and took both of her hands into his. He caressed her face and kissed her forehead. "I said I would never reveal the desires of my heart, but I cannot live another day without telling you of my love. I long for you with every breath I take. Your memory is always before me."

"And I love you," she said. "Before I knew the meaning of the words, you were in my dreams."

Again he drank from her lips and drew her tightly into his arms. At last they parted. She wanted to believe there would be time for them later, and she could not relinquish that hope.

"You could have been hurt," he said. "I don't want to think of life without you. What is the urgency for such a dangerous ride? I understand your father's hate for me—"

"He plans to commit this horrible thing when this day is over. And his vengeance is more than hate for you, it's the land." She stared into his deep, penetrating eyes. "What he will do is more terrible than I could imagine."

"Tell me." His hand still clasped hers.

"Some of his amigos have arrived from the States. They are evil men. Mid-morning Papa plans to inform those at the ranch that he and his friends are riding north in search of mustangs. But what he really will do is move westward and round up nearly a thousand head of cattle to stampede through the valley tonight after everyone sleeps."

A cold, angry stare replaced Armando's ardent gaze. "Has he no honor? Innocent women and children murdered in their sleep? And what of the old people?"

"I don't understand him," Marianne said. "Neither do I know how he can be stopped. I love him, Armando, but this is so wrong."

He paused and pulled her close to him. "If ever I needed *Dios*, it is now." He held her a moment longer. "The men from the village must be assembled at once and a plan devised to save our people."

Lifting her head, Marianne hoped she could find the strength for what lay ahead. "I will stay with Rosa. You do what you feel is right. I'm afraid for you and your people. And with what I've done, I'm afraid for Mama and my *tio* and *tia*. " She took a breath. "And my papa. I love him too, even with what he's planned."

In the next instant, Armando left her to summon the men of La Flor.

Silence met Armando's ears once he finished explaining what Weston Phillips intended to do to the people of La Flor. A few of the older men turned ashen while others wore grim expressions as they considered the threat to their friends and families.

"What do we do, Armando?" Pepe asked. He leaned against a live oak. Armando felt a swelling in his chest—not of pride but a heaviness that revealed his inadequacy. Felipe stood to his left, discontent etched in his brow. "In the beginning, we all talked of giving our lives for our valley," Armando said. "We believed our families and children deserved to keep their homes. I know this hasn't changed. I've made mistakes, and you've still allowed me to continue leading you. Perhaps it's because you know my heart rests with all of La Flor.

"We celebrated when Padre Bernardino Vallyo spoke to Governor Juan Bautistade Elguezábel, and he ruled in our favor. But Weston Phillips has not given up securing the valley for himself. This road we walk is hard. The Spanish cannot arrive in time to save us, nor do we have many weapons to fight. So once more we are alone to defend our families and our homes." Armando's emotion nearly choked him. He paused to gain control. For the first time in many years, he wanted *Dios* to be real. "As *Dios* reigns in the heavens, I never wanted to sway any of you in the wrong path."

He stared out over the gathering of men, certainly not a strong band of soldiers, but simple people who loved their homes and families.

"My allegiance is to you," an older man said.

"*Si*," another called out. "You give us your ideas, and we will listen."

Emilio stood, and the crowd hushed. He waved his hand over the men and faced Armando. "*Mi amigo,* we follow your heart. Let us pray and ask *Dios* to guide us."

"You pray," Armando said to Emilio. "I cannot form the words." Perspiration trickled down Armando's face. For the first time in many years, he craved *Dios* to be real.

"*Maria, madre santa del Dios,* hear our prayers. We humbly ask for guidance and protection from Señor Phillips. Save our children, we ask of you. Save our village."

Armando listened to his friend's prayer. He too had implored *Dios* to help. *Not for me, but for my people. I do not deserve Your attention. Hear the words of these humble servants and cast them not away from Your presence.*

How long had King David's plea escaped his mind and heart? The declarations from the ancient king tumbled from his thoughts like a waterfall rushing to meet the earth. Armando had blamed *Dios* for so many years for the unfortunate and tragic events tormenting his life. When he left the mission, he traded his fervor for God for the cause of La Flor. Both had emptied his life and left him impatient and weary. Yet somehow the answer had to lie in Armando's relationship with Him.

Emilio concluded his petition. "Grant our leader wisdom in how we can prevent this tragedy. In Your Holy Son's name. Amen." The men looked to Armando for answers as though *Dios* spoke through him. Their lives, their families, and their homes were at stake. He dared not lead them astray.

Help me, Dios. Por favor, I beg of You.

"I don't think a man here wants to abandon his home to Señor Phillips," Armando began. When they affirmed his statement, he raised his hands for their attention. "We will all need to work together against our enemy. Every man and boy, twelve years and older, is needed. First of all, the women and children must be taken to safety immediately. The older men can assist. Tell the women to take only what is necessary and what they can pack in one hour's time. Later, if possible, other important belongings can be carried out. The best refuge is our hilltop camp. It will house them sufficiently until the danger is over."

Armando cleared his throat. "I have an idea on how we can deter the stampeding cattle and keep our village from being destroyed. There is but one way the cattle can be driven into the valley, and we must be ready for them. If every available man is positioned behind a barrier with a gun or some method of loud noise, we can possibly turn the cattle."

"We have few good weapons," Felipe pointed out. "The 1757 muskets, carbines, and pistols were returned to Señor Phillips. *Belduques*—large, heavy knives—are not noise makers."

Armando ignored Felipe's cynicism and looked for any others who wished to speak. "We will need the remainder of the day to line the area with wagons, carts, rocks, and whatever else we might need."

The crowd murmured until Pepe stood. "Armando has good ideas, but I would like for you to consider something else. In addition to what he has suggested, a herd of mustangs driven against the cattle would also force them to turn."

"Why not stampede our cattle against them?" a man asked.

Armando cringed with the thought. "By running our cattle against theirs, we risk losing them all. Pepe is wise to consider the use of mustangs. Even if we lose the horses, we can still feed our families."

"What good are the cattle if we are dead?" Emilo asked.

"You are right. We shall stampede the horses and the cattle behind them." Armando clasped Emilio's shoulder. "You are wise, *mi amigo.*"

The crowd agreed, and Armando seized the opportunity to get started. He handpicked a dozen men to stay behind and plan the barrier while the others returned to their homes to alert the women.

"Help your women until you are assigned a duty from one of these twelve," he told them. "Remember, one hour for the women to gather up belongings, and these things must be hand carried or packed on burros to take out of the valley. What few carts and wagons we have must be used to transport the sick and lame and then used for the barricade."

The crowd quickly disbanded, and Armando stared grimly at the men before him. Some were loyal to Felipe. Others sided with Armando. Hours of backbreaking work lay ahead, and unless they all cast aside their personal differences, the village would not be ready in time.

"Are we together on this endeavor?" he asked.

The men either nodded or voiced their agreement.

He selected four men from the original twelve to begin the evacuation and gave them instructions on how to most easily move the women and children. Armando chose one man from the remaining eight to make sure the village moved as much food as possible. Even after the stampede was stopped, the villagers would not be able to return until all threat of danger had passed.

For every three families, an older man assumed the role of leader, keeping track of the number in his group. Older children were needed to return to the village and assist with the barrier until dusk.

Armando placed Pepe, Felipe, and Emilio in charge of moving the mustangs from a nearby canyon, but the task could wait until later in the afternoon. Right now, he needed help to build a wall on the eastern ridge.

Raking his fingers through his hair, Armando sensed the blood rushing through his veins and spurring his body and mind. If they couldn't finish preparations by nightfall, the village would be destroyed.

Chapter 27

Armando watched as Marianne mounted the hill where young and old worked diligently to build a barrier against the evening's raid. Carrying a jug of cool water, she stopped several times to offer a drink to those perspiring in the heat. He watched her slow ascent. Twice before she'd headed his way, only to be stopped by those who needed their thirst quenched. This time she'd reach him.

He shielded his eyes from the noonday sun and took in the amount of work completed. The progress pleased him. The women and children were safe in the hills, although many had returned to fetch additional possessions, to cook for those working, and to help with the barricade. Marianne had labored side by side with the villagers, just as she had done the night of the fire.

He captured her attention, and a smile passed between them. The mere glimpse of her eased his spirit. They'd not talked since dawn. In one breath, he regretted admitting his love for her. Nothing could become of his confession but heartache for both of them. She must still marry the don as planned. He saw no other alternative.

"*Hola,*" Marianne said as she neared him. She quickened her steps and offered him her jug. "I have water for you."

"*Bueno.*" He reached for the container and drank deeply. All the while he observed her, the paleness of her skin and the hint of pink to her cheeks. A smudge of dirt marked her forehead, reminding him of Indian war paint.

"So many people are helping." She glanced about. "The wall will be finished long before dark."

He nodded and rested the jug on the ground. "Let's walk a bit. I want to look for weak points in the barricade, and we need to talk."

Her lovely features clouded. "All right."

He grasped her hand and they moved away from those around them. "You cannot stay here, *mi señorita,*" he said. "This is too dangerous."

"I want to help," she said. "I cannot bear to leave you."

Sighing, he stopped and searched her eyes for understanding. He would not risk the life of his beloved. If she stayed, he wouldn't have the strength to make her leave when the turmoil of the day ended. But would she be able to put up with his restlessness?

"Armando?" She touched his arm. "I belong with you."

"In this?" He gestured at the busy throng of villagers. Irritation grated at him.

"*Si*," she said. "I love you and you alone."

He softened at her declaration and ached to hold her. Armando lifted her chin with his finger. "Without your bravery, these people would have perished tonight. I owe you my life for your single act of courage, but I'm still afraid that we cannot hold back the stampede."

She turned to watch the work. "I know, and I'm causing you more trouble with my insistence on remaining here."

"No, not trouble, but concern." He hesitated and dropped his hand to his side. "With all that has gone on today, I need to see a priest and make my confession, but it's impossible. I cannot leave my people." He hesitated. "I have turned my back on *Dios* for too long. Now my people need a miracle."

"Do you believe you must see a priest?"

Her question bristled him. He knew she believed in *Dios,* but she sounded ignorant of the way of faith. Then again, she practiced the Protestant religion, and he knew nothing of its doctrine. "I need forgiveness of my sins," he said.

She tilted her head slightly. "Why not go to *Dios* and ask Him to relieve the burdens from your heart?"

"For forgiveness, I need to make confession," he repeated.

She nodded. "I know you once studied to be a priest. And I see the unrest in your spirit. Only the love of *Dios* and the acceptance of His Son Jesus Christ into your life can give you peace."

"You are not a padre who has been educated in the way of the church." Instantly he regretted his harsh words. "Oh, Marianne, I'm sorry. You are the last one who needs to taste my bitterness."

She touched his cheek. "For a moment, listen to me. Jesus Christ is my Lord and King. When I acknowledged what He'd done for me and asked Him to live forever in my heart, He forgave my sins. Because He gave His life for me, I love Him and follow Him the best way I can. All of us are saved by His grace. Thank Him for sending His Son to die for you, ask Him to forgive your sins, and He in turn will give you eternal life . . . and peace."

He stared at Marianne speechless. Her words sparked both frustration and hope. She spoke of the one thing he so desperately craved. *Peace.*

Without responding, for fear of hurting her with his spiteful words, he pointed toward his people. "I must get back to work." His mind raced with what she'd just said. Could he have been wrong? Nothing from the padres or the books he'd read ever sounded like this. But he had seen this peace in some of the padres' eyes and in many of the people of La Flor.

Her troubled look touched his heart, and he forced a smile. "I don't want to quarrel with you. Your ways of worshiping *Dios* are not the same as mine. Forgiveness can only come through a padre."

"I understand your confusion," she said. "I'll pray for your understanding. I think you may need a little time with *Dios.*" Marianne turned to leave, then faced him again. "*Dios* loves you. You don't need a padre to go to Him. All He requires is a repentant heart."

Again Armando chose not to reply. Her words whirled in his troubled mind. He'd performed all the things the priests required, all but his priestly vows. He'd never felt the peace that she spoke of. What more must he do?

But the restlessness seemed to overpower him. In his reflections of the blessed Savior, Armando had always considered Jesus as a symbol of love and sacrifice, an example of total humility and an inspiration to do many things for Him. He'd died for man's sins. Was there more? What could have escaped him?

Armando realized he needed help. The prospect of one more hour with the agony so familiar and yet so hated settled like a heavy yoke. This yearning didn't come from his sense of duty and responsibility but from something deep inside him.

Heading to a secluded spot far from the others, Armando knew he needed quietness to mend his spirit. The moment he reached a clump of rocks, barren of vegetation, he fell to his knees.

Santo Del Padre, I don't understand how I can ask forgiveness of my sins without a priest, but I cannot live another day with the restlessness burning in my soul. My sins are more than I can name . . . greed, selfishness, coveting, allowing myself to look grand in the eyes of my people. So many faults, Dios, and I beg Your mercy upon me.

My heart aches for peace. What must I do? More prayers? Work harder for my people? Possibly return to the San José Mission? I beg release.

He remembered the placid look on Marianne's face when she spoke of Jesus Christ, as though she knew the blessed Savior as a friend. She talked of acknowledging

His sacrifice. Hadn't he done that every day at the mission? Must Jesus be asked to live in a sinner's heart? Was that all He must do for peace? How could a single young woman know more about *Dios* and His workings than a man who studied for the priesthood?

Questions without answers assaulted him. He felt beaten and battered more than if he'd built the barrier wall by himself. Tears flowed down his cheeks. He again begged for mercy. Burying his face in his hands, he saw no alternative.

Blessed Jesus, I know You suffered and died on a cross for my sins. I know You rose from the dead and reign in the heavens with the Santo Padre. I need Your gift of peace. I need You in my life to rule and guide me in all things. I need Your wisdom to lead my people and what You would have me do with Marianne. Come to me and give my spirit rest.

No sooner had the words left his thoughts than Armando felt an invisible hand lift the heaviness from his shoulders. The burdens of his heart vanished. He touched his shoulder. No one was there. Could it be his prayers were answered? The blanket of darkness surrounding him with despair for longer than he cared to remember appeared gone, and in its place dwelled a sense of freedom. And peace.

"Oh, Lord," he whispered. "*I do not see You, but I believe and love You. Thank You for filling me with this unfathomable joy, for I have received the salvation of my soul.*"

Rising to his feet, Armando allowed the moment to wash over him. *Si*, even to drown him. His *Dios* would be right beside him during the siege of La Flor. Now he could lead his people. Later he'd discuss all of this with his friend Padre Bernardino.

Marianne. Suddenly he saw his beloved with him as long as he held breath. He must thank her for urging him to see the truth and allow her to see all the love he possessed—for *Dios* and for her.

"Congratulations, Isabella, I'm so glad for you," Marianne said, as the two women filled their jugs from an open spring. "When is the wedding?"

"Two weeks," the dark-haired beauty said. "I know what is happening to our village is so very sad, but I cannot but feel happiness when I think of Emilio and me spending the rest of our lives together."

Marianne hoisted her filled jug to her hip. Her whole body ached from toting water and the lack of sleep, but she must continue to help. "I think love is supposed to make you forget bad things and be happy."

The two began the trek to where the men worked. "And what of you and Armando? With what you did for us, he will never let you go."

Marianne's heart lifted. "I'm not sure what will happen, Isabella. When we last spoke, he thought I should return home. He believes I have no future here." She gave her new friend a faint smile. "But in La Flor, I'm truly filled with joy."

Pushing back her raven tresses, Isabella frowned. "He loves you. I see it in his eyes. I saw it the night he brought you to the celebration."

"Even then?"

Isabella nodded. "I was so jealous."

"He thinks he must provide for me as Papa does."

"Don't listen to him right now. Wait until all of this," and she waved her hand around them, "is behind us." Isabella paused. "I feel I should warn you, though."

Marianne studied Isabella. "About what?"

"Armando is inclined to black moods. I'm not certain why. It may be due to his denial of *Dios*."

"Leaving the mission and not taking his priestly vows?"

"He doesn't believe in *Dios,* or so he claims. But I think his spirit wants him to." She raised a questioning brow. "Do I make sense?"

"*Sí.*" Marianne had seen enough black moods from Papa. Surely Armando did not have the same ill temperament. Mama's warnings sickened her. "I will continue to pray for *Dios* to touch his heart and give him peace."

"Emilio and I have been asking Him the same thing. Armando is like a brother to my Emilio, and he hurts to see Armando in such torment."

Marianne failed to reply. In the last hours, doubts had clamored in her mind. Mama's words about Papa's charm during their courting days, and his change after they married crept across her mind. And of course, she could never forget Angelina and Clay.

Marianne scrambled again to recall all of Armando's good qualities: the times he could have taken advantage of her naïveté or continued in his rebel ways to frustrate Papa. Armando kept his word to the padre at the San José Mission and to the governor. Shaking her head to expel the misgivings roaring through her mind, Marianne decided to pray and seek God's leading. If she returned to her home, Papa would discipline her severely for foiling his plans. And if he banished her, she could seek refuge with Don Lorenzo . . . if he still wanted to marry her after this. Guilt caused her to shiver. How wrong it would be of her to run to the kindly Spanish nobleman because Armando wanted her to leave La Flor.

I am spinning my thoughts when it's not necessary. Trying to think as God does and guess the future is wrong and displays my lack of trust.

"Marianne," Isabella said. "Emilio and Armando are walking toward us. They must have good news for they are smiling. Please forgive me for alarming you about Armando. Love often changes how a man sees things."

Marianne turned to her. "Don't apologize because you merely reminded me of what I already know."

The young women watched the two men approach. Indeed they looked happy—and in the midst of the pending gloom. Curiosity nearly overcame her.

"Here are the two most beautiful women of La Flor," Armando said, with a dazzling smile. He reached for Marianne's water jug and rested it on the ground. Gathering her up in his arms, he pulled her to him. "You were right, *mi ángel.*"

She searched his face for answers and saw a calmness not evident before.

"All I needed was forgiveness, a turning of my heart to *Dios.*" A smile continued to play upon his lips.

"You've found peace with the Lord." His admission filling her with elation, she encircled her arms around his neck and struggled with emotion. "Never have I been so happy."

"I came to tell you and met Emilio along the way. Peace, Marianne. I have true peace."

They laughed, and he held her at arm's length. She brushed a tear from her cheek. "I'm forever crying about something, but this is worth a river of tears."

Armando chuckled, then sobered. "All the years I have spent miserable and bitter." Shaking his head, he looked to Emilio. "*Gracias* for not giving up on me. How sad our village must face destruction before I can call upon *Dios*."

Emilio's eyes grew liquid. "*Dios* will protect us as He has led you to Him."

Armando reached to grasp the shoulder of his friend. "I now understand what you've been saying to me all these years." He glanced about him and on to the busy villagers. "At the mission, I learned about *Dios*, but not about knowing Him. Now he lives inside of me where He should have always been."

"Your face is bright with the love of our Lord," Emilio said. "Our souls are singing together, despite the evil that threatens to befall us."

"Tonight, when it grows dark, all of us will be ready to meet Señor Phillips and his cattle . . . and our *Dios*," Armando said.

"To die if necessary." Emilio wrapped an arm around Isabella's waist. "I'm ready."

Marianne shivered.

Chapter 28

With the sun fading behind the hills, Armando walked the length of the makeshift wall. The villagers had used carts, wagons, tree limbs, rocks, and personal belongings to barricade the entrance. It stood as a symbol of their commitment to their families and homes. The men had bade their loved ones good-bye and sent them on to the hilltop refuge before they assembled with Armando for final instructions. Now they must wait for Señor Phillips.

Emilio stood at the corral with Armando's horse. "*Gracias.*" Armando took the reins from his friend. "*Dios* willing, we'll save our valley and our people." He pointed to the moon. "Look, we have a light to guide us."

Emilio smiled. "As you told the men earlier, we are ready. *Dios* will fight for the righteous man."

The two men briefly embraced. "You are a true amigo," Armando said as they parted. "You and I are brothers. After tonight, we should see Padre Bernardino Vallyo. He'll ensure justice is done."

"The Spanish can be of use to us after all." Emilio chuckled. "We could use them in a few hours."

"For once I would welcome the sight of a blue and red uniform." Armando gave him a half smile and swung up onto the saddle. He peered down at his friend, wanting to say more in the event they never saw each other again. "I ask one favor of you, my brother. If something happens to me tonight, take Marianne to Don Lorenzo Sanchez. He'll not let any harm come to her. Do not let her father near her. I fear for her life after this is over."

"I promise."

"Instill in all of those staying in the valley that no one is to reveal to the gringos where our villagers are hiding."

"Most assuredly, my brother."

"Tell Juan I'm sorry. Thank him for looking after Marianne all the years she craved the affections of her father."

Emilio nodded, and Armando spun his horse around in an easterly direction where guards had been posted since early afternoon. There, a little more than a mile from La Flor, Felipe and a dozen others searched in every direction for signs of stampeding cattle. Armando rode confidently, his trust and strength in *Jesús Cristo*.

He wanted to study more about his Lord. All of his recollections about the blessed Savior pointed to a personal indwelling of the Lord in a man's heart, but he'd been blinded, spending all of his strength on doing things for other people. He'd believed that *Dios* counted him worthy to enter the kingdom of heaven by his efforts alone. How many others had fallen to the misfortune of believing heaven could be reached by accumulating good deeds? Marianne spoke such wisdom when she encouraged him to seek *Dios* with his heart. Later, if He willed it, when the happenings of this night were over and his people safe, Armando wanted to spend time with his Marianne and discuss the way she worshipped *Dios*. For certain, not all Protestants were pagans.

Marianne. The mere thought of her name invoked a passion never felt in him before. Her happiness and well-being ranked foremost in his life, and he shuddered at the thought of ever letting her go. But that must be the decision of *Dios*, not Armando's selfish desires.

He waved at the shadowy figure of a villager posted on a rocky knoll. Already, darkness gathered around them, but the brilliant light cast from the full moon would be their amigo tonight.

Felipe, riding a midnight-blue mare, stole from behind a grove of trees. "Armando," he said, "I've nothing to report. The señorita was wrong." His words edged with fire.

Armando ignored Felipe's obvious dislike of Marianne. "If Señor Phillips does not come tonight, it will be because he changed his mind."

Felipe turned his attention toward the east. "We'll see who is right. When you look like a fool, the people will elect me as their leader."

"If the people want you to lead them, then I will gladly concede to your leadership."

"That will happen before the night is over."

Armando bit back a retort. This wasn't the time to become involved in petty disputes. "And where are the other men posted?"

Felipe pointed to the various lookout points. Pleased, Armando saw the strategy in their positioning. He needed Felipe to support him and the plans for this night. "You have done well," he said. "You haven't supported me in many of my decisions, but you have done a fine job today. I appreciate your loyalty."

Felipe stared at him in the darkness, no doubt dumfounded. "*Gracias,*" he whispered and paused before turning his attention back to the vast prairie of the east.

Armando and Felipe dismounted, and for the next thirty minutes, they listened wordlessly. Insects and birds called out in an air of tranquility. Then a sound, like distant thunder, rumbled in the distance.

Felipe dropped to his knees and listened with an ear to the ground. "They're coming. And there are many."

In an instant, Armando sat in his saddle. "You know the instructions." He whirled his horse around to the north where Pepe and several others waited with nearly one hundred mustangs.

Armando's dun raced across the hard ground. The steady, rhythmic beat of his horse's hooves stirred his heart for victory.

"Pepe." He barely stopped his horse long enough to speak.

The round-faced man emerged from where the horses were temporarily penned. "Are they coming?" Pepe asked.

Reining in his horse, Armando slowed long enough to reply. "Yes. Be ready. I'll join you with the mustangs."

Armando spurred his horse toward the villagers who stood guard near the barricade. He repeated his earlier orders. "Watch for the cattle. Make all the noise you can. If we fail, fire what weapons we have to deter them."

He rode back to Felipe. None of his men would face danger alone. He intended to be with them every step of the way.

As his horse stood beside Felipe, the rumble grew louder. He could smell the danger and almost taste the dust accompanying their approach.

"Now!" Armando fired his musket into the air. The men at the barricade had boys and elderly men to reload for them.

Fourteen men sounded their weapons into the night sky. By the moon's light, they pursued the stampeding cattle, the village men racing their mounts along the far left side of the herd, urging them to swerve south.

From the north, Pepe and a handful of men chased mustangs into the advancing longhorns. Behind them followed La Flor's cattle. The men fought an enemy of sound—as though the thunder of hell beat down on the valley's defenders. Still the stampede pushed on in a deafening roar. Despite the futile efforts to turn them, Armando refused to accept defeat.

Oh, great Dios, we cannot do this without You. I beg of You, turn the cattle away from our valley.

The mustangs and cattle of La Flor rushed forward, a mere sprinkling against the force threatening to devour them. The men shouted and raised their weapons. How soon before the stampeding cattle pounded their homes into the ground?

Armando would not let his spirit wane. The valley must be saved. "In the name of *Jesús Cristo*," Armando shouted. "Do not destroy our homes." Suddenly, as though an invisible hand touched the sides of Weston Phillips's cattle, they slowly leaned in a southerly direction.

Elation filled Armando's being. He shouted at the cattle until his own throat stung with his screams. "Keep them turning. Send them back to where they belong."

Phillips's men fired into the villagers. Bullets whistled past Armando, and he felt certain he stood as the main target. Phillips most likely had offered a pile of gold to the man who killed Armando Garcia. He wished he could see if any of his men had fallen. Later, they would gather the wounded. Something stung his right shoulder, biting into his flesh like a swarm of a thousand angry bees. He winced but refused to cease firing and reloading his weapon.

The torch lights of La Flor flickered ahead, but Armando no longer feared for the valley. The cattle now raced south, but he and his men intended to veer them back east. The exchange of musket fire continued. He attempted to count Phillips's men and realized they were few, just as Marianne had reported.

With the cattle turned, the villagers bravely trailed after the gringos for another two miles, scattering the longhorns so they could not be brought together for another attempt.

Weary and weak with the loss of blood from his shoulder, Armando joined his men to return to the village. Victorious. But two men lay dead from stampeding cattle, and one had been thrown from his horse only to be speared in the leg by a longhorn.

Dismounting, Armando tore his shirt at the shoulder and wrapped it around his upper arm to stop the bleeding. The bullet had only grazed him, and he had full intentions of riding with some of the men to the hilltop site where the women, children, and elderly took refuge. There he'd speak to the families of the two dead men. Both had small children. Felipe volunteered to stay with additional guards in the valley in case the gringos returned. Perhaps Armando had earned Felipe's respect tonight. Swinging on to his horse, Armando bit back the pain. Much was left to be done before he rested.

"Let me talk to those who lost a loved one tonight," Emilio said. "You need to take care of your wound."

"I will . . . soon." Armando appreciated his friend's concern. "This is nothing compared to the grief our men's widows and children are about to face."

Marianne refused to relax for even a moment's reprieve from comforting a woman or a child. Many hours had passed since she'd last slept. Her body longed to be delivered. Her mind begged for its release, but she couldn't give in until she knew the outcome of the evening. Many people lay around her on pallets and the bare ground. Only the children slept. She and Isabella had held hands and prayed until their words were muffled by sobs. They all desperately needed to hear word from La Flor. The sharp crack of musket fire revealed that Papa had followed through with his plans. Oh, how she'd hoped he had changed his mind.

Consumed with haunting fear, Marianne knew the impossibility of no one being wounded or killed. Bullets would fly from the muskets owned by Papa's men, and the villagers must defend themselves. The thought frightened her, sickened her. She wanted neither side to taste injury or death.

The sound of horses and excited voices captured her attention. Instantly she and Isabella stood from their position near the fire and joined the anxious throng.

"Our homes have been saved!" a man shouted. "We turned the cattle."

Another man jumped from his horse and ran to embrace his wife.

"Thank you, *Dios*," Marianne said. She embraced Isabella, and they laughed.

Amidst more men, she saw Emilio dismount. Isabella cried out for him, and soon they were in each other's arms. Marianne searched the crowd for signs of Armando. Where could he be? Heat flooded her body.

"Emilio, where is Armando?" She hoped her voice did not sound as frantic as she felt.

He immediately released Isabella and reached for her hand.

Panic swept through every inch of her. "Where is he?"

"He first went to the families of two men who were killed."

"Oh, I'm so sorry." She released a heavy sigh. He was alive and not stricken by one of Papa's men. "How dreadful for those people. Are there injured also?"

"One man fell from his horse and suffered an injury to his leg, but he will recover. A few cuts and bruises, but nothing serious."

Isabella touched Marianne's shoulder. "Our prayers have been answered." Isabella stared at Emilio with tears streaming down her face. "Forgive me for being selfish, but I'm rejoicing that you are all right."

Emilio pulled her tightly to him. "Tonight was a miracle for all of us. We were outnumbered, doomed to die, but *Dios* had mercy on La Flor."

Marianne stepped back. The couple should have time alone, and she interfered with their privacy.

"If I'm not needed, I'll sit by the fire until Armando comes." She smiled. "*Por favor,* tell Armando where I am."

"No, wait," Emilio said. "We will stay with you."

"It's not necessary. I am comfortable alone with my thoughts." She offered another smile to show her words were spoken in earnest.

"But we want to keep you company." Isabella broke from Emilio and linked arms with Marianne. "I don't want you peering into the fire without a friend when we can talk . . . and laugh. I want to remember laughter forever, for it seems so long since my people were really happy."

While Emilio tended to his horse, Isabella and Marianne were too weary to speak. Marianne urged her new friend to rest, but the dark-eyed young woman refused. They would all wait for Armando.

In the distance, Marianne heard wailing and cries of grief. No doubt Armando had revealed the tragedy to the family. Shivers raced up and down her arms. She despised the discord raging between her father and these good people. Men had died tonight. And what of Papa's friends? Had they escaped harm? What of Papa?

The longer she reflected, the heavier her eyelids. She knew once she gave in to sleep, nothing would wake her.

Just as she drifted away, someone touched the top of her head. She lifted her gaze to see Armando kneel beside her. Immediately she saw a cloth tied around his shoulder.

"Armando, you're hurt."

He shook his head. "This is nothing, *mi ángel.*" But in the firelight she saw the bloodstains.

"Has it been dressed properly?" She vowed not to let her exhaustion summon needless emotions. Armando had seen her in tears too many times.

"I'm ready to clean it now," he said. "And it is merely a breaking of the skin. Nothing for you to concern yourself."

"I think you are wrong." She viewed the red stains through the makeshift bandage. When she attempted to rise, his uninjured arm forced her to remain seated.

"You haven't slept in two nights," he said. "I can take care of treating my arm."

"But I want to bandage it for you."

Emilio chuckled. "As tired as you are, Marianne, someone will need to rescue you. I have bandaged this *hombre* many times, and I can again. Both of you," and he gestured to Isabella, "need to rest. Tomorrow we can talk and celebrate our victory."

"And bury the dead," Armando said. "Two men gave their lives for their dreams."

Marianne understood. He would rather have given his own life than cause others to suffer loss.

Chapter 29

Marianne and Armando leaned against the corral fence watching the horses. She rested her chin on her hands, and although she appeared to study the animals, her thoughts were absorbed with the events of the past two days. After Emilio had bandaged Armando's arm, she'd slept until the sun reached its highest peak, but her body still ached. Her heart ached more for the families of the dead men—and Papa. Not knowing how her father was needled at her heart. She couldn't return, but she shouldn't stay in La Flor and leave her mother alone to face Papa's wrath.

After helping Rosa put her and Manuel's hut in order, she had accompanied Armando to bury the two men. La Flor had no priest, but Armando and Emilio led the people in prayer.

"Another day is nearly over," she said to Armando. "What happens to the hours?"

He shook his head. "The older I get, the faster time goes."

She eased up from the wooden fence and studied his injured shoulder. Only dried blood met her scrutiny. "How is your arm? Are you in pain?"

He pushed his sombrero back on his head. "A strong man like me? No, not at all." He gave a laborious sigh, much like an old man, and turned to her. Suddenly his dark eyes sparkled mischievously, as though he resolved to put the ugliness behind them. "*Dios* has given us a beautiful day to put our lives in order, and He's given me a beautiful woman to keep me company."

"And I thought you would need a kiss to stifle the agony in your shoulder. But I guess not."

"Oh." He grimaced. "It's throbbing like a torch has branded me."

She laughed. "Sorry. I have no more kisses left." But she did let him steal a quick brush across her lips. Her mood instantly softened. "I love you." She reached up to weave her fingers through his black hair.

"And I love you," he said. "I think I must hold you captive, so I don't lose sight of you."

"How long?" She widened her eyes just for him.

Before Armando could answer, Diablo snorted and demanded her attention.

"My prince is jealous. I believe Diablo should know you better to appreciate your fine qualities."

"He hates me," Armando said. "I think if I were him, I'd feel the same."

"I think the two of you could be amigos. With time, he accepted Juan."

She sensed him studying her. "How did you manage such a feat with Juan? I've heard the stallion sometimes gives him a difficult time."

"Juan had the idea. He gave me one of his bandannas, and I tied it on my wrist every day for two weeks. During that time, Juan approached him a little every day. He fed Diablo with me present and talked to him. Then I gave Juan one of my scarves, and he wore it on his wrist. It took a while, but finally Diablo allowed him near without me."

"I can try," he said. "He is a magnificent horse."

"You must talk to him, compliment him on his beauty."

"Like a lovely woman?"

"*Sí.* You know how to treat him already. If I love you, surely he will too."

Armando said nothing, and she sensed him deep in thought. A part of her wanted to know his musings, but a larger portion feared he wanted to send her back to her father's hacienda or to Don Lorenzo Sanchez. Teasing her about being his captive wasn't the same as wanting her to stay with him always.

They stood, and with his left arm around her waist, he drew her to him. "I feel it's selfish of me to ask you to stay." He pulled her around to face him. "You are *mi ángel*, and I love you more than I ever dreamed possible, but my love requires a responsibility for your happiness. Through your prompting, I know what it means to trust the *Santo Padre* with all my heart. I owe you my life and what you've done for La Flor. . . . Yet the rivalry between your father and me is not over."

He lifted her chin. "I fear it will never be resolved." His handsome features spoke of tenderness and compassion. "How can I ask you to marry me when it puts you in more danger than before? It wrenches my heart to think of you wed to Don Lorenzo Sanchez, but there you would be safe."

"No, Armando." She fought hard to maintain her composure, remembering her vow to be a strong woman. "Don't send me away when my place is with you. True, Papa doesn't give up easily, but neither do I."

A smiled curved at his lips. "You are a stubborn one, which is only one of the reasons why you are such a treasure to me." His features darkened. "What would you have me do? Ask that you spend your days in poverty? I can't risk your despising me one day because of a harsh life. Poverty shortens the lives of those who battle with its cruelties."

"I could never despise you. My place is with you." She swallowed the liquid emotion threatening to drown her.

Armando stroked her hair. "If you love me, then you'll heed my words and do what I ask."

"Then you're sending me away?"

He looked beyond her, as though viewing the future. "Soon, Marianne—to Don Lorenzo—not to your father's hacienda. This is real love, *mi ángel,* to put you above what my heart craves."

She nodded, unable to reply for fear she'd cry. "I've already spoken all I can. For you, I will do as you ask and go to the don's hacienda, but can you send word to *mi madre?* She will worry about me."

"*Si.* I can send a rider in the morning to Juan. I regret your *madre's* knowledge of me is only as the ruthless man who held you captive."

"We've talked about you, and Mama knows my heart."

He lowered his head and kissed her, at first lightly then deepening as she felt his passion flow through her. When they separated, she trembled.

"I believe *Dios* brought us together," Armando began, his voice but a mixture of the early evening and a light breeze. "You are *mi ángel*, a gift from *Dios*, a gift I cannot keep."

Marianne wakened the following morning to the peaceful sounds of nature unfolding in the splendor of another day. Last night she had cried in Armando's arms, despite her resolve for their time together to be filled with happiness.

Why must it be so, God? Her only comfort lay in knowing He wanted the best for her, even if she could not fathom another day without Armando. Far better to spend her life without her beloved than to live against God's will. Someday she hoped to accept that concept, but now her heart ached too much.

Today Armando planned to send a rider to Juan and then on to the Mission San José to seek Padre Bernardino Vallyo. He would inform the governor of what happened at La Flor. *What of Papa? How would he treat Mama now that Marianne was a traitor?*

No matter if Don Lorenzo still wanted to marry her or he, too, had turned away in disgust. Mama would be alone to deal with Papa's temperament, and to go through the months before the baby was born with no one to talk to her. Marianne considered the possibility of Mama living at the Lorenzo hacienda. She needed someone to care for her. And would Juan and Carmita continue working for Papa? So many questions, and the answers were yet to come.

"Marianne."

Hearing Armando's voice, Marianne opened her eyes to see him standing in the doorway with one of the vaqueros who worked for her father. She blinked and recognized the man posted on guard the night she left home. The vaquero mentioned her name, and she strained to listen to the low hum of their voices.

"I will have her ready within the hour," Armando said. "And I will accompany both of you."

"Señor Phillips's guests left yesterday. None will harm you."

Marianne raised her head. "What has happened?" She made her way from the pallet to Armando's side.

He brushed back a wayward strand of hair from her face. "Your father is sick," he said. "Your *madre* needs you."

She searched his face. Lines etched around his eyes, his telltale sign of worry. "Tell me about Papa. What is wrong with him?"

He gathered her hand into his. "He became enraged with the outcome of the cattle stampede. His heart is failing him."

She nodded and swallowed hard. How well she remembered Papa's temper and the way he often grabbed his chest. *Oh, Lord, this cannot be. Papa does not know You. He and I have never settled our differences.*

While they prepared their horses, Marianne's concern mounted.

"Talk to me," Armando said. "It will make you feel better."

She shrugged and tightened the girth under Diablo. "I miss what I never had with Papa. I've told you about him before. . . . We seem to make each other miserable. Besides, I envied how he felt about Clay. Many times I deliberately made Papa angry, and I know I wanted to somehow punish him for hurting me. This time, I may have killed him."

"You are not guilty of this," Armando said. "All of us are responsible for the choices we make. You're not the cause of your father's illness any more than I am."

She shook her head as though to dispel the anxiety pelting her senses. "My mind tells me what you say is true, but my spirit hurts because Papa has always been so unhappy."

"I understand unhappiness," Armando said. "Remember I once hated my father for deserting *mi madre* and me. So your father and I have more in common than you may think. Trust in *Dios, mi ángel,* let Him be your comfort."

"I will." She forced a smile she did not feel. "Thank you."

His loving gaze said more than words.

Within moments, Marianne, Armando, and the vaquero raced toward the Phillips Hacienda. She tried desperately to think of fond memories of her father, but they were few. She remembered one occasion, when a Spanish soldier told Papa she had eyes like his, and Papa had smiled. Another time, she overheard Papa tell Clay how proud he was of her ability to tame Diablo. But any other good recollections were vague at best. Papa had wanted a son, and she had disappointed him. Even if Mama bore him a male child now, the relationship between Marianne and her father would still be held together by a slender thread, if anything at all.

Marianne felt Armando studying her. She couldn't acknowledge him and not weep, so she kept her attention fixed on the trail ahead. How could she expect him to understand? He and Papa were enemies. But what if Papa died before she had the opportunity to say she loved him? Could she live with herself with such guilt? She shook her head. Papa had chosen to ride to La Flor that night. It was his decision. But her realization that his failing heart was not her fault did not ease the pain in her heart. She didn't know what lay ahead, and the unknown could be a formidable beast.

They were nearly home. A churning sensation swept through her. When they reached the front of the house, Juan met them near the stables. He hugged her close before taking Diablo's reins. His wide-eyed gaze locked with hers.

"Is he alive?" she said through a raspy breath.

"I think so."

"Go to him," Armando said. "I'll wait with Juan."

Marianne nodded and stared briefly at the house before walking toward it. Inside the heavy door, silence met her ears. Fearing the worst, she hurried to Papa's room.

Mama sat beside him, grasping his hand with both of hers. Tears streamed down her face, and her eyes were closed. Papa's face held the gray pallor of death. Marianne gasped and covered her mouth with her hand, her fears confirmed.

Mama glanced up. "He lingers still," she said. "He has been asking for you."

"For me?" Marianne repeated.

"Please sit here." Mama stood from the bed. "If he is strong enough to talk, you will want to hear him."

Marianne obeyed her mother's bidding. She hesitated, then picked up Papa's hand, limp and weak. Her fingers brushed over the many calluses, and she remembered all of the times she had wanted to feel the roughness. So many times she had silently begged those hands to touch her in love and acceptance. Those hands had built this land. His sweat had built this house and his empire.

"Papa," she said. "It's Marianne."

His lips moved, but she couldn't hear his words. She bent closer and heard her name. His fingers moved within her hand, and an onslaught of tears flowed from her eyes.

"I love you, Papa," she said. "Please get better."

His eyelids fluttered, yet they didn't open. Again he attempted to speak. "Marianne . . . the desk . . . hacienda is yours."

"Don't try to speak." She lightly squeezed his hand. "Just rest."

"Take . . . take care of your mother and the baby," he whispered. "You . . . you are my beloved daughter." As soon as the words formed on his lips, his body relaxed.

"Papa." She stared into his still face. "Papa, we can make up for all the times we quarreled. We can ride together. We—"

Her mother touched her arm. "Marianne, he is gone."

"But we—"

"There is nothing you can do."

Marianne sobbed on his chest—for his untimely death, for the wasted years, for the sorrow, and for the love. She felt her mother's arms around her shoulders, and they fell into each other's embrace.

"He loved us." Mama's body quivered. "He told me so."

They comforted each other until the weeping subsided. Mama pulled the coverlet up around Papa's neck as though he slept. She kissed him and whispered goodbye. "I pray you have a son," she said. Standing, she gathered Marianne's hand into hers. "In your papa's desk drawer is his will. He left everything to you. The only stipulation is, if the child is a boy, he shall be granted half of the estate upon his twenty-first birthday. If the child is a girl, you are to provide for her until she marries."

Marianne shuddered. "Why would Papa leave all this for me?"

Her mother took a deep breath and moistened her lips. "You two are so much alike, and he realized you could better manage our land than I ever could."

Marianne's mind spun with the news. Disbelief haunted her. She peered down at her father, his face free from bitterness and pain. "He did love me." She shook her head to rid herself of any more tears. "Did he talk of Jesus?"

Mama's face saddened. "I asked him if he had made his peace with God, but he did not answer."

Silence prevailed in the death room.

"Are you alone with the vaquero?" her mother asked.

Marianne paused. No doubt her mother knew the truth. "Armando is with me."

"Marianne." Her mother reached up to stroke her face. "You did the right thing in warning the people of La Flor. I see in your eyes the love you have for Armando Garcia." She kissed Marianne's cheek. "Your papa had me pen a letter to Don Lorenzo to ask him to release you from your promise. He also requested that you return his gifts. A rider left this morning with the post." Mama's eyes clouded for but a moment. "I want you to be happy. You have my blessings if you feel your life is with Armando."

"Oh Mama, thank you. Give him time, and you will see a good man. He loves the Lord."

She merely nodded, grief overcoming her once again. "Let me be alone with Weston for a while. I want to recall the way he courted me and his once-sweet ways." She glanced at Papa's peaceful face. "Then have Armando come inside. I want to meet this man who has stolen your heart."

Hours later, Armando and Marianne walked through the courtyard. Mama had been cordial to him, and when he apologized for past injustices, she stiffened.

"The only pledge I will accept is for you to love my daughter with all of your heart," Mama said. "And if you ever hurt her, I will not rest until you are dead."

"I give you my word. My life will never be filled with riches, but Marianne will have all of my love."

As they walked, Marianne had yet to tell Armando about the hacienda. She fumbled for the right words, trying to anticipate about his reaction.

"I need to tell you about Papa's will," she said. In the coolness of the day, the fragrance of flowers wafted about them.

"Are you certain?" He patted her arm coupled into his. "It can wait. You have endured enough pain for one day—for a lifetime. If we need to take care of your *madre*, then so be it."

"It's not bad news." Marianne took a deep breath. "He left me this hacienda and asked me to take care of Mama and the new baby." She lifted her head to meet his dark depths. "La Flor is now safe for all who live there."

"The prayers of so many are answered."

She glanced away, then back to her beloved Armando. "We could be together . . . here. Would you think about this?"

"What do I know of running a vast estate?" he asked.

"We can learn together."

A smile played on his lips. "Maybe I could learn with the help of a fine woman."

"You led the people of La Flor to victory. I think you could handle this hacienda just fine."

He lifted her chin with his finger. "I believe there is something unsettled between us."

She peered into his eyes. Had he chosen to return to the mission and take his vows to become a priest?

As though driving away her doubts, he drew her into his arms and brushed a kiss across her lips. "My sweet Marianne, in all the world, there is no other woman for me. No woman with your beauty, your spirit, your excitement for life, and daring for adventure. I know I am not worthy of your love and devotion, but I must ask. Will you marry me?"

"My heart is yours, Armando. Today and tomorrow."

Dear Reader,

Armando and Marianne's story first came to me a few years ago. I love Texas history and those courageous people who formed this great state. Soon I was enveloped in a love story that only God could orchestrate. I stepped into the world of handsome vaqueros and brightly dressed, dark-eyed maidens. I heard the sweet strum of a guitar and smelled the fragrant flowers. I tasted food seasoned with life and the toil of a man's hands. I felt the hot sun baking the clay at the mission, and I sat under the tutelage of the padres who instructed the people in the ways of God. Most of all, I saw two people separated by culture, religion, and social demands embrace the love that comes only from the great Creator.

At first I abandoned the story and told myself that it was a rendition of Zorro, my girlhood hero. But my mind kept journeying back to bigger-than-life Texas heroes, the strong men and women who dared to step over the line—those people who understood that God had a purpose for their lives.

I hope Armando and Marianne's story never leaves you, for their love story is a symbol of what helped build this great country.

DiAnn Mills

www.diannmills.com

And what doth the Lord require of thee, but to do justly, and to love mercy, and to walk humbly with thy God?

Micah 6:8 KJV

Discussion Questions

1. Marianne takes great pride in being the only one who can control Diablo. Why do you think she worked so hard to tame the stallion?

2. Armando believed he had abandoned God and turned his efforts to helping the people of La Flor. What evidence did you see that God had not abandoned him?

3. What character in the story could be compared with Diablo?

4. Marianne risked her life to save her mother. Do you think she really understood the gravity of her decision? Consider 1 Corinthians 13. Does this apply or not?

5. Armando is confused by his feelings for Marianne. He feels his heart has betrayed him. How does his past drive those feelings? Do you understand his hesitation?

6. Armando wondered if Marianne could force away his black cloud of depression. What happens when we think another person can play the role of God?

7. Armando and Marianne admit their love, but the social and political environment of the day frowned on their relationship. Forbidden love often pulls two people together, but what does God say is the foundation for His gift of love?

8. Although Marianne did not love the don, she planned to marry him out of obedience to her parents, and to try to forget Armando. Did you find this a strength or a weakness on her part? What is more important to God, our happiness or our obedience? Why?

9. Weston Phillips is a hard man to understand, perhaps an even harder man for his wife and daughter to love. Do you have people like him in

your life? How does God want us to handle this kind of relationship?

10. Marianne loved Armando and the people of La Flor. When she warned them about her father's plan, do you think she was obeying God?

Award-winning author DiAnn Mills launched her career in 1998 with the publication of her first book. She is the author of numerous titles including novels, novellas, and nonfiction. In addition, she has written several short stories, articles, devotions, and has contributed to several nonfiction compilations.

DiAnn believes her readers should "Expect an Adventure." Her desire is to show characters solving real problems of today from a Christian perspective through a compelling story.

Several of her anthologies have appeared on the CBA Best Seller List. Three of her books have won the distinction of Best Historical of the Year by Heartsong Presents, and she remains a favorite author of Heartsong Presents' readers. Two of her books have won Short Historical of the year by American Christian Fiction Writers in both 2003 and 2004. She was named Writer of the Year for 2004 at the 35th Annual Mount Hermon Christian Writers' Conference and is the recipient of Inspirational Reader's Choice Awards for 2005 and 2007.

DiAnn is a founding board member for American Christian Fiction Writers, a member of Inspirational Writers Alive, Advanced Writers and Speakers Association, and a mentor for the Jerry B. Jenkins Christian Writers Guild. She speaks to various groups and teaches writing workshops. DiAnn also belongs to Cy Fair Women's Networking, an exclusive professional women's networking organization.

She lives in sunny Houston, Texas, the home of heat, humidity, and Harleys. In fact, she'd own one, but her legs are too short. DiAnn and her husband have four adult sons and are active members of Metropolitan Baptist Church.

Website: www.diannmills.com

HARPER LUXE

THE NEW LUXURY IN READING

We hope you enjoyed reading
our new, comfortable print size and found it
an experience you would like to repeat.

Well – you're in luck!

HarperLuxe offers the finest in fiction and
nonfiction books in this same larger print size and
paperback format. Light and easy to read, HarperLuxe
paperbacks are for book lovers who want to see
what they are reading without the strain.

For a full listing of titles and
new releases to come, please visit our website:

www.HarperLuxe.com